Bed 18

....

Carrie Kacen

Dedicated to my daughter, Cailin Jane

I wore my belly as a proud pregnancy badge. It was the token to enter the wonderful world of motherhood. I yearned to become a mother for over six years. It was an absolute joy to find out I was going to have a baby of my very own. I grew and carried my pregnancy very well. I was healthy during the pregnancy with the exception of having an allergic reaction to lactose. The experience was extremely painful, and I only had two episodes to figure that one out.

I went to the hospital on Monday. I was concerned with two issues in my pregnancy and I wanted to prevent anything. I was examined with my dear friend, Fran, supporting me emotionally. The doctors saw that my cervix was closed in the examination.

"High and tight," they stated. I felt as if I had been leaking amniotic fluid and my discharge changed. Yes indeed, there was a yeast infection and of course we took the safest route to treat it. We agreed to rule out an oral treatment, but definitely the topical treatment would cure the infection. How embarrassing, I thought!

Fran says, "Car, don't worry, seriously it's nothing to worry about. Don't be embarrassed."

"I know Fran, but how gross!"

They checked my amniotic fluid on the ultrasound. The fluid was status quo. My baby was swimming with the placenta in the front.

I drove to work, and did hair feeling better about the experience. I was tired. I forgot the meeting I was conducting to award my girls. They have worked so hard. Where is my energy to pump it up for them? I found it and was home in bed by 11. I'm used to my 8 to 10 hours of sleep at night. I'm healthy and take good care of my baby. I'm just tired.

What's going on guys? Why do I feel the presence of three to four souls, large in size, in my bedroom? Are they the baby's guides? Cause I'm all good with that. I'm too tired. I can't make sense of it. I had an emotionally long day. Although there was a single presence the night before. Tomorrow will be a new day. Right???

The streets have homes and lives everywhere. No one is outside. I am though, by myself. What's new? I'm by myself a lot, by choice. I am strong. I am an independent woman. I'm not afraid. The trees have showers. I am showering and enjoying it. I have taken quite a few showers. The loud neighbor above didn't wake me up! I was counting on her to get me up by 6:30 a.m. I forgot my phone at work. I don't need it. Work, eat and sleep are my major concerns. Who is gonna call me? Well, maybe a friend. No biggie. I wake up at 7 a.m. I can get out the door on time. Just a little pep in my step. It's my shift with Allison. I love my Tuesdays. We work in sync. It's my back. Why is it hurting so much? Certainly,

Bed 18

I slept too hard in one position. The baby is mad and is resting on my spine. The placenta is in front of the baby. Dust it off. Get in the shower, Carrie. It's just gonna be one of those days. It's gonna get better. Face, hair, perfume, lunch. Looks like I'm locked and loaded. Let's go make some money doing what I love… hair! I love this new supportive brace I bought. It will definitely be beneficial to my back and stomach. I want to get back into my Victoria Secret's aqua bikini. I sported it last summer and looked fabulous.

I love my Pilot. I'm glad I purchased it. I am a mother to be. I need the safest SUV out there. I also wanted one. I'm strong and an independent person, woman, for that matter. I am accomplished, but still struggle. Who doesn't? But I do it all myself. Well, my dad does help in crisis. He knows I work so hard and things come up. He is helpful, but I'm strong and I can do it myself. Wow! Why does it hurt so much? It's just gonna be one of those days. Ouch! Music, music. We like music. Barbara Streisand is always played around this time. The greatest hits. My child needs to be around music and this is a great CD. I'll sing and you'll stop kicking my back. This is gonna be a long last four months of pregnancy. It hurts. Well, it's gonna get better. Carrie, chalk it up to one of those kinds of days.

I'm five minutes late. Thanksgiving is in two days. Holidays… family… people… they all need their hair done. I see my girl, Allison. She has come a long way. A bit of tug-o-war with her. The resolution is always compromise with lots of rules and regulations. She is frantic. I left my phone there. She called three times. "Where were you Carrie?" Al says.

"I would have loved to call you, but I left my phone here at work."

I was taken from the shop in her mind. She was so worried because that isn't like me. I'm strong and independent. I run a salon. My client is the one woman with the most hair in the world. We are going to make it big with her hair. Somehow, some way. Homeless people even comment on her hair in the Loop. The running inside joke is, "I got one, John." John is her husband with the poker straight hair. Great people! Joan isn't worried. I check her in and cut her hair. She cancelled one appointment on me. Why? She was sick and didn't want to affect my health or the baby's. That is the compassion I received from clients on my journey through motherhood. The joy of being pregnant! Tears, hugs and plenty of smiles were a typical response. How come I didn't make this happen sooner? This world of motherhood, gosh parenthood. The journey was long awaited. Just like me. Dreams of showers are just so darn refreshing.

My trusty dream book. I will figure my "shower dream" all out. There's always a higher meaning. What each dream was meant for. Water, bath: new beginnings. Yep! The thought comes to mind a few times for me. *My water is gonna break*. Really... no! *My water is gonna break*. It's my own voice. I'm working. It's the holidays, and this is the time to make my money. I'm strong, independent and a single mother. I need to make my money and have fun doing it. I have to hustle a little bit. I love the hustle of the job when it's busy. Private salons are too slow. My salon is busy, busy. Economy down? Whatever! We are making money! I'm fast cause I'm strong. People like coming in last minute. We like it too. Keeps it alive. Allison and I are hustling. I'm moving slower than usual. Why is my back killing me?

Dorothy comes in. She is such a nice Irish elderly lady. Dorothy and Ruth come to see me. They fill me up. I love seeing how long they have had a friendship. The two met in college and are now in their 70's and have the same hairdresser... me. I'm a chatty person. I enjoy gabbing for the most part. Certainly, don't catch me when I'm not in mood though. I have Diane, a nurse, processing with color. We are going a shade darker. It's fall. We will go lighter in the spring, when I'm due with my little one. What a great time of year to have a baby. Now there is a lot of input and influence on pregnancy. Are you finding out the gender? Absolutely not, people. I am due for a pleasant surprise in life. They are far and few in between. How are you carrying? High? Low? Cravings? Morning Sickness? Back pain? How do you handle standing on your feet all day long? I just do. I'm small, only 5 feet. I have no torso. I am all belly. From the back you can't see my pregnancy. I have gained 15 pounds. I feel better standing and moving around or on my couch in a fetal position. Yes, March is a wonderful time to have a baby. The winter will be coming to a wrap. A St. Patrick's Day baby would be cool.

I am now in a lot of pain. It's 10:55 a.m. and I watch the clock for the pain. I describe it as a cramp. It starts every 4-5 minutes. I am doing my yoga breathing. Diane notices my pain. Dorothy understands I am not feeling well. I apologize for not being very talkative. I should be wowing and delighting my clients. I have instilled the process of customer service at my shop. Dorothy checks out and wishes me well. I tell her it's just a rough day in my pregnancy. I'm doing my yoga breathing and waddling back to the shampoo area.

I say, "Diane, meet me over by the bowl."

Diane says, "You really are in some pain aren't you?"

I lean on the wall. I am teary eyed...what? Me? I am strong. I am independent. I am self-sufficient!?

"Yes, Diane. I am cramping every five minutes, and it comes around in my back."

Diane says, "Call your doctor right now! Carrie, don't worry about me."

I say, "Okay."

I am quivering enough to startle Allison. She turns to see me upset. Me? Yes, me! I sit and think. I'll email my doctor. She did get back to me yesterday in five minutes. I just am so tired and in so much pain that I don't have the patience to email with my iPhone. I'll call. The nurse answers and greets me.

I say, "I'm Carrie Kacen, Dr. Worldly patient. I am 23 weeks and I have some cramping that has been going on since 8 a.m. It seems to be happening every five minutes. Can I talk to Dr. Worldly?"

Diane peeks her head into the room to see how I am doing.

Bed 18

The nurse states, "She is in surgery. You need to go to the hospital immediately."

I say, "But, I was just there yesterday. I was diagnosed with a yeast infection and my cervix was closed, 'high and tight.'"

Nurse says, "You need to go to the hospital now."

I say, "Okay, I will."

I am crying. I am scared. I am confused!! I call Emma. I leave a message on the second try. Her stupid cell phone never works when I need to talk to her. My voice trembles into her voicemail, "Emma, I am cramping really bad and I need to go to the hospital. I know you are not starting until one, but can you come in now? I need to leave. Call me at the shop."

I try one more time... still no luck.

While I am crying, I rinse Diane's chemistry system out. She says, "No cut today, Carrie. I like the length of my hair now. I can leave with a wet head."

"No, Diane, let me cut and dry your hair."

"No, Carrie, I really don't need a cut."

"Okay, I'll just blow-dry it. Please Diane, it will help me relax."

"No, Carrie, really it's okay."

"Diane, I need to relax. Let me blow-dry your hair."

"All right."

I proceed to my station with Diane.

My Allison is ringing out her customer and being so very diligent. I say, "Allison."

She turns to me. She sees my face and she knows, "Yes, Carrie."

"Allison, when you are done ringing out your customer, I need you to call Emma. Tell Emma to come in now. I have to go."

"No problem, Carrie."

I begin to blowout Diane on my favorite dryer, the Chi Rocket. Hot, lightweight and a life-changer for my job. It takes me about 7–10 minutes... so about two contractions. Allison hangs up the phone, "Carrie, Emma was in the shower. She said she will be here in 15 minutes."

I look to her big, brown, sweet eyes and say, "Thanks, Al."

We say thank you all day to each other. Manners go a long way with coworkers. I try to create that pleasant tone for us each to meet. The customers feel it, breathe it and taste it. I head to the register. I ring out Diane with her favorite deep conditioner by Redken, Real Control. I feel really out of control and scared.

I move slowly and steady. In the nose, out the nose. In the nose, out the nose. I love my yoga and breathing techniques have been the largest benefit. Just writing about breathing brings me to a place in the summer. It's warm and sunny on a Thursday afternoon. I am off on Thursdays. Dad and I try to meet for lunch. We head to Wishbone in the West Loop. They have a great outdoor area. We valet the Pilot and grab a table. I am so happy to be pregnant. I am surprised to be doing it on my own. Not that I am not fully capable, but how everything went down. Word of advice ladies... trust your gut. My gut made me an investigator. When a male tells you that you're crazy. Be sure to pull up the rugs, show up unexpected. You know, get down to what is really going on. His loss, my gain. As Diane, my client and a nurse says, "We would be extinct if men had to carry and give birth." She is so right! Once a liar, always a liar. Once a cheat, always a cheat. Lesson learned.

The waitress asks for our drink order. Of course I get the strawberry lemonade. It's like a smoothie. We look over the menus. Us Kacens don't take long to decide... except Marie, but she's a Gemini. Our orders are taken. My dad says, "Carrie, I been doing a lot of thinking and I wasn't drinking." I am hanging on to what he's gonna say. He is not a man of deep commentary before his 5 p.m. Coors Light. He continues, "I know that you need someone in the delivery room with you. I think it would be best to be a man. I would like to be there for you when the baby is born. I figure we could take the parenting classes together." He has tears in his eyes, and I do too. We are committed to the plan of him helping to bring his third grandchild into the world. My dad is my best friend. He is my rock. Although my rock is so attached to me that it cracks a bit. That's what happens when you're so interconnected.

Emma walks into the back room. I breakdown. She has that affect on me. She rubs my back and says, "Are you okay, Car?"

I reply, "No, I'm not okay. I have been in pain all morning. The pain seems to come and go every five minutes. I called the doctor and the nurse wouldn't even put me through. She recommended getting to the hospital immediately. Oh, and would you grab my blow-dryer off my station? I want to sneak out the back door."

Emma replies, "No problem." She returns to ask, "Do you want me to help you to the car?"

"No, Emma." I am strong and I am independent. I can do this myself. Also, I am still concerned with following the policy to have two stylists on the floor at all times. There are two or three walk-ins still waiting.

I leave and waddle to my car. I drive to Canfield and hang a right. Pick up the iPhone and contact my Dad. He is crunching on lunch, which is funny to say. He has been receiving dental work and does not have his four front teeth. His goal is to have his teeth done by March when my child is born. Most recently, his floating disks within his spine are taking the drivers' seat. "Hi, Car," states Dad.

I have a quiver to my voice, "Dad, I am heading to the hospital. I am having cramping. The doctor's office told me to go. I need someone to meet me there."

He replies, "Who do you want?" We had a plan. He was my guy... my delivery guy... my dad... my friend.

"My sister. I want MY SISTER. FIND HER!!!"

Marie and I have had a contentious relationship throughout our sisterhood. We went through a lot as children and teenagers. She took on a lot of adult responsibilities when my parents split. My mom worked and directed Marie to her household motherly duties. I was her trusty assistant and tag-along sister. She dragged me everywhere afterschool. Her friends loved me, especially her friend, Julie. She hated it. I got all the attention, and she slaved afterschool as a very young mom. When I say young. She was only ten years old. Sure, she was good at it, but seriously! That topic is a whole different book.

Second phone call is to Fran. "Hey Sweetie," she answers.

"Hi, Fran. I am heading to the hospital. I have cramping. Where do I turn in to park in the garage?"

"Carrie, what did your doctor say? No, just park in Lot B. It will be way easier to get in the building and call me when you in with what is going on."

"I will."

I park my beloved Pilot. I get a spot that is in the lot. It is not so close. I think in my head. What if I am in labor and I drove myself to the hospital? That is so Carrie Kacen. I am strong and independent. I don't need as much help as the average bear. Ha! I am breathing in and out, in and out, in and out. No, I don't have to take a crap. I am scared.

I walk across the hospital breathing in and out. I know where I am going. I was just there yesterday. I reach the elevator bank and push three. I reach the third floor. I have to ring the intercom button and keep it together. I am ready to burst into tears. "Hello?" she says.

"Hi, I am Carrie Kacen I was told by Dr. Wordly to come up to the hospital. I am cramping and only 23 weeks."

She replies in a rushed voice, "Come directly to the left."

I enter the doorway and walk so slowly and carefully. I try to take a deep breath and keep it together. She looks at me concerned. "Weren't you here yesterday?"

I quiver and cry. Will the words spill out of my mouth? "I am 23 weeks along. I had a bit of blood in my discharge and I have been cramping all morning. I am sorry, but I am really scared."

"It's okay," is the reply. "We are going to take you back now to examine you."

Bed 18

I walk down the hallway with a nurse. We enter the examining room. I am guided to the same exact bed I was lying on yesterday. I was fine. My cervix was "high and tight" and the baby had plenty of amniotic fluid to live and swim in. That was yesterday, and we are here today. Live in the moment… well, there is something not right about how I am feeling. I know that for certain. They will figure it out. I was so embarrassed to head up to the hospital again! I'm a neurotic first time mother. No, I am very, very, very frightened.

I know the drill. Utilize the bathroom, change into the gown and use the step stool to get up to the bed. I am here again. The Emergency Doctor is on duty again! Ohhh, geez louise! His demeanor reminds me of a Scrubs character. Lots of questions, but no expression. Dry, dry and dry. I wonder, does he ever have sex? Cause that really might never happen to him. Lots of questions, but no pen, no pad to right the answers down. Again and again with him. I had to deal with him yesterday. Patience Carrie, you impatient Aries. Patience is a virtue in life. Yoga breathing… in and out, in and out. Relax. The nurse with me is amazed and bothered by my belly ring, as are so many others. Oh well, one less hassle to keep it in until my belly button pops. I will be wearing that piece of jewelry again. I do not want to pull it through the hole on a daily basis. Another thing to worry about and put into my daily routine. Besides, Jimmy Coleman and I had it repierced during my Dugan's on Halsted days. I am not looking for a charm the third time!

The Emergency Doctor and the nurse are locating my pain and conducting an ultrasound. The nurse is pulled away. I think it was probably a shift change. I have a new nurse who is short in build and dark-skinned. We talk and I take to her. Jessica arrives in the room. She has received the low down on why I am here again! Jessica, the doctor, has a Polish last name I come to find out later. I have a thing for Polish people due to being a Pollack myself. I have a real soft spot for the fighting Irish as well. I identify closely with both nationalities. Jessica asks me questions. I provide answers. I am told that they will conduct an exam on my cervix. I do not like getting them so very much. It is uncomfortable and I am tiny in size. It is extremely uncomfortable and hurts. Maybe, just maybe, that is where the tinge of pink came in my discharge. Yes, it has to be! No, no, put the soles of your feet together and let your knees slide open. I wish I were in my Yoga class with Francis doing this. I would have pants on, no socks with my toes well pedicured and polished. I am here though. Live in the moment of now, Carrie. Jessica knows I don't care for this. Her voice is so comforting to me, "I know Carrie, just let me take a few minutes to see what is going on." We are completed with this process after some painful moments. I go to the bathroom. I feel the energy high and a tone in their voices about some stats. I have an idea that it's not right.

They help me up to the bed. Jessica looks with her held tilted to her shoulder. The non-verbal cue is sympathy and compassion. I like her. "Carrie, you are dilated to one centimeter."

I lose it. I am strong and confident. Oh no, I am scared to the bone. Marge was dilated one centimeter and due in November with Nina, another Scorpio. That was fine. She

Bed 18

would be a week or two early. I am 23 weeks and 1 day. I am not supposed to be dilated. I cry and break. I am broken. I am frightened. I need someone. I am strong and confident. I am so sad. I call my sister. No luck. I try Max, my brother-in-law, but Marie, my sister, picks up.

Marie is having lunch. A celebration for my niece, Aubrey. She completed a few weeks of testing at Kiddo Hospital. She does not have Crone's Disease. She is going to be a healthy six year old that reads at second grade level. I am on the other end with another piece of the world. She answers with a happier tone. I haven't heard that tone from her in awhile.

I am hysterical on the phone. Tears are covering my face. The doctors are watching me as if I'm on television. They are engaged and concerned. It's not Grey's Anatomy. This is my moment, my life, and my now. "Marie, I need you to come to the hospital! I need you to come and calm me down. I am dilated one centimeter."

"Car, I'm being dropped off at work right now. I am grabbing something and I'm on my way."

I peer back at the doctors. Jessica says, "We are going to move you to a room."

Maureen Connelley, my client with a cute brown bob that has 95% gray hair is a delivery nurse at Resurrection Hospital. She told me I'm having a girl, and to request Room 16 or 17 when I have my girl in the spring.

They roll me to Room 16. I am here and I feel the energy of nervousness. Jessica says, "You are going to be here for awhile." I know this is not good. I check the clock. Yes, my sweet child, I am counting. I have a Type A and an obsessive personality. I begin on the new obsession. My sister will take 30-45 minutes to get here. It is sometime near one o'clock in the afternoon. I have the dark-skinned nurse going to put an IV into me. I hear Jessica saying, "Don't move. You are one centimeter and bulging." Bulging? Bulging? I am enduring cramps this whole time. I am breathing. In and out, in and out. Then there is a young nurse. She is a student. I wish I remembered her name. I do remember her and probably will not forget her, ever! The IV is being put into the top of my left hand. I am bony, but veiny. They are nervous. I am terrified. I am left alone a few times in Room 16 by Jessica, the ER doctor and the IV nurse. I am cold. The IV is dripping into my veins. I'm always cold, but this time I am really, really cold.

The young nurse student, let's name her Comfort, asks what can she do for me. I am strong and confident. I answer her question. I always envisioned music during my delivery. Music relaxes me and grounds me. For someone who is not a grounded person, I need music. I am strong. I am confident. "Please, put the television on with a music station," I say.

Comfort says, "Do you know what station you want?"

Now my girls at the shop would say, *Hello!! We always and only listen to XRT with Carrie.*

Bed 18

"XRT," I say.

"What station is XRT?" Comfort replies.

"93.1," I come back with. My shoulders relax a bit.

Comfort says, "What else can I do for you?"

I am strong. I am independent. I am confident.

"Stay with me. Hold my hand." I answer.

"Okay," Comfort says. She is on the right side. My legs are lifted up by the bed. We talk. We discuss what I do for a living, my sister coming and how scared I am. Comfort tells me I am doing so well and tells me about what she wants to do as a nurse. I know she is going be a great nurse, because she is already. I am holding her and breathing through my cramping.

The dark-skinned nurse of Indian decent comes to tell me that my doctor is going to be transferred to my phone. I think the IVs and the pills they feed me will make this all come to an end. "We are going to slow down your contractions and keep you hydrated. You seem cold. Do you care for a blanket?" they tell me.

I am shivering where my body is moving. I'm supposed to stay still. I can't. My body is doing things I've never experienced. I am not in control. I am strong. I am confident. I am independent too. "Yes, a blanket would be great!" I say.

When the phone rings, it is immediately handed to me. I am left alone. I am strong. I am independent. I say "Hello." I am quivering emotionally and physically. It's Dr. Worldly. She is lean, a Scorpio, has a strong accent and I like her immediately. She is the second doctor that is looking after my precious wee one and me. She talks astrology with me on the first visit. She is a Scorpio and I am an Aries. Two leader signs. One is more reserved… that wouldn't be me. Dr. Worldly always says 'no' with her strong accent, which actually means 'yes or right' in her lingo. She is always telling me how skinny I am. I certainly don't feel skinny, but yes, I am all belly.

"Carolyn, I mean Carrie. We are going to transfer you to Human Spirit Hospital. This is a good hospital. They are trying to slow your contractions down and will be transporting you there. If you have the baby, they will be able to handle the baby." Dr. Wordly says to me. I am crying. She understands my fear and worry.

I ask in a weak broken voice, "Are you going to come there too?"

She replies, "No, I do not have privileges at that hospital. I will call and check on you."

I say, "Okay, okay," through my sniffles. They take the phone away from me and hang up.

I know this is not good. I keep being told that they are slowing down my contractions. Although in reality they aren't slowing down at all. They are getting stronger. My transportation is on its way. I keep looking at the clock. I am about to call my sister. I have placed the phone to my face. I just want to say, where the fuck are you, as she walks into Room 16. She has arrived and I feel better. Marie can display a lot of nervous energy, but she can also get up to her elbows in a crisis situation. I hope for the best. She seems to be delivering her best. She holds my hand. I like a firm hold. No fingers together just hand in hand. That is the physical interaction I demand from her and any nurse or EMT during my contractions.

My feet are raised in the bed. I am 'bulging'! My ambulance is on the way! I think of Patrick O'Connell. I have a better understanding of his demeanor at this moment. I can hear him being calm and funny at the same time. The team arrives. First, is the shorter Italian from Addison. He is a straight-talker and is moving things around. Then there is Tom, the Irish one. I immediately have a crush. He is dark-haired with light eyes and I start to tell him I only have black socks on, just like any good Pollack. My sister is sharing how I'm the jokester of the family. I think my brother, Matthew, is more so. We used to be really funny together. Those days have been lost for some time. The 'Scrubs doctor' is moving and talking with his major lack of personality and normal expression. He comes over for a minute.

I smile to Tom. He asks, "What?"

I convince him to speak with his demeanor for just a minute. He does, and we lock eyes. Confirmation of the goofball. As Dad would say, "knucklehead".

Then there's the Black Angel, my male nurse. He says, "I'm sorry we have to meet this way." He takes a liking to me. I like him. He is the most masculine nurse. He makes sure I receive my third pill to stop the contractions. I am not allowed to gulp water or sit up. I am sipping the tiniest amount of water in my mouth. The pills feel like they are just stuck in my throat! I want a big glass of water or Gatorade. "We have you hydrated with your IV," they keep telling me. I want water!

I'm moved from the hospital bed into the transporter. I don't look forward to the rolling around looking up at the ceiling or straight on. We are in crisis mode. They all keep telling me that my contractions are going to slow down. They don't. I hope they will. My baby wants out. Why??? My sister is ready to follow the ambulance. Oh no, sister you are coming with me! We ask if she can come. "Of course." we are told. We are going through the hospital. Too much energy and stimulation. Faces, proceeding through the Emergency Room, out the door. I get very, very dizzy upon entering the great outdoors. The Italian tells me, "It's the exhaust, Carrie." They glide me strongly and swiftly to the back. My contractions continue every 4-5 minutes lasting 1-2 minutes. The Italian or Marie are on hand support duty. They are doing a good job. He ends up squeezing my hand harder than I squeeze his. We laugh and I smile. I do smile and giggle throughout this crisis. The whirlwind is still going.

We are in the elevator. Tom and I have a chance to speak freely about the goofball Emergency Doctor. Tom states,

Bed 18

"I was trying to make you comfortable and confident with the three of us."

The Emergency Doctor came over in the hospital when I was on the stretcher. He states the classic textbook response regarding guilt, "This is not your fault. Things happen." He goes on and on.

I just want to speak to Tom. He is Irish, cute, funny and has great common sense. I am more confident in his care than that doctor! Doctors are a breed of their own. A great doctor is a person that has been dethroned, has experience with loss personally and professionally and learned from it all. A humbled person is a great doctor and I will call by "Doctor". Otherwise, you will be called by your first name. You have not earned it quite yet. I will hold the bar a bit. I will peck at that ego a bit.

We are in the back. My Black Angel and Marie are timing my contractions. The Angel and I communicate. "Here comes another one." I breathe in and out in my yoga way.

"Braxton Hicks is what it sounds like," the Black Angel responds.

I'm diligent in communicating when the contraction starts and ends. I'm being transported because they have slowed down my contractions. Really? I'm in route to Human Spirit Hospital for the level of care I need and possibly my wee one. My contractions haven't slowed down. In fact, they are stronger and pretty close in time. I believe what they are trying to tell me. First, slowing down my contractions. Secondly, stabilize me. Thirdly, have me at the hospital I need to be at for the level of care we require, which is level three. Resurrection is level one. I wanted to have my child at Resurrection for many reasons. I was born there. I wanted my child to be born in Chicago. My family is located in the Northwest Suburbs. The hospital is located right off the Kennedy and Harlem Avenue. I had wishes and plans. I wished to go into labor at work, have a quick ride to the hospital (work is five minutes from the hospital), a massaged body, facial, manicure and pedicure with red toes. I am strong and independent. I am confident. Wishes, dreams and plans are the story of my life. Life happens when you are making plans!

Marie is timing the contractions on her iPhone. She is to the right, Italian to the left and the Black Angel behind me at my head. I am protected again by three souls. They have my best interest at heart. We travel down First Avenue. Very rocky and bumpy road... can we say railroad tracks? God allowed us to pass each set of tracks without a Metra train and those stinkin' freight trains. Blessed and not quite aware how blessed. We talk to the Italian about where he lives and where he grew up. He directs the same questions to Marie and me. He is all over my stats just like a hawk. Each EMT is all over their task. Efficient, friendly and kind. They are same at the bar. I drank with Paramedics before. Efficient in ordering beers and shots, friendly in conversation and kind in their demeanor. They are crisis savers. They need people that show their emotions. I am strong and confident. Not a match. I am independent.

Bed 18

I am swiftly brought to the ground on my stretcher. I am rolled across the Emergency Room at The Human Spirit Hospital. The Grey's Anatomy episode is off pause and on play. Only this is my life. The eyes, glances and stares I receive along the way to the floor of Labor and Delivery, frighten me. The ceiling is passing me oh so quickly. Overstimulation! I am strong, independent and confident. So, I can keep it together. I breathe my yoga breathing. No prenatal classes, but nearly four years of yoga. The ability to concentrate is from my dedication to centering myself through yoga. My painful life experiences give me the ability to stay calm in crisis and escalated situations. Nothing I would wish on anyone, but it is what it is. I am strong now! The friendly nurses say, "Hello, Carolyn!" in cheerful voices. I state, "I go by Carrie!" Let's get that straight, ladies. Little did I know how much I would be stimulated by conversation in the next hours to come. My shop business and my staff have nothing on this one!

The EMT team settles me in and is on their way out. Warm wishes are exchanged by both parties. I was having fun with those guys! Back to the crisis. 'A rollercoaster', is what I am told it is. Well, who bought my ticket to this ride? I am independent and I know I sure didn't buy it! The nurse has a half-empty glass in life. "I have two jobs," she states numerous times. Wow! Let's go there and get that off your chest. Who doesn't work their ass of in this economy? Geez louise! I've had two jobs the majority of my working life. I am independent because of it, lady! My sister rubs her skin like nails on a chalkboard. Marie looks at her with her baby blue eyes and asks the 2-Jobber, "Am I getting on your nerves?" Marie knows the answer, but loves the mental game of push-and-pull, no matter the occasion.

2-Jobber states, "Marie, I have been doing this a long time."

We have cleared the air in my tiny room with all sorts of equipment to help me and my wee one. The nurse has two jobs, Marie is protecting me with her bitchy ways and I am in the middle as usual. 2-Jobber has been doing this job a long time. Although she doesn't seem to keep my legs very elevated! That is a must... I am bulging.

The circus has arrived and I am the guest her at The Human Spirit Hospital. Clowns, acrobats, animal weirdoes and all sorts of peeps. The welcome sign wasn't read. I was rolling too fast into this place. Marie knows to ask for a Neonatal Specialist upon our arrival. I have worries and concerns! We need to talk people. Lord knows Marie and I can talk well with one another. Our communication isn't so great. I am getting a new IV cause the first shitty one on the top of my hand isn't good enough even though I was tortured! I say, "All right, where are you gonna put it?" They look and I am veiny... lots of veins. On your left wrist. Marie recommends a numbing, then the IV and I am game. That is all on the left. On the right they are trying to talk to me. I look at the lady... I swear her name was Marilyn. She is up in my grill. I look at her while she is talking to me with my eyes closed breathing while the IV is being placed in. "Marilyn you need to come back. One thing at a time!" I fiercely state. She gets the picture and it's clear as a blue sky in the summer. Bye, bye lady come back. Oh, she is back shortly talking and talking. I have repeated the process of why and when I started with this crisis. Over and over. Ouch! Then we proceed with talking and answering questions.

The Neonatal point person arrives to the left of my bed with my Marie in front of her. Here is the conversation. Raw and real begins around 7 or 8ish on November 24, 2009. She is dark skinned and shorter, but peaceful. She is calculated and has clear intentions. She is Jasmine to me from Aladdin. Jasmine is stating over and over to live in the now. Our conversation, contractions and cold IV are making me shake all over. She wants me to calm down while we talk possibilities. What are your concerns? Let's talk options. Stats. Probability. Wants. Desires. Raw and real. I am strong. I am confident. I am independent. What if you have the baby today? Do I want to resuscitate? Rock the baby to death or eternal life? Disabilities? Survival Rate? Quality of Life? Big deep water. I am a direct decision person. I am strong. I want to resuscitate. No question about it. If my child will not have a high quality of life, I will cross that bridge. I will not hang on for me. The baby needs a quality of life. Jasmine says, "Don't worry, this could never happen. It is just good to have an idea and direction. You are very clear on your decision."

Marie says, "Yes, that was a direct answer."

Yes, I have a clear answer and intention. The dark deep sea isn't awaiting. Oh no... I'm in it and have no stinkin' clue! I am in the now. Painful contractions and having the most important conversation of my life!

Jasmine departs. I am with Marie. We are back to the large medical attempt to put the red light onto my contractions. I am repeatedly told that they are trying to stop them. They are stronger and still quick frequent, usually 5-8 minutes apart. I am thinking how the heck I'm going to be on bed rest and still manage financially. Marie knows that is where my mind is going. She says, "We will figure something out." Your health and your baby's health are most important.

The three doctors keep coming back in and out. I am examined at least half a dozen times. I can't take it. I have contractions and they want me foot to foot with my knees relaxed and opened. I am not in yoga class. This is horribly uncomfortable alone, plus contractions equals NO FUN!!! I stated numerous times, "I hate this part... not again!" They did not have to do much convincing for I know their intentions are to help me and my precious wee one!

I am discussing with Dr. Rose, the sweet Philippino, that they would like to conduct an ultrasound. I keep telling her and the other two labor and delivery doctors that my wee one was measuring large at my 17-week ultrasound. My child was measuring anywhere from two days to two weeks larger. The head measurement was 20 weeks. I kept saying to Nana, Jane Kacen, that I was having a big baby. She agreed. The ultrasound was one of the best days of my entire life. I had my dear friend, Fran meet me at the hospital. "Carrie, you look so cute with your little belly." Fran would always say with a sweet smile and a rub to my belly. Fran and I draped me up for the ultrasound. We had quite a discussion of true friends and people's pessimistic attitudes. She just became engaged to a fantastic man, Sean Hayes, and only had been together a short period of time. Judgment allows us all to feel better about ourselves. For me, I have no right to judge, but do it anyway. Little did I know the magnitude of this conversation would be oh, so much greater. We were called into the ultrasound room at Resurrection Hospital. My wee one was one active baby. Two hours later with two technicians and a doctor they collected the proper data. The data did show that there was a concern of my placenta being low. My doctor, Dr. Wordly, told me later that day not to worry. Ninety-five percent of women are fine. The memorable moments were when my active baby was high-fiving us all, utilizing the pointer finger (I'm telling you) and kicking up a storm. Fran cried, we laughed and then needed to calm down to get the shots. It was such a great experience.

So, here Dr. Rose and I are discussing the ultrasound. I would like to go to the bathroom before this happens. They give me a bedpan. Never used one before today. Today is a new experience of urinating in a bed pan, about 10 times actually. Wow! I'm not elderly, just not allowed to move. I have nurses wiping me. I am insisting on wiping myself. I am independent. I am strong. I am confident. I am rolled into the ultrasound room with Dr. Rose, Marie and Katie, my angel. I did not know Katie had wings at this point. I was in the room with ice chips, sucking on them. Dr. Rose was very attentive and diligent. I was thinking I might just want to find out if my wee one is a girl or a boy. Marie says, "You are having a boy, no daughter would do this to her mother."

She wanted to find out and not tell me, so it still would be surprise. No way sista, this is MY life. Marie leaves the room for a bit. Dr. Rose and I discuss possibly finding out later in the ultrasound. Katie arrives back as well as Marie. My entire body turns burning hot. My mouth, my entire body. I turn to Katie and the doctor. "What are you giving me?! Why is my body burning?!"

They both said, "Nothing."

Another piece of the puzzle missing that is. Dr. Rose is completing the ultrasound finding out that indeed my child is measuring quite small! I am shocked and wondering, WHY? Well, possibly due to the internal infection, my child was not developing as well. There was no way of feeling, sensing or knowing I had an internal infection.

Dr. Rose turns to me and says, "So, do you wanna know?"

After keeping it a surprise for myself and others, I knew I needed to communicate by name to my child at this point. "Yes, I do."

She scrolls down and around. "See this?"

"Dr. Rose," I say, "Is that a penis?"

"NO," responded Dr. Rose.

"Is it a vagina?"

She smiles and says, "No, it's a labia."

Bed 18

I raise my right arm up so high, make a fist and pull it down with all my might. With a big smile and feeling relieved I exclaim, "YES!"

Marie appeared surprised while processing the new data. I am thrilled. I thought I was carrying a girl all along.

I am rolled back into my small room. Katie states, "I am doing my best to keep the other room across from you vacant." Privacy is always a good thing.

Marie and I are getting ready for bed. I need saline solution, a toothbrush and soap to wash my face.

I left my friend, Angie, a message earlier. She is my old neighbor. I met her on the first day while looking to purchase my second condo. I liked her immediately. She is warm and friendly. Angie is a Neonatal Nurse Practitioner. I left a message to talk to her as a friend and a resource. She returns my call. I tell Marie, "Give me the phone. It is Angie, my neonatal friend." Angie is so shocked and comforting. We discuss in length how I am at The Human Spirit Hospital, when it all started, how I am doing at the moment, what "they" are saying and what she can inform me on. "Carrie, there is something magical about 24 weeks. If you could hang on to Cailin for one more week the odds are better." Angie informs me. I hang up the phone.

While the phone is crossing my body to be placed onto the table, I inform Marie about how magical 24 weeks is. "We gotta keep the baby in for at least a week." I place the phone down on the table.

POP. GUSH. "Fuck, my water broke! Go get them Marie, and tell them my water broke!" I screamed and cried hysterically. Marie runs across the small room to almost hit the glass room separator and curtain simultaneously. She turns the corner only to bump into Katie.

I say loudly, "Cailin, WHY? WHY, Cailin? It's too early!!!"

Katie and Auburn-haired Doctor enter my room.

I ask, "Where is my sister?!"

They both state, "In the bathroom, in the bathroom."

I scream loudly, "MARIE!"

She comes back into the room. I say, "How the fuck can you leave me when my water breaks?!!"

She glares in shock with her baby blues that I am swearing at her.

"Get over here!" I say with my right arm extended for hand support.

Auburn-haired Doctor and Katie, my angel nurse, say, "Oh, just a little water," when they look at my sheets.

I know differently. For I know that my bed is soaking wet. They reassure me that the baby can survive for sometime even after your water breaks. I stare at Auburn-haired

Bed 18

Doctor. I scare and yell, "This is not supposed to fucking happen today, not today, she is too little!!"

His eyes show fright, fear and major concern. I come to discover Auburn-haired Doctor was fairly new to Labor and Delivery. I am sure he will not forget me. He is standing with his arms crossed, feeling shocked as well. We all know this is definitely not the ideal situation for my wee one. I have plans of a Valentine's Day shower, eating a lot during the holidays and having my family feel my wee one moving about my stomach. My wee one is a mighty wee one. My child has more control of how things are and how things will be.

I am wheeled into my delivery room. The teams of doctors are collaborating for this high-risk delivery. My wee one has a team of her own, the Neonatal High-risk Team. We are prepared. Ha! Ha! I have a request to take out my contacts. I don't know how long I will be in labor. They have been in my eyes since 7 a.m. Just too long. Save the eyes! Katie, my angel, and Marie give me saline and my contact case. Along with the hand-off comes four hands to try to help me take them out! No! No, ladies! I jerk my arm into my body and say, "Let me take them out!" Mission accomplished. Back to my peak contractions and breathing. I am moved to the labor bed. I have to slide side to side to get there. I am told that my water broke, but maybe the labor will slow down. Yeah, right people. My child has plans, power, control and a magnificent purpose here in life. Watch out! I am breathing and told the epidural is on its way. I wanted a vaginal delivery with an epidural. Thank you, God.

The annoying epidural man comes in. So it's Katie, Eppi Dude and me. Marie is behind a curtain listening to me. I keep saying I want it, but I am scared. I have heard too many stories of the epidural. I know that damn needle is creepy long and you must not flinch. Katie is helping me through my contractions that are at a peak. She says, "Carrie, I am going to have you cross your legs and sit up near the end of the bed. Then push the small of your back out."

This position is ideal. Most cannot achieve this. I am an overachiever. I am strong. I am confident. I am a rule follower. Katie asked and I did it. I have my hands on her shoulders. She has hers on mine. My idea. I look in her cute Irish face and say, "Katie keep me centered, keep me calm."

I tell her when the next one is coming.

Katie keeps responding, "Carrie you are just gonna breathe through it. Keep your shoulders relaxed. Keep your quads relaxed. Keep breathing. You did it again!"

She was my angel and still is with her kind heart. Katie has had so many kind gestures. She got me through the worst part of my physical delivery.

On the backside, I have Eppi Dude. I am breathing so much through my contractions that I am actually blowing Katie's hair. I say to her, "I am so sorry Katie. I am sure my breath smells so bad."

Eppi Dude is knocking on my back and proceeds to say, "All I smell is the alcohol back here."

Bed 18

I respond in a bitchy tone, "Are you almost done back there?"

During the peak of my contractions, he already asked me what my height was and now he asks again. Check my fucking chart. I have enough to concentrate on. I don't want my back screwed up. The Eppi Dude discarded one tray and requested another one. I originally thought he dropped his tray. I was very annoyed with him. I am thinking... can't you handle the pressure dude? Really, that is the way it is given? Eppi Dude just needed another tray. Finally, that was over.

Marie comes out from behind the curtain. I am lying in the middle of the bed. She is on the left. Katie is on the right. Eppi Dude comes back in for the kill. He has this tiny pin that almost looks like a tack. He is poking me and saying, "Is this sharp?" He is on the left and proceeds to right. Not that gently though.

My mouth and attitude are flying. "Of course it is sharp! It's a damn pin. All right already! Yes, some spots are sharper than others."

Does it really matter? My wee one is on the way dude! You are done, and I am moving on. I am breathing through the contractions. Marie is on her iPhone and getting it ready for pictures. We don't know exactly what to expect. My child is extremely premature. Both teams are getting ready. I am stating, "I am crowning! I am crowning!"

Marie wants to see. I say, "Don't look at my vagina."

She looks at me, "But I gotta see."

She looks all right. When has she ever listened to me? I'll give her this one too! She had c-sections with Aubrey and Jackson.

She is the one that ultimately gets the doctors attention. "She is crowning, guys!"

The doctors are asking me to get to the bottom of the bed. "I can't. I can't. She is coming."

The doctors ask, "Why?"

"Because she is coming!!" I push just a little bit and I feel her. Her head and then her little shoulder.

She is here. Cailin Jane is here. My girl. My daughter! I am so happy and so very scared and sad. She is only 23 weeks and 1 day. My weekly pregnancy book that Kiki gave me describes a 23-weeker (as the neonatal peep say) of being a small doll. Well, they weren't lying.

I am staring to the left at Marie. She is up at my shoulder. She is starting to see the expressions of the Neonatal Team. She is blankly staring. I am fixated on her blue eyes. My placenta! It is not coming out. The cord snapped. Apparently, it's a common theme in pre-term delivery. I have Auburn-haired Doctor trying to get it out. No luck. They keep telling me it's gonna hurt. They have a hand inside me and a hand on my abdomen. One hand pushes on the abdomen while one hand is trying to pull. No luck. Round two.

The young female doctor is doing the same thing. No luck. Dr. Rose is on it. She still has no luck. I will be going into surgery to remove the placenta.

Jasmine, Neonatal point person, is approaching me on the right. She does not come too close. Time is of the essence. She looks with her brown eyes. "She is badly bruised, much smaller than anticipated and we had trouble with the smallest breathing tube with her. It does not look good. Marie will come with us while you go to surgery."

Of course, my sister gets to go see my baby before me! So typical. Actually, she is getting prepared to prepare me for the worst. I see it in their eyes. Their eyes are medically, scientifically and factually fixated. I am so drugged up. I start to really listen to everyone. It's only been God and myself for sometime now. I am on the bed with Katie at my side.

Eppi Dude is back on the spot. Right when I thought he was gone for good. Nope! I believe at this point I let him know my thoughts by saying, "Not you again."

His boss laughs and asks me, "Do you want a 'forgetful drug' during your surgery?"

"Yes, I do."

I am wheeled off again to the surgery room. I see a lot of equipment and everyone is taking his or her station. I am in and out of it. It was successful. I lost a lot of blood. I lost a lot blood. I am told this frequently. Well, people I am not dying. I do know that for certain. In Labor and Delivery, Marie worried that I would choose my baby over myself. She asked me hours ago to pick myself. I told her not to worry. I know I would have picked Cailin. I would have. I just would have.

Picking your child over yourself is something I face along this journey. I discover an unconditional bottomless love for my child. I love Cailin Jane more than anyone here on earth. I love her just as much as I love God. God has kept me together all my darkest days and nights. Cailin is just a symbol of his love. I melt. I am in love. Love that I have never felt before. Mother and daughter love. She is the truest blessing and gift I could ever ask for. Thank you, God. Thank you.

I am out of the operating room. Marie is in my delivery room. Katie is helping me go to the bathroom. She places large comfy underwear on me with a pad. She wipes me. Wow! "Katie you just wiped me. Thank you so much." Katie does this daily and does not think twice. I know she is a remarkable woman!

There are three women after a major crisis situation. What are we worried about? How we look? But, of course. There is a large mirror and we look into the mirror. My sister, Marie, has her Lush Victoria Secret's lip gloss. We both use it. I check my eye makeup, not to shabby for just having 15 hours of labor and a baby, huh? I fluff my wavy hairstyle I just started sporting. Katie and Marie both tell me how I am looking pretty good. Really? Katie checks herself briefly and Marie is all set. We are off.

Bed 18

I discussed during labor how I would like my child baptized. No matter what, she is willing God's light. I want her protected from this crazy world and all the bad juju! The Chaplain, that I will never forget, goes to the NICU with us. Katie and Marie are taking turns pushing my wheelchair and taking photos. We take a picture of Marie and me, then one of the Chaplain and me, Katie and me. Marie is trying to make memories. She knows how I am always taking pictures. She is not that into pictures. She rises to the occasion of making my memories. This is my first child. It is not a usual story, hence the book. Our story is incredible! She takes a picture of a piece of art on the wall upon entering the unit.

We enter the unit. It is a blur. Little do I know. I know myself, but it's still a blur. A big blur. My baby is so tiny. She is a small doll. She looks so fragile and not ready for this world. She is bruised. I am scared to touch her. Katie takes pictures of us looking at Cailin. Marie looks with concerned eyes on me in all the photos. I love my daughter, Cailin, and Marie is loving me. All the pictures show love. Love. Love at Bed 18.

I reach into the incubator to touch her foot. I am scared to touch her head. The breathing tube, lines, IVs. So much stuff on someone so little. My wee one is wee. I feel she knows it's me touching her foot. She had her first sacrament. She is in the light. If God wants to take her back home or have her stay on earth. I did the right thing. I never regret giving her a chance of living.

I am wheeled in a blur, back to the delivery room. Chaplain, Marie and me. The Chaplian and I have a deep conversation.

I am crying. I am not sure Cailin is going to make it. Everyone is telling me how critical she is and the 23% chance of her survival is slim. She is bruised. On and on. Factual. Real. Scientific. How about the unseen? God's will? Our true path and journey in life? The lessons we are served that cannot be measured by medicine? These are the hurdles I have to face here in the NICU. I am unaware of the next chapter, challenge and layers beyond layers of our life. Cailin Jane. The Chaplain asks me questions and I answer. I express my thoughts. You are thinking, what are your thoughts? Here they are: I am afraid. I am so very frightened. I cannot imagine burying a child that I just carried and gave birth to. I have to watch how people are treating me. I need to think for myself. I am blurred with emotion, medication and hormones. I know myself. I will do this. I have no idea how, but I will. God has a plan. If Cailin is called back home to him, she will go in the light. I did my part. I want her though. I wanted her from day one! I love her. I miss her. I miss my belly. I miss her long skinny legs hitting me. I miss being uncomfortable physically. I am so out of sort. I am so uncomfortable with the magnitude of this! The Chaplain has lost three children this young. He understands loss. I am on the brink of something. What is it? I will not know without moving forward. Living in the now. Our life is so scary and uncertain. We talk out all my thoughts. Real and raw thoughts. Real and raw is how I become. It is not fun for everyone. Cailin's birth has thrown all my closets out in the open and my curtains down. Mommy, clean it all up? Clean what up? I am strong. I am independent. I am a single mother. I am. I am. I am me. I am on a journey now. The journey is ours. The journey entails making things better, people better, cleaning up messes, not tolerating certain relationships, setting boundaries, discovering who in my life is good in my life. Yes, Cailin. Yes, God. I am in!

I am in. How long? How long will this be? I am wheeled to the room I will be in until I am discharged. Marie is sleeping in my room. No question. She is with me. Thank you. We get ready for bed. Wow! What a day! Marie and I have had many days and nights together. November 24, 2009 will be on the top. The icing on the cake. The flower in your hair. It is unbelievable at this point for many peaks and valleys to come. I sleep. I pass out for about an hour, maybe. I am up. I am in a fetal position on my right side. I don't have Cailin in my belly. I am not sure if I go to see her she will be there... alive. I am crying like a baby. Shaking all over. Not the shake of an IV. A shake of my world being ripped from me. I am confident. I am strong. I am weeping as I never have before. Many more to come kiddo. Many more. I am separated from the love of my life. OHHHHH! I call the nurses stations. I want to go see my daughter. Marie lies still. I know she is not asleep. I am wheeled from my corner room. Thank you, God. Some privacy and respect during this fragile life situation. You picked me. You picked her. We agreed. Right? I am praying. I am crying. I am rolled to Bed 18. I don't remember the few tasks to do before seeing your child her at the NICU. The tasks I will be doing for a long, long time. I turn the corner. Pocahontas is her nurse. I cry and I say I am not sure she'll make it. I want her. I feel so bad. My stupid infection! Pocahontas looks at me with warm kind eyes. She is the taste test that I think I will have here in the NICU. She listens and is quite comforting. No questions. Just ears and heart, and she hears me. She feels some of my pain. Pocahontas is angelic to me.

My labor and delivery nurse of Philippian decent is short and petite like me. She grabs my wheelchair. I am in the wheelchair with a blanket, blue hospital socks and a hospital gown. I do not remember much on the way back. I cried. I was not talkative on the way back to my corner room. I crawled into my bed. I lay in my chosen position. Fetal on the right side. I lie there and cry. I weep. I weep and weep. Then I am silent. I lie there and try to sleep. I hear Marie on her pull out chair move. We have been lying still for about twenty minutes.

I say out loud, "I can't sleep."

Marie replies, "Me neither."

I ask her to spoon me. I love being spooned. Any person I dated knows I love a good solid spoon. I am strong and confident. I want to be held. Marie is not very affectionate. She crawls aside me. We discuss and process the day. Remember this. Remember that. What did you think when this happened? When that was said? How about that nurse, Katie? Wasn't she amazing? The questions went on and on. We laughed, we spoke with quiet voices, we cried. We were on the brink of major life changes. We had been challenged and stuck together as sisters. We would be challenged and not always see, think or feel similar...but this time we did!

A new nurse was on duty for my care. She came in and asked, "Where is the patient?"

Bed 18

I raised my hand and Marie scurried into her fold-out bed. We were caught. We were comforting each other, showing our weakness, our humanness and our true selves. We are Kacens. This does not happen. We are warriors in life. We are fierce. Cailin and God knocked all that bologna right out of us. We are real. We are scared. We are hurting. We are females without males handling yet another major, major life challenge. Challenge, Lesson, Test, Difficulty. The list goes on and on. It is called Life people!

Life. It is precious. It is scary, daring, sweet, bitter, dark, light, friendly, mean, rude, unpredictable, enjoyable, a journey. My daughter, Cailin Jane Kacen is here living her life. She is chosen. She signed up. She picked me. God planned her life. I was chosen. I agreed. I am here. She is here. God is everywhere.

The phone is ringing off the hook. Marie is fielding my phone and her phone. Word is out. People know. People are different. People have energy, intentions, will and I am on the receiving end. I am used to action. I am used to multi-tasking, handling many challenges and many people in a very short period of time. The message is slow, scared, small, love, quiet, love, help, guide, small, chosen people, guidance, small and sacred. I do not hear this message. All the energy, hormones and drugs cloud my mind, heart and body. I am uncertain. I will learn the hard way through living life. Chaos then clarity, they say. I know. For my life goes from chaos to clarity. Disagreements occur. Intentions are not clear. People say they care. They talk. They tell. They share. Are they on the way to church? Are they lighting candles? Are they meditating? Are they sending positive thoughts and prayers? Are they being aggressive with rapid and frequent texts, emails, phone calls and voicemails? Are they taking their emotions and searching for me to clarify them for a short moment? Are they worrying and being anxious? Are they searching for me to answer and address those concerns of themselves? Are they adults? Are they parents? What does Cailin need? What do I need? What does this situation, our life, need?

My father will be coming to the hospital. He will come see his grandbaby and me. He will watch his child go through a life experience that is so very magnified. He doesn't have to say much. I feel him. I know. Anxious during transition.

Margaret calls. She wants to know where I am. She asks... asking is key. For many want and feel they deserve. She asks. "Carrie, can I come see you?" She is weeping with me.

I say, "Yes, around noon."

Margaret is a great friend. She is a stable mother and Polish, gosh darn it. She is tough and very loving. I love her. She loves me. We are true friends. I nap. I eat nasty food. I have a smile when I see Margaret. She came to my room with a ton of prayer cards, a small prayer book and a pink saints bracelet. All things that do not leave my side. I tell her the story above while my dad sits and reads. He has a hard time listening. He needs to know how intense this was. We talk. I cry. Marge always compliments me. She tells me how good I look. I thank her. I sure don't feel great. I need to pump for Cailin. I am still not producing much. My dad gets so uncomfortable knowing that I will start

Bed 18

pumping. He goes for a cigarette break. Margaret and I are great friends. I am not one-ounce uncomfortable. She assists me in pumping. There is a knock on the door. It is Marie and her friend, Cling. Cling drove from Cary to The Human Spirit Hospital. They drove to Resurrection Hospital to grab my Pilot. They drove to Oak Park to my condo. Marie grabbed a few necessary things. My Ponds lotion, contact solution and a track suit to go home in. Marie grabs my fav Chuck Taylor shoes with my black clovers and red cherries all over them. We giggled when my dad arrived because of Max's, my brother-in-law, way of packing. Task completed, but the rolling and twisting of clothes. Ha! Marie is onto her usual ways wanting me to cover up cause Cling arrived. I asked Cling if she felt uncomfortable. She said, "No." Sorry Marie, I am just a little stressed and don't give a shit about my boobs sticking out sista! Pick your battles my friend. I produce a few drops of gold. We take a picture. I am so impressed that Marie is taking pictures of all of my first baby's moments. She just isn't much of a camera person. Where I love, love pictures and love being in them.

Margaret is on her way home. She and Josh, her husband, her family and the Kustras all prayed for Cailin Jane at the beginning of their Thanksgiving dinner. I give thanks to her. My daughter did not want to miss the holidays. I am feeling better that I saw Marge. I sent Kiki, also known as Chrissie, a text regarding Cailin's birth. She is in Oregon with her in-laws. She is texting me. I respond a bit and cease. I am receiving a lot of contact from many people. My dad and I go to see Cailin Jane. We arrive at the NICU. He wheeled me up there. We arrive and have a nice visit. The nurse is peppy and her name is Priscilla. We are spending time with Cailin. Cailin is very critical and I am still very scared to touch her and listen to all the issues she has. The doctors doing their rounds greet me. Dr. Bolt is on Cailin's medical case. He speaks to me about what is going on. I do not recall what he is saying. He is talking medical jargon and I am confused. I am out of it, scared and he is fully aware of how bad I am feeling. He speaks gently and to the point. This happens quite a few times during the first few visits. My dad really liked him. He said he really likes his profession; he is kind and a good man. I agree as I watch the characters unfold. Are we bad? Are we good? No. We have intentions. What are yours? Is Cailin a medical case? A statistic? My daughter? A living child? A human being fighting for her life?

We are going to head back down to my room. Priscilla asks, "I have to ask this. I know a Jane Kacen that has a daughter named Jackie Kacen. Are you at all related?"

"Yes," I say. "Jane is my grandmother and I named Cailin after her. Jackie is my aunt. My dad is the oldest of the six Kacens."

My dad proceeds to ask where she lived and what school she attended, only to discover she lived on the same block, went to high school with Jackie and Nana, and would drive them to school. Small world. Our world.

The next few days I bring visitors in and out to visit Cailin. I feel a lot of pressure. I am going through the motions. I have to pull it all back to have it the right way. Our way.

Bed 18   45

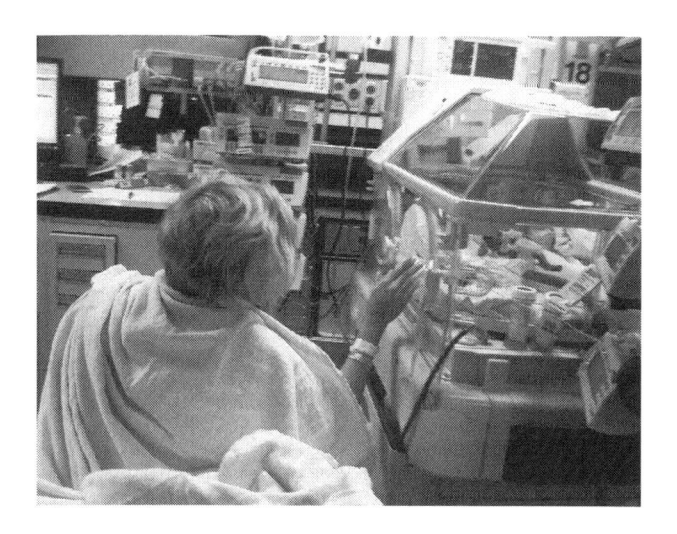

God, I'm In

Here I am with the premature delivery of a precious, little, fragile daughter, Cailin Jane. Why? Marie, my sister, wants to figure it all out. How it happened and why? It just isn't fair. I do ask why in my hospital room.

I have thought, meditated, cried in the sense of losing Cailin, cried in the fear of losing Cailin, I have talked a lot to get all the thoughts to come out and not haunt me.

Here I am again in the deep blue sea. I thought I was drowning, but now I have to tread water until God completes his healing process. I understand everything is a process. This is much larger than a process in life. I believe that God served me and Cailin this journey on a spiritual level. He trusts both of us entirely. I have kept to my faith. I do not recall being mad or angry with him. I know that He is the man with a plan. I am granted the honor to endure the medical healing of her premature body and emotionally healing myself. I have required healing for sometime. I neglected many of my relationships in my life. I have tolerated things that do not make me feel safe. I have tolerated being treated poorly.

I cleaned out my closets, although they weren't too messy. I was preparing. I was thinking what I would be like as a mother. All the hats, scarves, sweaters, accessories and so on were going to change. Cailin arrived unexpectedly early, sick and in need of major medical care. I required the proper type of love and support. I had energy from left, right, center, from the back, jumping, screaming and crying. I felt as if many monkeys were trying to jump on my back for a ride. My question became, what is their intention? How do I feel when certain people approach me? I have neglected my feelings and emotions and justified how people spoke to me as well as treated me for way too long. God wants me to stay strong and centered to Cailin through my faith. I am truly committed, entirely. I was granted a chance to be a mother to a very precious blessing from Him. Cailin's illness is one of the lesser worries. For I know, He will heal and challenge those who tend to her. Doctors, Fellows, Residents, Medical Students and our Beloved Nurses. The nurses get the brunt of it. My presence frightens and alarms many of them. I step back and stop to justify my stance, presence and faith. The approach from the many family members and friends is another layer. God wants me to stay centered. When I have demands on Cailin's status and updates I know that is not what we need. Cailin and I need love, understanding, prayers, positive thoughts, spoken masses, lit candles, cards, notes of encouragement. Those gestures are the love we desire, need and embrace.

On the other hand, the calls, texts, gasps of breath, despair, anxiety and worry are only distractions of his work. God provides light for the dark, strength for life, embraces for the tears and love that always ends with a happy ending. The distractions will only take us away from the purpose of our journey. I can't and will not update folks on Cailin's status. It is private and intimate. I need all my energy for Cailin. The distractions and me justifying myself is a waste of time and spinning around. For what? To make someone outside our journey feel a bit better only to need more information shortly. It is not necessary when you have true faith. God will serve his grace daily. We must approach each day gratefully and gently with the daily lessons.

I have many lessons I learn each moment with Cailin's health. I love God and Cailin so very much. I will receive what God grants me each day. I must do his work. His work is not always understood by outsiders. I must stay centered and loyal to my faith for He shall grant us a long lovely life as Mother and Daughter.

Viva Las Vegas - NICU

Room and board is $10K a night. We have shows including drama, horror, happy endings and everything in between. What stays in Vegas, stays in the NICU. You must sign in with the infant you're visiting and who you are. What bed and your relationship to the occupant. Privacy. Clip the badge, so we know where you belong and to whom. Enter upon the clicking large doors. They swing open. I enter. Wash your hands to the right. The sinks are large enough for surgery. Sanitize and dry hands. Push the next door-opener. Click. The next set of large doors open. The front desk divas will watch if you washed your hands, check the last time you came, how long it was, what you're wearing and your demeanor. Nothing they haven't seen. Don't think you're the first or last on this trip. To the left the Nurse Manager station is present. The charge nurse is there. The captain of each row, bed, baby, shift and nurses. Enter your row. Do not glare at the other babies. There is a privacy issue. No, it's not a private stripper room. It is where your baby is being nursed to good health. Breathing, eating and temperature control. There is a list of each show and story on the dry erase board. Kacen, Bed 18.

What is your story Kacen, Carrie, Ms. Kacen, Baby Girl Kacen, Sweetpea, Angel, Peanut? We are asked many questions.

Where do you live? What was your due date? When did you have Cailin? Where is the father? Is that man the father? A child does not have a father where there is a lack of presence. She does not have a father. A donor. End of story.

Each nurse has a schedule. Princess shift equals 4 hours. We have options of fun, drama, horror and happy endings of 4, 8, 12, or 16 hours. Pick your vice. We have showgirls. Some shows are a bit of dancing to the routine. I like the dancer that puts her heart into her glides, twists and turns with a smile and true expression with each dance number. Cailin's dances are ballet, tap, jazz, meditations, hip-hop and some good old country.

We have Pocahontas who is a ballet dancer. Elegant, pure and angelic. She is precise with her delicate movements and perfect formation. Her work is a piece of art. Pocahontas will voice her frustrations, advocate Cailin's needs during her two 12-hour shifts and the finale of her of 16 hours. She chose Cailin as her caterpillar that will become a beautiful butterfly. Pocahontas will rub Cailin Jane's head when I am not here. Telling her to relax and stay strong.

Princess Aurora does a bit of tap dancin'. She is entertaining with her commentary, gestures and sweetness. She has been on the floor for about 20 years. She knows her shit. Princess Aurora is that warm tap on my back, the warm towel for Cailin when she changes her bedding. Princess Aurora will run right up to the lab counter and hit it to get her blood work to the technician. No clotting. No clotting. Damn. Pick line people. For Princess Aurora will not tap Cailin's skin over and over for blood draws. I trust Princess

Bed 18

Aurora. I laugh with Princess Aurora. I confide in Princess Aurora. I confirm characters with Princess Aurora. She gets me right away. She is a dealer that knows the game. She knows the odds and how to change the odds with her tappin'.

Priscilla. Plain and simple describes this Capricorn. Levelheaded dancer that is just good old country. Let the song speak, Carrie. She trusts the guitar strings to play and if not well and out of tune...tweak. Tweak. Tweak. She takes the song and easily manipulates it to have a smooth rhythm. Priscilla will go to bat for you. You won't even know she is doing it.

Snow White is on the jazz side of things. Trust was what she wanted from me. I wanted respect. We meet in the middle of that horn playing verse that evolved to smooth jazz.

The babies are having all their stats followed. The machines ring just like the slot machines. The nurses yelp at the machines and gracefully cheer their baby on to good numbers. Good numbers is a win of stability for a period of time. Unknown amount of time. It reminds me of a craps table. Everyone is there together for the game. People have their own needs, desires and intentions of winning. What happens here, stays here.

Until I write of this strange world. A different planet. Vegas. A circus. The words can only give you a taste, just like a good teaser. The doctors are a different breed. Fellows. Half of them are a "hey fellow" the other half "hey foe." Residents. The brain of gathering experience and knowledge.

As I wonder through this NICU at The Human Spirit Hospital I am here for a while. My daughter, Cailin, is depending on this wild, wild world. I have to find the layers that we need around us of care, comfort and security. I have to learn what is what for her medications, body functions and difficulties, machines (each number when, where and how) and stats of breathing. Desat. How long? Bag her? How low? How high? How many? Calculations, just like gambling. Her gamble is her life. Not money.

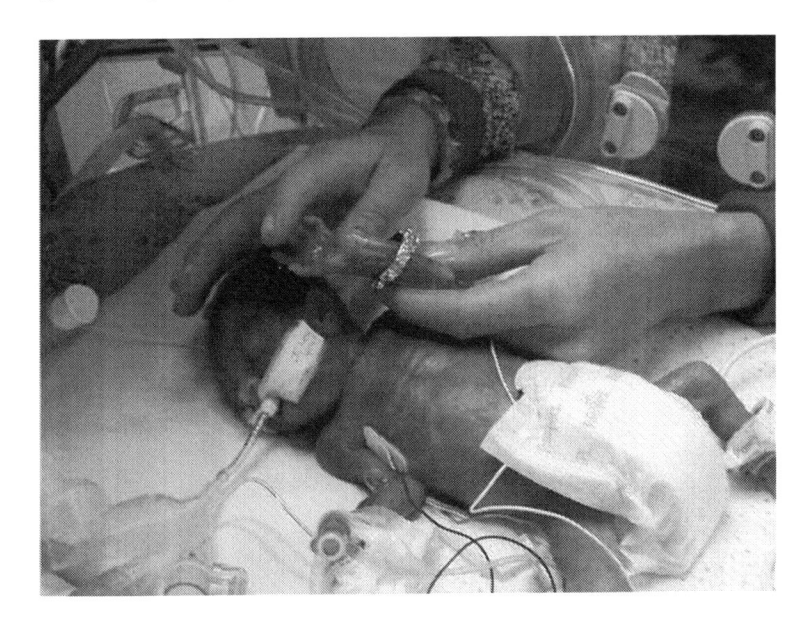

The Call

I felt the energy knowing he would call. Marie and I knew. She wanted to know how I wanted it handled. I said it was an easy answer. Simply tell him he is calling the wrong person. She is determined that he is going to reach out to her. Really? I don't think so. He will contact me. I know he will. I feel it, but still very distant. I break down and I confess my sins. I feel that I have forgiven him in a way, a way of the higher level. The earth level I am still holding on to. I have anger toward him and myself. Why did I give him another chance?

I gave him a chance for many reasons. I fell in love for the first time with him. He was the first to break my heart... many times. That is part of love. Joy and pain. I had joy reconnecting with him. I loved the good side of him. He was a very stable force for me during my youth. He protected me from the abusive homefront. His family was educated and worldly. I knew there was more out there for me. We liked to party though. He was an athlete and threw it away to addiction. He ruined his potential. We all knew. My P-town girls knew he could have been someone of higher magnitude. He sought me out. He contacted me. I was hesitant. He was a liar. I knew he fibbed often. Did I want a child to be around his lies? How would I protect my child?

He lied, I cleaned. He lied, I organized. I would shower him with love by helping him get his house and life together. He drank, did drugs, sold drugs and lied. I felt some of the lies. I became suspicious when he became distant. She emailed him and he replied. He lied. He was going to get a job and live with me and rent his house out. His house became a whorehouse. Nasty was the first. She had a long-term boyfriend that became a short-term boyfriend. There were three in her bed in the short months I was his girlfriend. I was his cleaner. He would say, don't you want to finish that upstairs? He would lie, text and cheat. I would clean. I saw what he told me. No marriage for now. He was divorced. Lie. He had the house in his name. Lie. I would clear out the marriage energy. We would paint and recarpet. He would lie. I would clean.

She emailed him just between you and me. He would say I left. He left in May. He entertained and screwed her. She lived with someone else. Our weekends turned into nights. He worked late and would just want to sleep. He lied. He cheated. He told me I was crazy. I felt it in every fiber... Nasty, Nastier or Nastiest?

She walked in with Nasty. She was shocked that I was in his room in my nightie. I knew. She was trying to get in his bed where she had been when I was gone. He lied. He cheated. I obsessed and investigated. She texted him, "Me and Nastier want to go dancing." I thought he likes going out, he is recently divorced. No, she had a boyfriend. She would hang out at his house only when I wasn't there. Nasty would ask when I would be leaving. Nastier would backstab and play

The Call

the victim regarding Nasty and Nastiest. He manipulated. He enjoyed it. He liked the game. Luke and Darth. He showed me Luke. He was Darth.

I wanted to believe him. I wanted him to get rid of the whorehouse and lead a good life with me. He pretended and played his game. I saw evidence that he was doing something sexual with someone else. I knew it was her. He started erasing his messages, except outgoing. The incoming would have really hurt me. The outgoing had the answers I was trying to pull out of him. He lied. He cheated. He texted Lucas two messages which read, "Baby with Carrie," and "I don't want anything serious with anybody." Answers I needed to hear, but he is a coward. He can't share. He played. He lied. His other outgoing message was, "I am on my way home. Do you need me to pick up anything?" To HER!!

He knew I was pregnant. He put me at risk. He put Cailin at risk. He hurt us. He lied. He cheated. He played the game. I knew there was not a chance when he did not take a step back. He played the game continuously. He lied and cheated. I carried a gift. He lied. He cheated. I confided. He lied. He cheated, even though he knew I was pregnant.

I woke him. He hates mornings. I read all the messages. He still lied! He is a coward. The mirror hurts his eyes. He commented on the mirrors in my home. Evil doesn't like mirrors. When I think of him and his family there is mirror. They turn away. Curiosity brings them back to wonder and drift... the mirror is at the end.

He lies and cheats. I discover. I confront. He reaches for the phone. I pull it close to me. He moves in. We are in the doorway. I slap him across the face. He runs out of the house. The Pilot is behind his vehicle. He is on foot. Calling me. Just to know I am gone from his house. I am trying to calm down. I call his brother. He listens with an open heart. His brother tells me to call him during the week to talk. I do. He doesn't return the call. I know what is going on. I place the mirrors around to protect my child and me.

I receive two messages from Nastiest and her buddy, Nastier. Take him. Have him. Don't think he won't do this to you. Please, he knew me since I was 13. He was my first love. He was my last mistake.

I carry my pregnancy well. I am healthy. He calls. I don't recognize the number. I listen to the message. I call and leave a message. I texted him. I tell him a number of things he needs to do. You need to call back, don't be a coward and turn away. You need to call me, for Cailin and me. I leave the same message on the text. He calls. I answer.

"Hello," he says softly. I am furious and emotional. I told Marie he would call me, not you. He will call after the baby is born. He did after Cailin was born. We would joke about how funny it would be. I will be ready to rip his face off. He would think that I would need him and be emotional. I tell him everything I felt I needed to tell him. He still denies what he did to me. I tell him I'm not surprised. He is a coward, not a man. A man would admit his faults. He says we would never work out because it has to be my way. I let him know that I'm not crazy. Crazy is a 20/20 report on

TV. I am doing well for all the pain and suffering he put me through. I know he did all the lying and cheating cause he doesn't love himself. He tells me all lies still. He tries to hold back. He can't.

The main things he said to solidify his stance were quite bold statements. He wants to not have me in the middle of Cailin. I am not in the middle. I am by her side. His addiction, lifestyle and lack of morals does not equal stability, let alone becoming a parent. He says he never wanted a child. I already know this. He was angry when I found out I was pregnant. He denies and lies.

I ask him, "What can you do for Cailin?"

His response seals our story, "Nothing." Wow! He is right about something.

I wish him well, to find peace in his life and accept his apology. His apology is not really sincere. He anticipated me to be a mess and need him. He told me I would never be able to raise a child financially. I do not respond. His drug addiction cost him enough money. I will buy diapers, wipes and food just fine because I am sober.

He texts me shortly after. "What day was she born? What hospital is she at?"

"Wow!" I respond. "Really? She has a name, a parent and family that loves her. We have been committed to her since day one of her entering the world. You have made choices. You have consequences to live with. Have a nice life."

He really thought it would blow over and he would enter as he pleases after I had her. A child is born when you know you are pregnant. Would he be calling me at week 24 of my pregnancy? No. So don't call, don't think and look into your mirror!

Sunday, January 3, 2010

I wake up at about 7:30 a.m. I was able to sleep in today. No work. Well, no financial earning work. I have tons of work to do today for Cailin and me. I roll and go. Coffee, burn that soundtrack for Magenta, wash up, automatic start the Pilot. I am out in about 20 minutes. I put the awesome soundtrack Ami made for me in the Pilot on track six. *The Promise* by Tracy Chapman is my song to Cailin. *After Midnight* by Eric Clapton is her theme song because she was born at 11:38 p.m. My dad looks like Eric Clapton a bit. The second track is *Up On The Roof* by James Taylor. He is a smooth singer with deep meaning in a simple manner. This is my song on how I deal with it all! Our life right now! I try my best to live in the moment, Cailin. Not spend so much time on the small details... really hard for me.

I drive to the hospital. It is about 11 degrees out. Bitter cold. Heading to be with my sweet girl, Cailin Jane! I arrive to do a few things. Check on Cailin, analyze the nurse, address concerns, talk to Cailin, read to Cailin, pump and pee. Off to 9 a.m. church. Upon my arrival Kate is her nurse. Kate is small in build with a petite tiny face. Cute. She thinks Cailin looks great due to comparing her to her first week. She is right about that. Cailin's coloring is off and she needs blood. I know she does not look horrible, but she will by night. Cherry, the respiratory therapist, agrees. Cailin looks pale. We talk about her "Pottery Barn" shelves with all her trinkets and books. Kate wants to see my house. I say, "I am not a Pottery Barn person. The only high-ticket item store I want something from is Land of Nod. I have picked out an artist design I love." My dad is buying Cailin's bedding. I am not much of a name brand type of person. Cherry comments that it is due to her line of work.

"Yep, we are not Disney or theme type of people." I say. I am off to pump.

I pump and relax for my 15 minutes. Still only getting quarter of an ounce. I clean up. The routine makes my hand so very dry. Especially on such a dry cold winters day. I head back to Cailin. I pick the "I Love You How Much" book. I read a book to her. Kate is asking me a bit about how and what I am all about. I answer some of her questions and fill her curiosity. She is interested and likes me. I like her. She tells me she will be working until 3 p.m. Then I will have another face. I say with Cherry still here, "I don't care about the face. I care about the new set of hands and heart." That is what is important. We all have faces. We have many faces to get through each day and life itself. I want a steady, loving and kind set of hands and heart for Cailin's care.

I head to church. I am late. I get in the back. I am single. I am confident. I am independent. I find a single space by a family of four, parents and two cute dark-haired Irish boys. The sermon is about epiphanies. I grasp the concept of how and why we gather knowledge. How as adults we are confused and have problems with our needs. Although a baby

Sunday, January 3, 2010

is not. So dependent and expressive for their every need. There is a baptism for a 4-week-old baby boy. I love the sermon and the sacrament for the baby boy. There is a lady with a decent voice behind me. She is just too loud for me. I am distracted during my singing, but find concentration during each song. It is challenging though. I scoot through the pew to go to the quickest communion line. I get my communion and head to the back of the church. I noticed that Cailin's name was not announced for the sick list, but is still in the bulletin. Thank you, God. I place three dollars in the candle collection slot. I pick a candle on the left. I light it for Cailin and her neighbor that is a sick baby boy. I pray for them both. I head out of the church almost missing a step. Story of my life. My new eyes allow me to laugh at the analogy.

I head to Magenta's Office for my third healing session. I texted and called. Is it 10 or 1? The holiday and my current life situation have me very screwed up. I head over there. Knowing very well that it is one. I ring no answer. She is sleeping. I head home. I can eat and take a nap. I arrive home. Home is warm, cozy and peaceful. I love the home I created for myself. I can't wait to bring Cailin home.

I make a turkey roll sandwich. I open mail. I get Cailin's new outfit from my client, Diane Price. I putz around. I take off the tracksuit and get back into my pjs. I call Margaret. I have not called her in awhile. I miss her. I speak to Josh in length. Happy New Years, Nina, Jack, work, holidays, Cailin, my work and me. Marge is giving her mother a bath. Josh thinks she will probably call me back soon. I crawl into bed. I get all my pillows, body pillow and Cailin's blanket and snuggle to take a nap. Marge calls. I pick up. We talk at length. It feels good to talk to her. She gets me, and I get her. We really have a great connection. We talk about my family, my issues, Cailin, her family, her issues and her Nina and Jake. She invites me over. She has a sinus infection and I have Cailin to see. I take a pass.

I put away clean laundry. I start more laundry. I take a nap for almost an hour. I can't believe I stayed home and took a nap. I wake up. Start the shower to steam up my bathroom. I make coffee. I make my bed again. I blast Tracy Chapman's third CD. *Start All Over* is the first track. Would you change your life…? Yes, Tracy. Yes, Cailin. I have already begun. I get ready with my new MAC Cosmetics. Love my makeup. I diffuse my hair curly, wavy. I need a cut and color. Soon. This week. I'll get it done next week. I am ready and off to see Magenta.

I arrive ten minutes late. My child is not even home and I am always late. I have so many bags. Blame. I am just slowing down to make sure I have everything I need. Magenta is greeted with the CD of Cailin and my soundtrack from Ami, my bud. Magenta pulled cards for Cailin and me at 12:30 a.m. on January 1, 2010. They are right on. Cailin's cards: Raven- open yourself to miracles. Use new eyes. Believe in magic. Embrace life wonders. My home is a peaceful haven (the hospital bed 20), Healing Heart "You're a Powerful Healer. Keep up the Good Work." I Will Do My Best to Make the Best of It. Openness. The journey. Understanding that the journey is as important as the destination. Enjoy every moment, and live life fully. This is Zen. A key to regaining your feeling of empowerment is to decide, right now, that no

Sunday, January 3, 2010

matter how good or how bad you are feeling, you are going to do your best to make the best of it. Do that again and again, and in a short period of time you will find yourself in a very good-feeling place. Cailin's cards for the new year are right on and so positive. She is so much and more.

I have good cards and a card I am not going to be happy with. Well, some will, a lot of resistance. Father Healing. "Your personal power increases as you give any father-related issues to Heaven." Turkey: Let go and away of the past. Share your gifts with generosity. Feel the freedom gained. I trust the intelligence within me; whatever is happening out there is only a mirror of my own limited thinking. Self-Acceptance: your true nature is neither good nor bad. It is newfound in enlightenment or lost in delusion. It is the spotless beauty of all creation. Who then is the self you are accepting or not accepting? The Most Powerful Law in the Universe: every thought vibrates, every thought radiates a signal, and every thought attracts a matching signal back. We call the process the Law of Attraction. The Law of Attraction says: that which is like unto itself is drawn. Willingness.

So, my card and my message from Cailin are to let go and be willing to open up. Then I can come to the place where we can "Play". I envision a castle. She says it is her home for now. She wants me to just be and not be so detailed orientated in the small details. Also, she wants to have her father come to see her. Not for me, but for her. She will receive the DNA acceptance from me of her entire makeup. I understand. But there are a lot of buts. I will contact him. I will invite him and I will see what happens. He will come slowly and probably run or transform his own life. Over there, away from us of course. I receive my healing session. We clear the energy that attached to me when he contacted me. I also figure out that my family is not in this situation on a daily basis. I am the giver and I need to give to myself and Cailin, not them. I am always feeling like they just can't meet me there. There is where I am. Well, because they can't, they don't know how to, they have their own work to do, and many are resentful toward me. I accept. I was a prisoner. I will now move through the tunnel Cailin to the castle and play with you for the rest of my life.

I feel great. I leave. I am in the Pilot. I am on a hunt for his number. I threw it out. Who needs his number? Well, today I do. I call Uncle Wally. He gives me two numbers. I call both. His cell twice and text him once. He will talk to his mother. He is a mama's boy. Just like all the men...boys I have dated. He will call. I feel it.

I get gas. I get Portillo's. I love the onion rings. I am on my way to Cailin. I need to have more fun and open up to her more. I get there and pump, eat. I spend time with Cailin for the rest of the evening. I write, I read. I share some of my writings with Pocahontas. She cries and I cry. This is such heavy stuff. It is life. I have a lot of work. Boundary setting. I need to take care of myself. I need to do this for Cailin. I will be back home for my 9:15 p.m. massage with Marvelous Mindy for 90 minutes. He will call later tonight or tomorrow. I think tonight. It depends on him speaking to his mom. I pray that this will help Cailin. She wants and asked for it. So I will do it for her.

Sunday, January 3, 2010

Today was a big day for my growth and new life with Cailin. She sneezed twice. It was awesome. She weighs in the 800-gram area. A lot of the weight is fluid, not proper weight gain. I pick out the bedding for Cailin and give my new set-up options to Pocahontas. I visit. I read. I share. I am tired. I go home. I get ready for bed. Still no response from him. Maybe tomorrow, maybe not. It will be what it is.

January 4, 2010

I wake up at 6:38 a.m. I hit snooze. I should shower and push myself. Not today. Not feeling it. I let it go to one more alarm. I call Pocahontas. She worked 16 hours. She changed Cailin's entire bed, rather incubator. It was long over due. She had to scan and time it so Cailin would get a clean one immediately. Cailin had an entire team of nurses to move her. One pound and yet so incredibly influential over large adult human beings. You are amazing, Cailin Jane! Pocahontas said Cailin had a good night and everyone liked her new bedding combo. Yep, I am pretty creative and outside the box. It's much more free outside the box. I ask about her output in her diapers. She had some high-measuring dirty preemie diapers. She also pooped although it had blood still in it. Not frank! Just maroon. Belly is still measuring big, but not worsening. We will wait and watch for your guidance and needs, Cailin. I will see Pocahontas tonight. She is heading home in traffic on the Eisenhower to hit her pillow.

I head to the bathroom then crawl back to bed until 7:30 a.m. Anytime around 7 a.m. is sleeping in to me. I just feel better. I wash up, grab a to-go cup and dump my coffee. I am off to see my "Bug-a-boo". I get a weird 847 number... maybe it is him. The donor. Nope it's Ami. I accidently called her yesterday. She is worried. Most people are worried these days when I call. I catch up with her briefly. I will call you in a week or so. That is my new thing. Less talk, more action. Action for my healing and growing and focus on my Cailin. I call my dad. He gives me my horoscope and Cailin's. I pull into The Human Spirit Hospital... the castle... Cailin's home. Let's play Cailin. Shit, there are so many characters. How can't you play?

I need to be playful. Priscilla is up to bat for Cailin. She is on 12-hour shift. We have an ultrasound of the belly. The mystery goes on. The pictures are done and she has the correct ones. I change Cailin's dirty diaper, clean her mouth and wipe the jelly belly from the ultrasound. She is feisty today. I love it! She is grabbing her tubes and breathing tubes. I go and pump as well as to see Princess Aurora. I head out to see Ms. Soundboard.

I wait for about 20 minutes. I have sometime to kill. I am happy to get to the place Cailin likes. Playtime in the castle. I pop on my iPod to Indie Arie's first CD. It is helping me relax and make sense of it all. My work, my healing, my new life. I wait and breathe, tap my feet to the music. I read our card information for the year. Ms. Soundboard greets me. She always takes a big gander in on me. She is trying to grasp me. We welcome each other with New Year's greeting and proceed to her room. Room 227.

It was a successful session. I was able to disclose quite a bit of information. Information on our family, medical staff,

January 4, 2010

friends, work, the donor and Cailin. I disclosed how I do not feel that my family is providing for me, my needs are not being met. They don't know how to. I am the glue. I am the middle child. I help them heal and do for them. I just don't feel complete when communicating with them. I am an enabler. I have allowed them to be the way they are. I need to move forward in my life with Cailin. Yes, I will communicate my new boundary. It will definitely not be taken well. Anything that I say is hard for them to swallow. When you are a giver of your energy to do for them and take some of that away naturally people will grasp. The grasp is the usual projection, manipulation and rude comments. All are attempts for me to change my mind. It is already made up. I have done this with people that are friends in my life as well. I have to. It feels like it has been a long time coming. Ms. Soundboard confirms that I have been doing a lot of thinking and set my intentions.

Intentions bring me back to the day Jake, Margaret and Josh's 4-year-old son, and I had a deep conversation. I believe God spoke through Jake that day to me. I simply asked Jake, "Will you be Cailin's friend?"

Jake stated clear as a blue sky, "It depends on her intention. If she warms my heart then I will be her friend. I have to know her intention."

From that moment on during this spiritual journey I look at other's intentions. What are they? How do their intentions make me feel? For feelings do not lie. My compass of my feelings has been blinded a prisoner of many relationships before. I have new eyes, clearer eyes and a motherly heart.

I am better. I can acknowledge and do what is necessary with each intention.

I head home. I start the shower to steam it up. It is so chilly out there. I make a quick turkey sandwich. I turn on the tape from my last healing session. I listen and laugh. I laugh at myself. A good-hearted laugh. I don't hold back like I use to with certain things... my feelings. I like the new me. Raw and Real. I am strong. I am confident. I am independent.

I reach the hospital and check on Cailin. I attempt to file her nails for the first time. I was able to do two nails. Then she was desating. No go. Half of the long nails are done. I read some of my writings to Priscilla. Priscilla gave me the update on Cailin's plan from the doctors after rounds. I read Cailin a quick book. I am off to work. I hustle through my shift with a few pumps in between. I speak to Priscilla. She gives me the low down on her IV nutrition and the bowel output tube. She tells me that she discovered her hands and was sucking on them. How stinkin' cute! She is a big girl now. We laugh. Well, developmentally, yes, she is a big girl. We still have a long way to go. She is resting and having a stretch out. She got really comfortable when The Animal Tamer and Priscilla were vibing her. She gets vibes on her back now! She is a big girl now. I can't wait for Kangaroo Care time. I am so excited.

January 5, 2010

I had to open the shop today. I rose about 6:15 a.m. I popped on the shower to steam it up. I was able to get to Cailin about 7:45 a.m. Princess Aurora was on her bedside for the past 12 hours. I was happy to know that. She is such a breath of fresh air for me. She was a bit tired this morning. I stated, "Princess Aurora, I am here to bring a piece of sunshine this morning." She giggles. Cailin has a big dirty diaper. I am once again relieved by her diaper measurement. I am able to talk to Cailin, and she is awake. I love when she has her awake moments. I then go to pump for my wee one. Wee pumping with my tatas. Such big boobs, but such little production. I am just amazed after each 15-minute session. I come back out to talk briefly with Cailin and Princess Aurora before I am on my merry way. It is 8:30 a.m. I must put a hustle in my bustle to open the shop.

I arrive to work with Joy. Joy is a stylist from another salon that is saving us. She wanted more hours, and I have had a few jump ship. I provide Joy with some shifts. She is a true Joy. She is already trained, has manners and respect. I am happy to have her join the team. She is around Allison's age. So great to have two young chickies for each other. We have a smooth day. I have a few customers come back and see me for the second time. That makes me happy. I enjoy all the referrals coming my way from my many, many efforts. You always get what you give. I proceed throughout my day. Knowing that today is the possible day of Kangarooing Cailin. Kangaroo Care is a way to bond deeply with your preemie. I am so bonded with Cailin already. I will just melt some more. Bring it on.

I am not a very patient person. Although here we are, Cailin Jane. You are 6 weeks old today and 29 weeks and 1 day gestational age. Always many details for such a tiny baby. So little. So very important! I love you sweet pea. I have my purple zip down sweatshirt. I arrive to Cailin. Princess Aurora has a staff meeting. I am going to hold Cailin in one hour. I throw all the butterfly stickers I just bought today on her sound machine and nametag. She is my butterfly. Having a child allows the child in you to come out more freely. I am free to actually play more. It feels good and brightens things up. I wait knowing that this wonderful time is coming to us. Princess Aurora gets out. I pump and change into my purple sweatshirt. I am so excited that I feel like crapping my pants or throwing up. I need to eat something. I open my long awaited box from my Auntie Kathy. It is a box of lemon shortbread. Nope, people. I open to bright colored striped socks. So funny, warm and cozy. So my Auntie always recycles all sorts of boxes. This is the topper. We are paging The Animal Tamer to come do her respiratory treatment. She is busy in Pediatrics with an emergency. We are on the second page. The Animal Tamer picks up. She is on her way. I give her a hard time.

We chuckle. The Animal Tamer is unaware of the Kangaroo urgency! She is like, "Oops, I didn't know." No, she didn't know. She gives Cailin her vibe treatment. She is doing quite well with it and considering her medical difficulties. We are all happy. Princess Aurora, The Animal Tamer and I are so very excited and concentrating on the plan.

The plan is to stay centered and calm. I plant my laptop to the shelves to play my yoga CD dad gave to us. It is relaxing and energizing. Princess Aurora is going to hand Cailin to me. First, she has to have free tape ready to tape down the tubing once I have Cailin. The Animal Tamer is on the right with the bag and the respiratory equipment. Cailin is handed to me. Then The Animal Tamer bags her. I feel Cailin. She is fragile but not nearly as fragile as when she was first born. She is crawling on me a bit. I can only feel her thoughts. Where am I? Why do I feel elevated and laying down? Why do I feel a warm body and a warm hand? There is a smooth transition for Cailin. As smooth as it can be. She settles in shortly. We are holding each other for the first time. I love every feeling. She is breathing on me. I hear her hole in her tubing. I feel her chest. I feel her little legs. I hold them with one hand. I hold her body with another. I feel her little fingers, hands and arms. She is feeling me out. She is always active with her limbs. She is discovering and breathing really well. We take many photos. The Animal Tamer lost her common sense from all the excitement. Princess Aurora was so determined to get everything done. They were awesome! I have such a great relationship with both of them. It was so special for all us. Sharing is caring. There is a ton of sharing when you have a preemie and caring is endless.

I have never had such a quick amazing hour go by. I felt tired after. I know I will sleep so well tonight. It was just amazing. I have to immediately print out pictures and tons on my phone. I am grateful for this moment in our lives. One of the top five moments in my life. Number one was finding out I was pregnant. The second was the first ultrasound. The third was the second ultrasound. The fourth was giving birth to Cailin Jane. This is the fifth. She is just going to keep adding on to my greatest moments. I have to thank her and God everyday for these moments. I am so very grateful.

Pocahontas comes for her tonight. We don't have to change her bed. She changes a dirty diaper and weighs her. She weighed 770 grams. She still has her belly issue, but she is growing. She smiles, sneezes, cries, almost rips her tubes out and finds her hands. She is alert… sure sign of intelligence. She is feisty and sweet. My girl is amazing. I hope for a quiet night for her. I will finish this pumping session and then read to my love bug. I am then heading home for some sweet dreams. I want sweet dreams of her and me… the feeling of having her for a lifetime.

January 5, 2010

January 7, 2010

I am off work today. Yippee. I have plenty of personal work to do. I wake up to speak to Priscilla. She replies back that Cailin had an okay night. Her oxygen is up, but she did have some desats. Priscilla comments on my voice. Well, hello Chickie, its 6:30 a.m. and I'm in bed. I am always a mystery to her. Cailin will have another set of hands during the morning shift until 3 p.m. I roll and go to the hospital. Yes, the "big snow" arrives today. It causes traffic to move slowly. Well, at least I am only commuting on Roosevelt. Snow, rain, sleet, cold… weather is not my major concern. I will reach Cailin, rain or shine or snow! I reach her by 7:30 a.m. The rate of driving did indeed take some time.

I am not able to do Cailin's diaper or mouth this morning. I have to pump my preemie palletes and be on my way. I have three appointments to go to. The times are as follows: 8:00, 9:00 and 9:40. I get to my 8 a.m. appointment at 8:30 a.m. I called to tell them I was running late. I am confident. I am responsible. When I arrive, they ask me if I have an appointment and they do not see me in the system. I show my booklet stating the appointment. They move me along. I am out the door a little after 9 am. During the appointment, my 9 a.m. appointment calls me. Where are you? Well, I tried to contact the Social Security Office and return the message twice yesterday. I was going to be able to have the appointment over the telephone. Different story today. I reschedule for January 13 at 9 a.m. I am flexible. I am responsible. I am confident. I head to my 6-week postpartum appointment. I do not suffer from depression. I did struggle with post-traumatic stress disorder. How is that a disorder? That is what happens to her mind, body, heart and soul to repair. It is a sign to process emotionally, mentally and physically your traumatic experience.

I speak to the Cailin's nurse briefly with 20% left on my iPhone battery. Cailin is doing okay. She has her oxygen up and I want to voice my concerns about her fluid retention. I tell that to the nurse. She can relay my concerns to the docs. The nurse comes out to call me. I hang up and head in. I am weighed at 127 pounds. Not too shabby, Miss Carrie. The aqua bikini is only a season-and-a-half away. Yoga, yoga, yoga. Water, water, water. I am only taking prenatal vitamins. All others are eliminated. Nice. Less toxins and dependents. The doctor is long and lean. She checks to see if she can take me. The intake nurse is not finished. She asks me questions about Cailin. Date? 11-24-2009 Weight? 1 pound, 0.02 ounces. Length? 10 3/4 inches. She sighs a bit out of the side of her mouth. Quietly and gently. She knows the stats. I am lead to my room. I am supposed to get a pap smear. I do not want one. That brings me back to being examined on November 24, 2009. I am not ready. I feel nervous. The nurse relays the news. The long and lean doctor will see me. I make a face. I was not feeling her demeanor. I undress. I am ready. I am nervous. Dr. Compassionate arrives in. He is a surprise. Not long and lean, nor a female. He reads my nervous demeanor immediately. He sits down. He slides into his chair. He knows my chart and energy. I take up a lot of space and only invite when I feel safe. I am upbeat and friendly to most. I am an ice princess to others. It is easily felt. I do not hide it. Dr. Compassionate is an African American male, bald, few earrings, earthly, spiritual, with a wide spaced toothed smile. I am happy. He was my surprise. He states, "You look nervous."

I reply, Yes, because I do not want to get a pap smear."

He says, "Then you don't have to. You had one when you were pregnant. How are you?"

I say, "That is a complicated question." I then pause. He looks at me. I look at him and look away down to the left. "Dr. Compassionate, I am not okay."

He says, "I looked at your chart. I know you have been through a lot. That is why I am asking how you are doing."

I look at him dead on with a mellow serious tone, "You don't have time, you don't have the will. I have a journey here and I'm doing the best that I can."

He looks at me with a nod of yes and a smile, "Well, that is an honest answer. I just have to check your belly and breathing."

He proceeds to examine my belly and back for my lungs and lastly my heart. During the short exam, I state, "I am just not ready for an exam. It will remind me of the day I had Cailin. I was examined so many times."

He is quiet and truly heard me. He proceeds to sit back down in front of me. Dr. Compassionate asks, "Do you have any questions?"

Does Carrie Kacen have questions? Ask Jerre McPartlin about my questions. She laughs at how many I ask.

"Yes, when will I get my period?"

We discuss in length that yes, Nana was right about all that she told me. I miss her right now. She is in Texas with Auntie Jackie. We also discuss how I may be breastfeeding for two years. I also disclose how I feel edgy like PMS. Now and the last two days. I am agitated. I have had two to three situations that did not agree with my inner voice.

Dr. Compassionate concludes, "Do you have any other questions?"

"Yes, is Dr. Rose here today?"

He replies, "No."

I ask, "Can I have a piece of paper to leave her a note."

"Yep," Dr Compassionate responds.

I am going to change. The nurse that was probing me when I came to get my physical for my leave of absence knocks in two seconds.

"Hello, I am just changing."

All the excitement of my case draws this unneeded energy. It is not wanted, nor needed. I am continuously shooing the flies away. Flies are gross and bring nothing good. They actually throw up on things that they land on. I am not a landing surface nor is our life. Right, Cailin? Right, Mommy! I grab the paper. I know this chick will just read this private note. So, I proceed to outsmart the lassie. "Please, can I have an envelope?"

"Sure," the nosey chickie nurse responds.

I write on a yellow long sticky note: *Dr. Rose, I was here for my six-week checkup. Cailin is six weeks old and three days today. I was able to hold her for the first time at six weeks old. It was wonderful! Have a happy and healthy New Year! Carrie*

I place my jacket on and lug my large purple bag over my shoulder. I am on my way out. I have to stop at KMart for a 2010 day planner. I have a quick call to Ami. Wilson, her dog, is performing doggie yoga on her mat. Smile. She will provide the baby shower favor. The best loving CD anyone has every created. I have been thinking of Courtney a lot. I want to talk to her, but just working shit out. She calls. Okay, we are meant to talk. Absolutely, she is a great listener and we have similar family disappointments. Let go. Let God. Radiate love and light. Energize Cailin Jane. Courtney is down with helping for the shower. Maybe she could order the flowers and bring them. I buy new bedding for Cailin's arrival home. I must take away all clothes, bedding and blankets with all my cats' dander. I am slowly transforming my home, my heart, my life and my will. I have a large reason… my tiny one pound girlie,

Cailin Jane. She rocks and spins my world. Stay centered in my thoughts and feelings. I head home. Place everything away, washes the dishes, change the laundry, pump and hit my pillow. I definitely checked on Cailin. The nurse was unsure on what happened with rounds. I am not content with the feedback. I proceed to hit the healing tape and relax each body part and breathe deep. I relax and work my energy to Cailin. I will pray and focus on healing her and myself. I am her mother and have such a deep-seeded influence. I will not take that for granted, my child of God.

I wake up slowly and realize that Cailin's fluid complication is directly parallel with my life. Saturated in the wrong areas, and highly dehydrated in the right. I have to let go and grow. Growing pains are uncomfortable and you step out of your box. I visualize for her. Yes, Cailin, I will do my work. My work, your work and our work. It is not your "job" or "role". It is what your spirits are to learn and perform. Others will have a hard time when your spirit has movement that takes away from their energy. Transformation. Cailin is transforming and I am too. We are on such a magnifying journey. I have to change my outward action so quickly for others. I need to check in with my internal body. I need to use my inner voice for navigation. That will be changing who, what and how I am to many relationships in my life. Work. Personal acquaintance. Close friendships. Mostly, importantly family. Yes, the family is my largest task. Smallest motion, energy and intention. Just let it go. Take care of myself and Cailin. That is my will, my intention and energy. My energy dissipates from others here. The grasps, laughter out of what they are needing, what will be lost and how life has changed. I must focus purely on my life, Cailin and our family of two.

I arrive to the hospital. I want to speak to a doctor. Oh, I am told Dr. Second Resident is in surgery and Dr. What's-Her-Face Fellow... Foe are in surgery. I don't give a shit. I need information and feedback. Cailin needs medical assistance for her fluids, people. I like to speak to the Attendee anyway. Well, he might be out of the unit. Page him. This is exactly why I don't like the rotation. New face, new ways. Now I must break them in. This fellow Vague does her job. Her heart is not into it. I don't feel a sense of urgency or true dedication. It is called Intensive Care for a reason. 24/7 medical attention and care. She does not remember her notes. She has no sense of urgency. She was not friendly or respectful in the beginning. Here we are again. So, she will know for certain this is not her game. This is Cailin Jane Kacen's life. Don't fuck with me. Oh, it's to late you have. I forgive you, but your leash is tight and assuming now. I have a good vibe about Dr. Wise. I told him I expect consistent feedback. If he does not find me, I will find you. We discuss her infection, belly, weight and so on. He asks nothing of me, such as building rapport. I am not sure if he has a bedside manner. I hear he is brilliant. Must supersonic smart folks do not have great social skills. Let's talk, medical staff.

Building rapport, trust and relationships are a huge part of caring for a patient. It so happens that you have to meet me. I expect communication. Do not give me half-ass answers. I don't know... I just arrived. Get up on my child's chart. You are here, right? Work is knowing what is going on. You recieved her case. Well, if you choose to treat Cailin like a "case" your job here at Bed 20 is gonna be rough. I will not tolerate the 'I'm not sure' answers. Show some connection and conversation. I know it is hard to handle a bulldog like me. Well, any bulldog is extremely loyal and loving, but it goes right back to building relationships. That is how care is full circle. Circle of trust. Are you in or out of the circle? I will know. I feel. I see. I taste. I touch. Emotions do not lie.

I sit here typing a bit bitter. Dr. Vague, the fellow, in my opinion is a half-asser. I see Cailin all tucked in. I see her Oxygen support is 62%...way to high for my liking. Pressure 25. Rate 45. Weight 860 grams. She looks like a little budda baby. She is wearing her white lace headband with a bow and pink accent. As Kitty, the nurse, states, "The bow is wearing her." Well, when you have a preemie princess, like Cailin you have a lot of cute stuff. Washcloths, tiny washcloths, receiving blankets. I can't wait to share with her that all these tiny clothes are her blankets. Yep, tiny baby girl. My baby. I love her so. She is definitely not lacking in the love department. I sprinkle her shelves, name tag, and incubator. Yep, she is a Kacen. We do not go under the radar. We are above the radar. She not the typical preemie they tell me. Well, she is her mother's child and a Kacen for that matter. Today I feel like a Kacen more so. I have had to bring out my vocab, assertiveness and energy. Do you hear us? Do you see us? Take care of your part already!

January 8, 2010

I rise at 3:17 a.m. Should I call my daughter's nurse? It's just about 6 a.m. I thought about the call and felt my inner self. I choose not to call. I then hit the bathroom to just crawl back into my comfy bed. I speak to Cat, the nurse for Cailin. "She loves to desat. She has been up to 66% and down to 64%." I say nothing. I am not crazy about the tone or the lack of effort to make a vent change from Dr. What's-Her-Face. What's-Her-Face suits her demeanor. *Oh, I'm not sure, you can speak Carrie and I still can't hear you, I don't feel you or Cailin.* I know. I will state what I need to once I arrive to see Dr. Wise at 8 a.m. He will enter smoothly about his day being such a seasoned Attendee. Little does he know I have an ear, heart and mind to express until my expectations are heard, felt and taken into action. I do my daily morning routine. Coffee and banana. Hit the dryer to heat up Cailin's clean linens. Shower, listen to my last healing session, makeup, hair, automatic car starter, oral hygiene and clothing. Lug all the bags on my tiny frame and hit the door. I turn on the relaxation CD. I need to be centered for this conversation. What is my intention?

Intention is large aspect of life. As Cailin struggles for her life, I must be present with my inner self. My inner self will navigate my intentions and pick up on others. That is my guide for proper care for Cailin Jane. Dr. What's-Her-Face does not have a clear or meaningful intention. Unfortunately, Cailin's difficulties and my intentions are to help Dr. What's-Her-Face. We will teach her a hard lesson.

I arrive to find that my usual nurse was not on Cailin. Just the soft touches and my likes are not complete. That is not here, nor there at this point. Her belly is measuring 23 centimeters, her urine output is only 10 cc, she is desating. So, here we are again. Let's make it happen. Intensive Care means 24/7. I have a sense of urgency in general, being an Aries. Where is everyone else's? Patience is a virtue. Breaking points bring the truth out and eliminate the fluff, right Cailin? I change her diaper. I clean her mouth. Put on a new headband bow. She smiles. Cailin smiles. Not often. She knows Mommy is going to bat for her and it will be a home run. Once I have my mind on something. The intention is quite crystal clear. So, don't mess with an Aries of my breed. I speak to the Diva at the front desk and Jem, Cailin's nurse, that I need to speak to Dr. Wise.

I pump and head to leave for work. I am running late. What's new? I have a sick, cute-as-a button daughter. Work, schmurck. I ask Jem to relay the message. I head to the exit and ask Diva if Dr. Wise is here. She says, yes. Now hold up, peeps. Staff will protect one another as any tribe would and should. I am not a tribe member. My tribe is Cailin and myself. Dynamic duo. But, they will not lie too often when probed. Diva would not have told me if I didn't ask. So sad that I have to be one hell of a detective… another great Aries trait. So I walk back to Bed 20, Cailin's haven. Jem tries to page and it doesn't work until the second time. I trust

January 8, 2010

Jem. She is strong, grounded and gentle. She knows I am pissed, as I told her so. Dr. Wise comes over and is not sure where I am going with this. Welcome to the land of clarity, Dr. Wise.

Dr. Wise stands and does not touch anything due to the isolation. I sit with my gown on.

"Dr. Wise, I have a few concerns," is how I start.

What I say next cuts through all the fluff. I tell him, "We had a great conversation yesterday. Then Dr. What's-Her-Face, was on call last night. She did not know what the hell was going on, I stated what we (you and I) discussed, she did know if the orders were made and completely disregarded what I said. She boxes me out nonverbally with the nurses all the time, even at Bed 20. I am Cailin's mother and will not be treated that way. I will be part of the team for Cailin's care. I know that there are a lot of babies here. Cailin is here as well. I do not feel comfortable having her on Cailin's team. Cailin is not a scientific case. She is my child. I will be up your ass and down your throat until we are discharged."

Dr Wise, nods in agreement with what I say. He comments on fellowship. Part of it is working with them, and he will talk to her. I state that she needs a lot of work. Either she is in the loop, or needs to get out of the loop. Step aside if the proper care is not provided. I add that a good doctor is one that uses their heart, hands and mind. When one area is lacking it is not good enough here at Bed 20. Dr. Wise takes it all in. His eyes widen knowing that I am extremely upset. I end the conversation as Cailin needs help. Would you help her? I leave it as that. I will contact Jem after rounds to find out what the plan is for Cailin. He agrees that is a good plan. Jem winks and smiles. I breathe and begin to pray.

I pray for guidance, strength and protection for Cailin. I listen to the relaxation CD all the way to work. It is a slow day. I am running late. For work, that is. I am on time and in the moment for Cailin. The daily routine humanly tasks always interrupt good work. Spiritually, I would have loved some yoga and a deep quick nap to connect with Cailin. I am a human and need to pay bills. I am on the way to work. In my head, I am visualizing playing with Cailin. I visualize myself as an angel. I throw green vines and flowers all around her bedside. I call all the Saints, Mother Mary and God. There are doves flying around her bed. She releases from her bed. It disappears and goes into her water. At times, we are mermaids. I paint all the colors in deeper colors for serenity. I try to create this serenity for her and me. I do my best to get out of my head. I spoke and fought for her. God's will. God's time. God's grace.

I arrive at work. A slower day after the holidays. We are getting back on track. I clean and do my organizational work. I used to thrive on it. Now it keeps my hands and mind in motion. My mind is busy with Cailin. Conversations, concerns, smiles and thoughts. She is in my heart all the time. I miss her so. Time is going by. We are into January already. I want it to go by quicker. Although quicker will not happen. Each day is a large lesson with many small lessons for the purpose. The purpose is for me to grow. Growing means to let go and let God. I continue to check myself. I am reading the book about The Law of Attraction. Nothing new to me

January 8, 2010

just means more. It has some space to meditate and journal. I usually journal in another book. I don't want anyone to see what I write. I might lend or give it away. Those days are over. I will write and underline and work it out. Work it out in a playful manner is what I really need to do.

I leave work to get a facial. I need to relax. It is relaxing when I get to the facial table. It's a journey when you get a facial at beauty school. So many questions and then the instructor is all over the student. I just want your basic $18 facial. The girl, Jocelyn, did a good job. She was not completely involved. She forgot moisturizer. I don't say anything. Unusual for me not to speak up. The caretaker in me is outshined. The feedback queen has to save it for bigger battles, Cailin's health. She is my battle. She is the biggest fighter in this battlefield of life. One of the quotes in the book is: Love is life. If you miss love, you miss life. Isn't that the truth! There are a lot of truths unraveling before my new set of eyes.

My new eyes are clearer, kinder, protective and guided by my intention. I see the world as a mirror of your thoughts, but my mirror does have characters that need to go away. Although I am learning that I have to let some things unfold, trust my higher intelligence and connect with my inner-self throughout the day. My purpose is a big one. My spirit soars and I want it to be positively influential. I want my daughter to be in good hands and benefit from me as her mother.

I head to Cailin's bedside. I arrive after I ate McDonald's for the second time today. I weighed 127 pounds, but I need to watch my intake. I need to work at losing my baby weight. I want to be healthy and lean for Cailin's arrival home. Being in great shape will help my endurance and thoughts. I am a lean machine. Well, I keep up on my comings and goings. The balancing act I learned a few years ago. Balance and flexibility in life situations are important. I know Cailin is sating (breathing and heart rate) well due to my brief conversation with Jem before my arrival. She is short and sweet on the phone. I tell Jem that I am writing a book. She laughs about it. I let her know that as long as your true character means well, you're fine. For those who mistreat... yes, family members, medical staff, friends... I will write. My new eyes allow me to separate and disclose. Oh, freedom. It rings. I hear the gurgling brook on Cailin's sound machine. I talk to her. I read to her. I have a present from Ruby, the Chaplain at the NICU. She gave me a journal. Now, how sweet is that? I write a quick thank you note. Give it to Jem and go pump.

I return to see The Animal Tamer. We smile. We laugh. We connect. Yes, she is on the level. Transformation. I will have less connections but more quality. Annie Marbach always says, "It's quality, not quanity." Amen sista! Although the tone of transformation can be different at times. Upon my arrival this evening, there was a baby, nurse, Chaplain and Respiratory Therapist coming in. I said, "Hi, Mickey!" I knew this was not good... just the people, their demeanor and the Chaplain. I am getting a journal from her. She is on the other side of a curtain bringing a baby girl to eternal life. I have not confirmed it yet. All the signs and symbols are there. Does the nurse go home? How do they carry that energy? Does that bedside 13 have a third event coming?

January 8, 2010

A nurse got really sick and was taken to the ER one night, the death of a baby girl and now what? Baby girl 13 was just stable earlier today. She had surgery yesterday. One previous neighbor was a 23-weeker, Daisey. She went home. Baby Girl… she went to home in heaven. This unit is such a heavy load. Cailin's complications and care, communication, staff personalities, shift changes, doctor rotations and other parents. Wow! I have the wind knocked out of me with all this reality.

I finished doing the bedding with Snow White. I vented to her. She is in our corner. What is so bad about asking for updates on my daughter care? Hello! Hospital, Care, Medicine, Doctors and Nurses… communication people. That is what I need. Do not try to pull the wool over my eyes. I have a new pair. No fool here. Cailin is definitely not fooled. She knows when I am there. When her core nurses are caring for her. She feels, hears and sees a bit with her immature eyes. My child has an enormous spirit and connection. Take notes, get involved and enjoy her ride. You haven't bought a ticket… too bad she added you to the list. Yep, that's the kind of girl she is.

I finish my day with a pumping session and some text messages to read. I have a lot of new ways about myself. Peace and serenity is a must. Although I have never been more popular. Excitement makes people flock. Well it's not an invitation, only a major life event. God signed up Cailin and Carrie. If you do not see your name on this event list then you have your own event or events. Don't worry, we all have porches. Sweep yours, sit on it and stay. Your energy of entering my porch right now is not uplifting for me. There are a few guests that I welcome, but the key word is few.

I will sleep well tonight. Snow White has my Cailin, the conqueror, the challenger, the charmer. My preemie princess is decked out in new bedding and a new purple headband bow. I will pray for me, her, Baby Girl 13 and her family tonight. I need to keep asking for peace to the others all around me that look, wait and watch. When really all I want is prayers from everyone.

I go to exit the unit and I soon discover that my keys are missing. Yep, I went to the Jazzy Coffee Cafe to get coffee before I went up to the unit. Accessory, the front desk diva, calls downstairs. I search the pumping room and speak to Snow White. I end up going downstairs. The games begin for me. I am so exhausted and emotional. I speak to the security desk representative and he has a call out for the keys. I take initiative to go out to the parking lot, only to really have my emotions come to head. I look for my vehicle and it is gone. There is Gray, security officer, in his van. I see my car is gone. He rolls down his window and I tell him, "I lost my keys and I think someone stole my car."

Gray responds, "You got to be kidding me!"

I explain that I am a NICU mom and lost my keys although I just discovered they were lost. He has me enter his van. We go around the first level. While, going around he asks me, "Would your husband or boyfriend have taken your keys?"

I yelp in tears, "No, I don't have one. I think someone stole my car."

Gray is trying to calm me down. Good Luck, buddy. I have hit another wall. I need to cry. There is my Pilot. I parked in the other spot in the morning. I have just come to another breaking point. Now we declared my car is not stolen. Thank you, Lord! We head back into the building. I call two neighbors. They do not return any of my messages. Thanks, guys. Gray leaves to seek out my keys and returns with the prize. I am so grateful! I am ready to walk to my car. Gray will not allow that. He drives me to my car. We talk about a few major life stories and the miracles in the hospital. I have one miracle of my very own. Time for rest. I'll tend to her needs in the morning.

January 9-11

I have an intense conversation with Miss Priscilla, Cailin's nurse, as usual. I don't know who starts them but we always seem to have them. I believe this will be the last one I have with her. Priscilla does not get what I am looking for or need. I had been thinking about Ruby, the Chaplain, and that I needed to talk to her. Well, I am sure Priscilla let Ruby in on her concerns of "my concern." Priscilla and I spoke on the telephone about Cailin's health and the lack of compassion and communication from her now fellow, Dr. What's-Her-Face. Well, Priscilla made some comments about how I needed to respect her and trust and so on. I do believe both are very important in life. When your inner-self alerts you of someone and then that someone confirms the alarm bingo… we have a red flag! I actually really expressed my inner-self to Priscilla. Hence she notified Ruby, the NICU Chaplain. I love Ruby by the way; she is truly here to help me. I expressed to Priscilla that she does not know this side of the bed. My defensiveness is very relevant in having a million people coming and going on my precious daughter. Trust is earned as well as respect. What I will trust is my instincts. She asked me in our lengthy conversation if she told me she trusts Dr. What's-Her-Face and her medical experience. Well, good for you that is your business. Three types of business, my business, your business and God's business. Your trust does not overlap with mine Miss Priscilla. You are around a quarter of the time Cailin and I are going through this journey. Also, you love Cailin as her nurse. I am her mother and I am protecting my young. I know Priscilla told Ruby. She did it to help me, help her and the staff. Well, we are still back to square one... communication. I am only asking for the common courtesy of communicating my daughter's health updates and concerns. I find it disheartening to have someone's ego get in the way of updating me. I am Cailin's voice, advocate, ringleader and her mother for goodness sake. Shame on you for always defending the medical staff. They are human and make mistakes and have disregarded me as a part of Cailin's care. That does not mean I am going to give up. Nor does it mean I should be getting so much resistance when it is all for the good of Cailin's medical journey. Bed 20 we present Cailin Jane and her mother, Carrie. Her mother is present every waking non-working moment possible. She will call. She will ask questions… why? Because she is her mother.

I arrive to the hospital drained and heavy from all the relationship work, disappointment and unnecessary stress. There is Ruby with Priscilla. I know what the score is. I need to talk to Ruby. I open up as much as I can. I cry and get teary. Ruby drapes up to communicate with me. Priscilla dismisses herself just enough for a small amount of space and close enough to have her much needed ear-full. I am fully aware of Priscilla's need to gossip and her own emotional needs. That appears to be why I need to back away from her. She causes more stress with all of her, "I feel…

January 9–11

you are, you are." The line has been crossed. The justification of unprofessional, lack of communication and compassion is not to be justified. It needs to change drastically. I do not work with 'these people'. I am the mother of one of their patients. Different ball game, Miss Priscilla. Different Angle. I feel Ruby get closer to me to communicate. She asks and presents that I am having a hard time with the change of the medical team. The answer would be yes, and I know Priscilla has discussed this with you. Ruby asks me of my fears, why I am teary, to shed some tears and take some of her advice. I present to Ruby the following. I find it unnecessary stress to receive such resistance, lack of communication and lack of compassion from certain members of the medical staff. I am told by Ruby that I am the first to be 100% involved in the care for a NICU premature child as a parent. Well, I am sorry for all the others lacking such support. That is not here, nor there. That is the explanation of the resistance I have received and continuously am receiving. I am simply asking for communication and respect in presenting updates, status and any changes or concerns for my daughter, Cailin Jane. The last medical team of doctors were informative, compassionate, available and assertive when informing me. They would call and come to the bedside. I very rarely would have to ask, page or track them down. This new medical team is on day 11. There has not been one single occasion or time they have approached me to provide what I need from them. Communication. Wow, how horrible, unacceptable and unprofessional. I will not tolerate it. That is only one layer. I have nurses particularly, Priscilla, and a few others that want to know where I am going, what I am doing, when I will call and when I will arrive for their own preparations. I will not communicate or let them know. I will come and go as I please during my 21 hours of access to my daughter. Worry about Cailin. I am at the hospital more than not. It would be one thing if I were being inappropriate by yelling and swearing at the staff. That is not the case here.

I have asked my father to support me emotionally. Hug me, encourage me, embrace me. My being, my inner-self. Be flexible to my needs. He replies by asking me aggressively, "What the Hell are you talking about? Give me specifics. I want to "throttle you." I want to "kick your inner-child to the curb."

He proceeds to tell me to seek a Psychiatrist here at The Human Spirit Hospital, and discontinue seeing my "spiritual advisor" and let him and my sister back into my life with Cailin. I send him a text message that I am seeing a counselor, "asshole." Get some support at AA. I want to hug his inner-child. That is the difference between us. Thanks for making it harder on me, Daddio.

I asked my sister, Marie, not to share Cailin's medical conditions, complications or status to keep it private. Her response was hours of text messages name calling (lonely "black horse, I am "sick", seek help). She disclosed that it is not about Cailin and I, nor Cailin for that matter. Wow! Who is the sick puppy? Quite malicious and sick to treat and talk to her sister in such an aggressive, negative, destructive and non-supportive manner. I asked and presented my needs. I was denied, rejected, name called, advised and not acknowledged. Well, I have been digesting and letting go of them and all their hurtful ways. The middle child that has provided the warm, worn-in, emotional comforter has pulled the cover off and burned it. The blanket will not return.

Ruby is surprised by all the layers I am experiencing. She asks how I feel with all the resistance I am getting from the staff, family and Cailin's illness. Well, I am having a real hard time with it. It is so heavy. I feel very much alone. Ruby confirms that I am alone. I know I am. If I didn't think or grasp that I was before, I know now. I am alone. I am strong. I am frightened. I am independent. I have heaviness all in my head. I am confident. I am on a plank all by myself. Ruby advises me to let go. Well, I am trying. I am trying to let go of the hurt and disappointment. I am trying to give space with Cailin's medical development. Ruby says it is hard for a control type person like me. Hard is not the description. I am lost. I do not know how to let go. I am trying. I pray for peace, guidance and serenity. I write and ponder on letting go.

Let go and let God. I think of Cailin's GI exploratory surgery. Do the benefits outweigh the risks? I hope that the doctors will be in God's presence with His child. Cailin is a gift to me as my child, and to the doctors a patient. God's plan and will is and has been in place for sometime. I have been distracted and hurt by all the turmoil. I am asking and communicating my needs. Knock, knock... nobody's home. I need to switch gears and keep praying. I pray for guidance. God, guide me a peaceful direction for I feel I keep encountering turmoil. Isn't it enough that I am struggling with Cailin's medical journey? Apparently, those are not the lessons God has for me and others. I am your instrument.

I am your ears. I am your heart. I am being kicked around and I still believe that Cailin will survive. I am believing God does good. Good will shine through. It does through all of these times too. It is just hard to see at times with my heavy heart.

I think of the ways. Ruby is his work of goodness. She is kind, sincere and real. Kind is key. I am having a real hard time with the lack of manners and cruel behavior. I don't have the heart or stomach for it. Unfortunately, I will express myself. I will ask for help. I will pray. I will show how lack of manners, rejection and cruelness affect me. Why should I not say something? I need to be strong for Cailin and express myself to stay strong. Keeping all this in will make me crack. Ignoring all the let downs and disappointments won't help me process. Letting go after I express will help me. Ruby hugs me, rubs my shoulder and encourages me to let go a bit. I trust her and know she really means well. I agree with what she says and speaks to me. Priscilla is right on my back. "Isn't Ruby great? She just knows." Yeah, she knows, cause you told her our conversation. How about a breather, lady? You are right on me to see how I feel about Ruby and my conversation. Priscilla is God's goodness, but needs to back off a bit. Give me some space. She doesn't understand me because her emotions are too highly involved. My mom is God's goodness. She heard me out and laughed with me a bit over it all. My home is His grace. I can sleep and be at peace.

During all these recent relationship developments and declines, Cailin is suffering from bowel issues. She has been passing blood in her stool. "Not frank," they say. Amen.

Older looking blood. Her stomach is measuring big, anywhere from 21-24 centimeters. She ends up throwing up bile, about 19 cm all over her face. Priscilla was on that shift. When I look the mantra up in Louise Hayes' book, *You Can Heal Your Life,* the mantra is, "I digest life with ease." Well, isn't that something? Cailin has green bile on her face, and I have bullshit on mine. So, here we go baby girl. Let's keep breathing in life with ease. How? Change directions. I have spoken plenty of my frustrations. What did you say Ruby? I feel you, I carry you and I hear you..."Carrie just try to let go." I am letting go. I am shedding the energy of dismay.

I went to take a break. My intention was gift shop, coffee, yogurt, bathroom and Chapel. At the gift shop, I discovered an amazing frame for $4.50. It is in my budget. It says, "Some of the greatest times are the times spent with my daughter." I am confident. I head to the cafeteria for coffee and yogurt. I always pick the register with the Asian lady. She calls everyone either young lady or young man. She is silly, always smiles and winks. I enjoy her presence. She has no idea how much she lifts my spirits each visit. I go to the trash to see the large Italian mustached Security Officer. We wave at each other and he asks, "How are you doing?"

I reply, "I'm hanging in there."

He responds, "Keep it up!"

I cross the hallway to obtain a parking sticker. I see the Interpretive Services along with Public Relations. I ask if they could interpret English to some of the doctors? I am being sarcastic. The lady tells me if I have issues, that is where I would go. I think about it. The next direction of whether I am getting the information I am seeking from the docs. I will use the avenue if it presents itself. Presently, I have to excuse myself to the ladies room.

I head to the Chapel. I discover a booklet with meditations and prayers. I love it. I sit by Mother Mary. There are about 20 different cultural Mother Mary statues, ceramics and pictures. I read through all the different ones. Where they are from, their heritage and other mystical facts. I am praying to Mary. I see Ruby come out of a small room in the Chapel, the room where I disclosed many of my sins. I waved. I am unsure if she will stop by me. She does in her pretty pale yellow sweater. We talk a bit about how I am feeling. I disclose more of the history of some inappropriate comments I have received from the staff. How I do not think Priscilla is helping me even though I believe that is her intention? I have to let her go. Ruby expressed compassion toward me and guidance. Ruby is allowing Cailin and I to digest life with ease. Her presence puts me at ease. I can confide in her and get to a better place. I feel better communicating with her than I do my counselor. Ruby has the spiritual connection. Here is another ah-ha moment. I connect with more consciously aware folks. My dearest friends are the ones with a spiritual connection. So, the different angle is digesting life with ease. Ruby and I say goodbye to only reconnect up on the unit.

Now don't think for one moment there are not amazing people and gestures up on the unit. I had Delight, mother of four, two children getting married off this year and her beloved dogs. She has been great with me all day. Kind and attentive. She is pretty silly and funny too! She waited for me to move Cailin. I arrived back up to the unit. We moved from Bed 20 in the second row to Bed 34 in the third row. How nice was that? A breath of fresh air. She did not have to do that for me. Delight did.

Ruby and a Medical Student arrive at the bedside. We talk, smile, laugh. I ask to share some of my writing with Ruby. She accepts. I read two passages. She is impressed, touched and feels it is me. Deep and light laughter. Then she asks, "Do you want to pray?"

I say, "Yes, can we pray to Mother Mary?"

She says, "Yes," with a smile.

Ruby describes in detail the importance and the connection to Mother Mary. Mother Mary was chosen to carry baby Jesus. She helped tighten her faith during much gossip, doubt and despair. Similar to my journey with my Cailin. We pray to Mother Mary and bless Cailin with the holy water my Mother provided for me. I feel lighter. I feel guided. I feel presence of life. God's life. My daughter Cailin is in his presence.

I await Cailin's 8 p.m. routine, which includes labs, new bedding, weight, exams and story time. At around 6 p.m., Auntie Angie arrrives. Angie is one our Angels. She is sweet, kind, an Aries and a Neonatal Nurse Practitioner. She brings Portillo's, our usual dinner. Chopped salad, fries, onion rings with extra dressing and two pops. We spilt. We catch up in the waiting area. Patience, the Pick Line Nurse Practitioner, comes in to bring me a card. A card for a company that is for "the greater good." Symbolic. Says funds go to various causes. We all three chat. Patience is an inspiration as well. She has had quite the journey with her son. She was a huge advocate for his needs in the school system. She rocked the boat a bit. Resistance allows for and creates the rocking of the boat. Then there can be some smooth sailing.

Angie and I work through Cailin's 8 p.m. routine with her nurse. We change her bedding. I helped weigh her and discover she is 950 grams. Cailin's blood gas comes back fabulous. They decide no changes in order to give her a good night. Angie always fills me up. Comfort, understanding, education on more of the medical side, encouragement and praise as a NICU mom. She is so great to both of us. I am grateful. We both head out of the hospital and go home. It's an early night for me. I will have an early morning and long day tomorrow. Time to get rest.

January 15

The number 15 is significant. My mother was born on the 15th of November. A true blue Scorpio. She was late with me and had to be induced. My mother, Trish, choose the fifteenth of April. Today is January 15, a decision day, for Cailin Jane's possible, "penciled in" surgery day. I awoke at 5 a.m. I called to speak with Angle, her nurse, regarding Cailin's night. She had a good night. I arrived at 6 a.m. I waited patiently for Dr. Glamorous Gladiator, the surgeon. I prayed with my little prayer book that Margaret had given to me. I prayed, rocked in the glider and breathed. Today is a big, huge day.

Now all the last 52 days have been big days. Today, the fifteenth, is one of those crossroad-changing days. I hear Dr. Glamorous Gladiator coming down row three with her high heels. She greets me with a smile and says, "Hello Carrie." Angle, the nurse, notices Dr. Glamorous Gladiator and she arrives back to our bedside 34. Dr. Glamorous Gladiator notices that Cailin's stomach looks better. She asks Angle about Cailin's night, her diaper and stool. I mention a few important details to Dr. Glamorous Gladiator. I talk about how she has 22.5 centimeters. She had a large stool with the same maroon color. The stool would be large due to no stool output since her episode of throwing up. Cailin vomited 19 cc of green bile two days ago. That was alarming for Dr. Glamorous Gladiator. She stated, "Cailin does not appear to have had NEC (bowel disease) and there maybe an obstruction of scar tissue in her intestinal tract. She really has everyone scratching their heads. I think we should have an upper GI performed to see where the blockage is for her. Then we could determine on surgery or not."

The procedure is discussed between Dr. Glamorous Gladiator and Angel. Dr. Glamorous Gladiator is asking Angle if Cailin is stable enough to be transferred to Radiology for a 20-minute procedure. Angle is hesitant. The shift change is occurring so the buck will be passed. The buck stops on the right advocate and nurse for this situation, Jem. Jem had the honor of comforting me when I thought I lost Cailin for 15 minutes. Jem is a no mess, no fuss kind of gal. She is warm, funny and just very real. I head to go pump and hit the bathroom. I arrive back to Cailin's bedside to have Jem come back through the row with all Cailin's IVs and medicine. She smiles and looks at me to say, "What a day already. I told them they need to come up to the unit to do the upper GI, or if I am going down it is not alone. I will have to have a doctor come with me. I was supposed to be row leader. I delegated that too. I am not afraid of speaking my mind." I gave her a big hug. She laughed and hugged me back. The buck is on the right pair of shoulders today, the fifteenth.

I called my mom to come at 7 a.m. The surgery decision was a long process. I wanted and needed her here with me if she was having surgery. She puts her clothes on and heads to the Human Spirit Hospital from Palatine. I wait patiently knowing it will be close to two hours. She was in

January 15

bed when I called her. I helped with Cailin's 8 a.m. handling including a diaper change, measurement of her belly, temperature, weigh diaper output and tuck her in. My mother arrives shortly after 9 a.m.

Peggy, the slender tall front desk diva, says, "I can just send her back." I wait and she arrives. I stand up and say, "Mom, I will wait for you to put your cape on to hug you." I lean down and grab one for her. I assist her with putting it on. Then I let her hug me. She hugs me for a long time. We rock very gently. Gentle tiny motions just like the size of our baby girl, Cailin. I let myself weep a bit. I am so relieved to have a hug from my mother. Our healing process for our relationship started the day Cailin was born. We are much further along in the process.

We spend about a half an hour with Cailin. My mom asks, "Is she sucking her thumb, Carrie?" I step over to the incubator to see Cailin has discovered her thumb and placed it in her mouth. She has her petite slender hand covering her face and her thumb under her tubing. Wow! My baby girl is becoming a big girl. She is so very mature for a 30-weeker and quite alert which is a clear sign of intelligence. She is quite active which is another good sign. Cailin you are a smart fighter! She is no fool. I am so happy and comforted by the fact she has found how to soothe herself. Another small step for us Kacens.

The unit does not allow the parents be present for "rounds" between the hours of 9:30 a.m. to noon. I am starving and already exhausted. This is just the beginning of a heavy and very critical day. We head downstairs to the cafeteria to have breakfast. I am fed but not satisfied by the taste. It hits a void, just not the expectation. We talk a bit. I have to call the bank. I screwed up this past month. Last month I was fine. I had more issues come down from last month. I am delayed with a screw up. I give myself a pass. Damn, no one else will. I am strong. I am confident. I am independent. I am human. I can make mistakes. I can fumble. I can stop cry and ask for help. Does that mean it will be delivered... no. Surprises are always pleasant.

We head back up to the unit to pump. My mom is reading Nicholas Sparks' book, *Dear John*. I love his writing. He is so in tune with his emotions. I keep asking her "How is John, Mom?" She talks about the characters as if they are her friends. Just as my characters develop. My interactions here at the NICU will shape how I write. My story is real and raw. We head back to the waiting room and keep the lights off. Upon heading there, I see a silver-haired man with a Radiology stitching. Jem won the game for Cailin. I love when common sense overrules! I lie down and sleep for about 15 minutes. I wake up on my right side with a sore shoulder and some drool. Such an attractive new sleeping trait I acquired during my pregnancy that has yet to seize. Cailin and I are very, very similar.

I hear my own voice, "It's time." I need to get up and see my daughter. We arrive back at the bedside. She has had an x-ray every 15 minutes since 11:15 a.m. I know that this is a heavy day. What do I mean by heavy? Well for a confident, strong and independent mother of a 23-weeker it entails much. Heaviness is what my soul, mind and heart feels. I feel that worry is creeping in all areas. Doubt is smiling around the corner. Interdependence is required. I have to truly let go and let God. It is a mantra I hear often. I say often. I work hard. The heaviness is the hurdles and layers I have to jump and peel off. Since November 24, 2009, I have felt heavy. I can get to a lighter place, a less worrisome state, a faith-driven sense when I do certain things. I have to discover the oasis through my inner self.

My inner self is just like this upper GI procedure. The clear dye is ingested to show a "contrast" through Cailin's digestive system. The "contrast" is the way I see light. I feel light and trust light in this deep dark sea. Some moments are fast and completed. Some times are long or come to a stop or just move slowly. I have to hear and feel my inner self to heal. My relationships are changing. I am transforming. Cailin is growing and being challenged. I am going through the most painful and joyful growing pain in my entire life. Why? Because God granted me Cailin as a gift and all she brings and all she destroys. The cycle of life. Out with the old, in with the new. I have to step away from the comfortable large door and keep walking to the sunny breezy welcoming window where I feel and hear my daughter calling me. I am coming. I am coming. I am strong. I am coming. I am confident. I am coming. I am not so independent. I am coming. I want to be with you, Cailin, where all my journeys end. My true love.

Love conquers all. We have all day to work with Cailin's updates and have her know and feel her family. We are here for her. I will not leave you alone, my daughter. I am here and will always be here in your heart... forever. You are surrounded by so many folks that love you and me. The countless prayers are what we depend on. They are working. They are transforming. They are saving. Prayers are a way to show love for God and his return is always goodness. I pray for many people these days. I pray for the loved ones that understand and support me, those who are hurting and hurting me, those who care for Cailin, caregivers hands, minds, hearts and souls to be directed to help Cailin. Cailin is in the grace of God.

The prayer circle grows and her procedure grows. We are here watching her stats sail and her x-rays are conducted. Mom and me. Cailin has two major supportive females physically fighting for her. Mom is doing Reike. I am doing visualizations. I have visual signs come to me or physical pains during Cailin's fight. I see visually two tubes or "loops" the docs would say. Right side, yellow and green. Not good. Not good coloring. I breathe through them. I imagine working the energy through her urine track. I breathe. I place light through it.

Enrique, Respiratory Therapist, is wearing Belief. I questioned him earlier about the scent. He commented on my sense of smell. All my senses are heightened. I have a good nose. I am Polish. Smiling. We discuss this earlier with Jem. Then Jem smells my scent. Pink. I mention this conversation to my mom when he arrives back to Cailin. I let Enrique know my mom is a massage therapist. She, he and I start on an uplifting conversation. We discuss Reike. My mom is invited to do it on Cailin physically. I voice it to Enrique that I am open to it. Enrique, "Good, then when I am here I will do some on Cailin."

The Consciousness Club keeps growing in numbers. "Carrie, try asking it what it is, what it wants, what you should do," the Animal Tamer states. I remember all these fragments, moments and statements that help me along the way to heal Cailin and heal myself. My soul sister, my daughter. I imagine a huge breeze by the water and the ocean blowing.

That is my visualization. Let things go. To feel. To release. To pick myself up. To keep going. Visualizations are so powerful for my mind and body. I envision many colors, themes, wonderful sites to protect, play, heal and relief Cailin from this medical reality. My micro preemie princess deserves the most wondrous places to come to her and to go visit. We are only a thought away from all of this, Cailin Jane.

Jem sits on Cailin's blood and starts to laugh. She thought I put it under her butt to play a trick on her. Cailin definitely needed blood to help her. I love when she gets blood. Her coloring is just so much better. The x-rays are scheduled now for every hour. At 3:15 p.m. they changed it to every two hours. I paged Dr. Wise to come to her bedside. He appears twenty minutes later. Dr. Wise. How can I describe this man? I am told he is brilliant. I know he is. I trust his medical knowledge and years of experience utilizing his gathering. He has sweet eyes. He is a gentle man. He has a nervous giggle and funny, quirky jokes. I like his jokes. I find his commentary helps lighten things and protects him from the intensity of emotion. He avoids me. I have to call him to the bedside. He will not approach me first. I see that now on the fifteenth day with Cailin on his team. That does not make me happy. Reality is not always happiness, but it is what it is. What it is, is what you have to work with. I can verbalize all I want and be present for updates. I cannot make someone deliver it to me. I can page and draw the doctors to the bedside to obtain Cailin's updates. Dr. Wise explains the process that Cailin's upper GI is through her left side and small intestines. This could take two hours to two days. Her own sweet time. He and the others can give me all the facts and scenarios of Cailin. I desire and have a right to know. Does that mean what it will be? No, because it is between Cailin and God.

My new team has knowledge. They should, as they are Neonatologists. I am not impressed with the communication. Dr. Wise does come out and entertains my questions. He keeps his distance from me. I called him out. He is responsible for shaping his Fellow, Dr. Vague. I am not impressed with her at all. I can say that she actually says hello and acknowledges me now in the unit. I am not seeking a friendship nor expect them to chat when I am on the unit. I expect Cailin's daily updates when I am at her bedside. They know I am here. Dr. Fine, the Resident, resides well with me. He was eager day one. He came to the bedside to meet Cailin and talk to the nurse. Oh, I so happen to be there! Ha! He asked me at the end of our conversation, "Is there anything I can do for you?"

I said, "Use not only your mind but your heart. That is all I ask of you."

My new team has big shoes to fill. They had huge hearts. Dr. Glee, the Resident, resided well with me. She was calm and comforting and extremely informative. Cailin was extremely critical. I had many critical conversations. She was a delight on such heavy, scary conversations. Dr. Jasmine, Fellow, was amazing and continues to be amazing since

January 15

November 24, 2009 on the Labor and Deliver floor. She is kind, informative, realistic and extremely compassionate to her patients and passionate of her work. Cailin. She blew me away. I hold her. Jasmine, will be in my heart forever. Dr. Sensible, the Attendee, is a remarkable woman. She reminds me of a tribal leader of this unit. She walks out and there are all eyes on her. She directs all of us; nurses, doctors, medical students, and parents with grace. I feel so secure with she was on Cailin's case. I embrace her. I can communicate well with her. She knows I will voice my opinion and finds a middle ground. She explains medicine, procedures and staff to me. She gets me. She will actually cape up and sit to talk to me in isolation. Not my new team though. Sitting with me is a larger commitment. Emotions? Time? The new team does not grant me. Am I just another old hat here? The hat that was shiny, new and fun before. Now, still the same song just different instruments. So, I find it is out of tune.

I am exhausted and restless. So, just imagine how Peggy, Front Desk Diva, feels. I need a pillow. I need a blanket. Yes, we will go to the quiet room. I lay down on the love seat. My mom is back to reading *Dear John* with the light on.

I fuss, "It is too bright."

She replies, "Do a Cailin and put your scarf over your eyes."

I have not felt very funny or much laughter lately. She was working it out of me. We laughed our tails right off. I repeated it to the nurses Jem and Snow White. Oh, they both understood the joke right away. It was joined with laughter! Sarcasm has a bit of truth in it always. My mom is full of sarcasm. I get back to her bedside to be part of the 4 p.m. handling. I missed it. I was so out of it. I went back to the quiet room. My mom laid a bit on the loveseat. Now I got a laugh.

"Mom, I am tired. I want to go home and lay down for an hour or so." These moments of pure exhaustion result in me surrendering. I am then asleep for only 10-20 minutes to wake up in full anxious thoughts. I drive my mom and I home. There is no place like home, except Cailin's home. We settle into my family room. Lights are dimmed, water fountain going and pine candles burning. I am all about environments. Hence, Cailin's colorful collection of receiving blankets, incubator covered with blankets, small washcloths and large ones available for props, blankets or an eye mask. I had on my two new piano CDs for our nap. I mention to my mom how I have always wanted to play the piano. I plan to purchase a piano and learn along with Cailin as she gets older. The sound of piano rocks my soul gently.

I try to wake my mom gently. She was snoring. I awoke and laid there for about three Tracy Chapman songs. I rose and called to my mom. "Mom, I want to go see Cailin."

"Carrie, she is fine," my Mom replies.

"I know she is right now, but I want to see her." I go into the kitchen. What can I do to keep myself busy while she wakes up? She is a much slower mover than I. I want to be patient. I decide to do the dishes and make a sandwich. I glide swiftly through my condo to the living room.

January 15

"Mom, I am going to make a sandwich with horseradish spread, mustard, tomatoes, Munster cheese and turkey. Do you want me to make you one?"

"No, all the salad and soup at the hospital made me feel pregnant."

I reply, "I miss being pregnant." I do consistently make this sandwich and miss being pregnant. Cailin was safe within me and I could feel her. I never got the chance to feel really fat, annoyed or swollen. For all you fat pregos... don't complain. Breathe. Most likely, your child is the 90% of full term birth statistic. I would rather have fat feet than see Cailin fight for her life each day.

We arrive back on the Neonatal Unit. Jem looks at us with confusion, "I thought you were going to lay down for a while?"

"I did and had dinner," I reply.

"What did you have to eat?"

"I had a turkey sandwich." Here I am justifying my calorie intake to Jem now. I am strong. I am confident. I am independent. She cares. There is not nearly as much privacy one would want around these neck of the woods. Snow White arrives out of the woods for the evening shift. I am always so happy to see her. "Hi, Snow White! How are you feeling?" We talk with my mom. Mom and I read to Cailin. We do some Reike. We proceed to leave the unit around 9 p.m.

We walk out. "Mom, thanks for being there for me. Being peaceful and just being."

My mom responds, "It was a good day. I enjoyed spending the day with you and Cailin."

I dream off to more days and memories. More good days to come. Night, night Cailin Jane and to the fifteenth. Hello, God.

January 17 - Promise

The sermon at 9 a.m. mass was about Promise. My song to Cailin Jane is *The Promise* by Tracey Chapman from her New Beginnings album. The album keeps me centered and grounded. Did Tracey think she would soothe someone with her lyrics, melodies and voice? She has brought such harmony to my mind, body and soul. Tracey, thank you. For you I am grateful. Promises are made and broken. The lyrics of the song describe the scenario of how I will come for Cailin as long as she waits for me. You wonder how can Cailin wait for me? Am I waiting for her? No, I am not waiting for her. She is waiting for me. I am her mother and I need to complete my healing process of life. As her body hits rocks and hard places during her growth outside my dark warm uterus, I cross the hurdles of my life. I promise to Cailin, God and myself to be true to all of us. Where is the end? There is no end in a journey. There is no destination. The promise is what carries us through life and the promise is the land of God.

I ponder on the promises I have made. The truest is the promise to be Cailin's mother. It started the moments before my pregnancy test that I knew it very well might be positive. Joy. Pure joy was the promise that she made when the cells were dividing and making her body. God promised to me a gift of life. He provides goodness. We have the choice to serve him or doubt him. I choose to follow him. Belief. Faith.

Today was a wonderful day. Cailin has been sleeping heavily and doing really well. Her grandma came to church with me, had breakfast, cleaned for me and read to Cailin. Thanks, Mom. I have a surprise for her up my sleeve. I am going to hold Cailin for the second time. My mom is so surprised and happy. She kept saying, "I have a feeling that today is going to be a wonderful day. Cailin is going to be doing so well." Well mommasita, you are right! Princess Aurora, our nurse, is discussing the plan.

"What, what?" my mom says with her head and eyes displaying confusion. "Carrie is gonna hold Cailin?!" she asks with her mouth wide open and eyes tearing.

We had a wonderful time together. I was able to hold her for one and a half hours. It was wondrous. I should have had my eyes closed to be able to feel more centered. I had my mom's energy along with Princess Aurora and Cherry. It was really nice for both of us though. I long for the next time I can hold Cailin.

January 18 – Disappointments, Letting Go

Today has much in store for Cailin and me. Manic Monday. I arrive to the hospital early enough to pump and change Cailin's diaper before "the visit." Betrayal is a door that hits me in the face often. I will explain what I mean, how I feel and what I do with it all. I told the donor to arrive at twenty after eight. He is typically late or cancels. He arrives at ten after. I am paged with his name at the bedside. That is all anyone knows at this point. I arrive in the hallway to see him. He buzzed his hair. His eyes are bulging out of his head. He is breathing heavily. He is nervous. I ask him, "How are you?"

He replies, "Okay, how are you?"

I respond, "I'm just hanging in there. I need to go to the bathroom. I will be right back."

He is wearing his black leather jacket that is too long for his arms. He has a stocky build. His jacket smells of cigarettes and his travels. He is wearing a Blackhawks shirt I should have thrown away while I was cleaning out his drawers. His jeans are the ones I purchased along with his shoes. He has all fresh undergarments, shoes and jeans from me. I had forgotten about all of that until I write of this. I sign him in.

Relationship. I put a cross through that one. Peggy, Front Desk Diva, nods with a sincere glare. We walk through Row 2. I do not look at the nurses. He is following behind. I wonder how he is taking it all in. Then I smile. This is a full circle moment. Completion.

I give him directions to place the cape and gloves on properly. He takes sometime with his shaky hands. I place the two rolly chairs by Cailin's isolate to sit down. Shortly after sitting, Dr. Glamorous Gladiator and her crew arrive. Oh, nice. He steps away to the far right. Princess Aurora is in the center of the outside circle. Dr. Glamorous Gladiator is wearing her hair down. I compliment her and she tells me that she had another one earlier. I believe it was Peggy. We discussed Dr. Glamorous Gladiator's hair before. Dr. Glamorous Gladiator needs to seek the most recent x-ray and talk to the Radiologist. We resume back to our visit. How do feel about that, donor? You are shitting your pants right now. I am sure of it. How about the last few months, I don't know, since July when I discovered I was pregnant? Oh, I remember so dearly. You were a selfish, lying sack of shit. Here we are though. I am letting go and letting God. Most advise this, yet never go to the brink and do such. I am here. Allowing someone that has known and grown with me. We grew apart many times. For many higher reasons we are here with this child. I stay separate from "his business." "My business" is mine. For "God's business" takes care of it all!

Princess Aurora is reading how baby Cailin is doing and she is putting in her data. I wonder if this is necessary. I let go of expectations and let God. Can you document that fact or gossip about it? Spread that word of the Lord, people. I ask if the donor would like to read a book to Cailin. He chooses one. A Dr. Seuss book from Christina. He has so much trouble separating the pages to read the book. He is sniffling. He has watery eyes. I have no idea what his thoughts are. Does he have a lot of regrets? Hurts? How can he lie and manipulate this situation? I have no cares. I am happy. I am relieved. I am strong. I am confident. I am independent. I am Cailin's mother. I am a good mother. I am doing a fabulous job with this wild, wild west we are dealing with.

My business is taken care of. I opened the door for a visit, completed it and am now letting go. Resistance gives him the power. I let go. I let God. I give way. I bow. I praise. I am complete. I move forward. I leave it in the past. His roads are at a dead end. He will have to construct new ones with his heavy load. Our heavy load is healing. I gave her what she deserves an opportunity and a visit. Princess Aurora provides information to the donor. What machine is what? What tube is what?

We leave because the doctors are about to conduct rounds. We walk through Row 2. We grab our coats. He thanks me. I have pictures for him. We enter the waiting room. I pull up my pictures. I say, "Have a seat." He sits. I show him pictures. How big I became during my pregnancy, Cailin right when she is born, when she is in the incubator, her Baptism, me after birth, after surgery, before seeing my daughter. I turn, "Do you have anything you want to tell me or ask me?"

He replies, "I can't even think right now."

"I can understand that," I say quietly.

We walk into the hallway. He turns, "Where is the bathroom?"

I say, "There are two to the right."

He replies, "Thank you." I walk to the elevators. I know him. He is throwing up. Crying and splashing water on his face. He will forget to do what he misses day after day. Look into the mirror. Look at yourself.

I proceed to the elevator bank. I get out of the elevator. I see his father. We make eye contact. Hello, Mr. Poor Role Model. He literally covers his face with his hand, his face is fleshed red and he turns. Shame. Guilt. Raw. Reality. The mirror is within for him. Life. It will always catch up with you. Run, drink, lie, cheat, play, smile, betrayal comes to a head. Always.

I proceed to the bathroom. Head to the store. I purchase food. Eat. Sleep. I take a nap. I wake up. I am still cramping horribly. I take a few bites of macaroni salad, two Tylenol, drink and crawl back to bed. I call Princess Aurora. Here is where trust begins and ends. I tell her I will not be up by noon. I have to have the Tylenol kick in to relieve my abdomen. She agrees. "I have to ask you, was that, Dad?"

"Yes, it was. Please do not share that with anyone," I reply. I believe that was English. She drew the information out. She asked. I replied. She took and documented. Shame on her for asking me. I proceed to be caught in a trap again. The

January 18 – Disappointments, Letting Go

game. Here in the NICU. Is it Vegas? No, it is a deep woods infested. Infested with many, many offerings. Your choice of how you want to react or proceed with care or caution. I get a check or a chip in Vegas. In the woods, someone tried to hang me a bit by my ankle to expose me. I will not be caught. I am a warrior. My work is larger than a few shifts and home arrival for my child. My child is my work, my purpose and my passion. I will win.

January 19

The surgery day. The opportunity to change things for the better. To be able to get Cailin to eat. I awaken at about 5 a.m. without my alarm. I tossed and turned to go back to sleep. I decided to go ahead and make the call. Smile, her nurse, filled me in on Cailin's night. Cailin had a good night and was on her belly. Belly time is a great time for Cailin. Her belly is hurting. Who wouldn't like to be on their belly when they do not feel well?

The debrief during the shift change disclosed a very disturbing and interesting piece of information. Smile asked Priscilla is she was aware of Cailin's surgery and her progress. Priscilla responds, "Yes, I have been calling for updates." I take it in. I want to scream. I must not. I breathe. I am pissed off.

I arrive at quarter to seven to visit and stand by Cailin's side. I am not interested in having a show. I keep saying, "Peace, Love and Joy." That's our mantra of the day. I change her tiny diaper to a more comfortable one. The surgery resident comes to mark her belly for her surgery procedure. He forgets to wash his hands upon leaving. I warn him and anyone else that is she not happy. It is displayed in her breathing. Do your peace soft, swiftly and get the hell out of her bed.

Priscilla approaches me from the left, "How are you? Are you a wreck?"

I look at her with a cocked head, "Really, what kind of question is that? No, I am not. This is the break that Cailin needs to get healthier. I trust Dr. Glamorous Gladiator and she is a good surgeon."

Her question displays the hard place we hit often. What a negative way to phrase it. If I told her how I really felt about today she might cry. I am concerned that her energy needs to be kept at bay. Too nervous and chatty for the situation. Her business. Her emotional capacity not mine.

My business is where the heck is my mamma? I text good ol' Trish. She is entering the building. Priscilla is a bit surprised by the page of my mom coming in. I am strong. I am independent. I am confident. I am a single mom with a sick premature baby who needs her momma. I know when to call in my support. I asked Courtney to come. She was unable. The way it should of been. My mom, Cailin and I. Three generations. Good things come in threes. Father, Son and the Holy Spirit.

My mom comes around the left of me to kiss me hello. I say, "Hi, Mom." I am relieved. I proceed to type a bit. Then I ask my mom to read to Cailin. I excuse myself to the bathroom.

January 19

Upon my short journey to the bathroom, Priscilla approaches my mom. "I know Carrie is strong and likes to be strong. Ruby is coming up."

My mother nods her head.

"She has a good rapport with Ruby," Priscilla adds.

My mother nods.

"We really need Carrie to express that she is scared," Priscilla finishes.

My mother does not reply. She does not give Priscilla anything. Priscilla's business. My mother's business. God's business.

My business is how the hell are you going to tell a mother of a 35-year-old grown woman what you need. Be a nurse not a family member. Her business is becoming a bit of nonsense. I am shocked and once again feeling my stomach. Feelings do not lie. I cock my head. Breathe and think. Make a plan.

My mom finishes reading to Cailin. I hand her my laptop to read my writings from yesterday. I wanted to tell my mother everything that has happened. It is too exhausting. So she could just read it. I read Cailin a prayer book. I talk to her about her surgery. I send her off with love. My mother and I head out of the unit at 9:25 a.m. We head down the south bank elevators and walk to the cafeteria for breakfast. We run into someone very special, Dr. Rose. She delivered Cailin. Our encounters are priceless and timeless. I love them. We hug and I fill her in on Cailin's status.

Scone, yogurt and coffee are my mom's breakfast choices. I choose cream of wheat with a ton of brown sugar, a cup of fruit and a cranberry-apple-raspberry juice. We sit at the same table we had last Friday. I discuss my concerns with my mother. I'm concerned with how things are going for me on the NICU floor. I decide that I am going to Public Relations. I have been thinking about it for a week now. Today is the day. I am done. My mom thinks we should wait until after the surgery. She is a person that waits until it is too late. I am an action person. Wait for what? Exploding. It is not worth it. I need a resolution for my tribulations.

I enter the Public Relations to tell the front desk lady I am a mother of a premature baby and I have concerns of the communication I am receiving from my team of doctors. She gracefully places my mother and I into a conference room. I sit down and watch where my mother chooses to sit. She sits across the table and down one chair. I place my two bags on the chair next to me. I put my feet up. Mrs. Resolution enters the room within five minutes. I am impressed. I think I found a pair of ears.

Note pad, pen, brain and ears. I proceed with my intro: "My name is Carolyn Kacen... I go by Carrie. My daughter's name is Cailin Kacen. This is my mother Trish Irwin. I was transferred here, to the Human Spirit Hospital, to have my daughter on November 24, 2009 at only 23 weeks, gestational age. I have been at the NICU unit for eight weeks.

January 19

I think that there are advantages and disadvantages of being at a learning hospital. They advantage is the amount of knowledge and brains for input. The disadvantage is rotation, miscommunication and dropping the ball. I believe that the hospital is great medically for Neonatal Medicine. My concern is communication... well, the lack of communication. I had a team that was so communicative with me. Dr. Sensible (Attendee), Dr. Jasmine (Fellow) and Dr. Glee (Resident) were all so informative. They came to the bedside, contacted me by phone and really were amazing. I have a new team now. Dr. Wise (Attendee), Dr. Vague (Fellow) and Dr. Fine (Resident). I have had them for two weeks. Not once has the Attendee or Fellow updated me without paging them. Dr. Fine, the Resident, was the only team member that has provided proper communication. Upon receiving our case, he walked over and introduced himself. He studied her chart and conversed with me. He is present whenever he in working at our bedside. I have to page Dr. Wise. I received hesitation on paging him in the beginning by the nurse. I still would not back down. He would eventually arrive. I spoke to him on two different occasions regarding my request of daily medical updates for my daughter, Cailin. Dr. Vague was unprofessional, rude and seemed bothered by my questions and interaction of Cailin's medical care since our first bedside. I spoke to Dr. Wise regarding the behavior and gave him specifics of the unprofessional behavior. I am concerned that when I disclose information that my nurse Priscilla thinks I need to respect the doctors and change. I do not feel heard or that I am receiving what I need which is communication. I have asked, requested and complained that it is not being received. On the flipside, how does my nurse obtain medical updates when she is not working? My own mother and family members are not to be receiving updates. That should be against the privacy policy."

Mrs. Resolution asks me a number of questions. Your telephone number? How do you know your nurse is calling for updates? Do you feel your daughter is receiving proper medical care? They are all easy answers. "Priscilla, my nurse, verbalized it to Smile, the last nurse, that she is calling for updates. How is that legally correct? I do not need to transfer my baby due to lack of medical care. Although here is where the bucks stops. I will seek legal counsel if updates are being given to a nurse that is in fact off duty. I feel that one party is too emotionally involved, Priscilla, and the other is lacking concern and care, the current team of doctors. I am sure that medically they are all very capable. That is not the only piece of good care. Your logo is, 'we treat the human spirit' and all you are posting is 'Care,' 'Concern' and so on. Correct? I am done trying to obtain and communicate I need to be informed on Cailin's progress. So here I am."

I am heard. There is a plan. Mrs. Resolution is going to document, speak to her director and check on the HIPA policy and see if it needs to go to the next level. She is apologetic that I am experiencing the resistance and fight. There is work to be done. The learning hospital is to receive feedback. Backlash is my mother's concern. No need to worry it will end. The gray area is large, but there is a fine line indeed. It has been crossed. The memo will do something. It is out there. Time to let it go and see what happens. I have had enough and took the next step. My mind, heart and head are cleared to focus on Cailin and her surgery.

January 19

We enter the unit to pump. My mother and I proceed to the waiting room. Ruby, the Chaplain, meets us. I fill her in on all the conversation I had with Public Relations. She encouraged me to seek a solution with them. Communication, change and work are what it boils down to. Ruby is proud, laughs at the humor of human ways and understands my journey. She is dedicated to us. Dr. Glamorous Gladiator, the surgeon, seeks me out. We meet in the hallway. It is my mom, Ruby, Priscilla and myself. Dr. Glamorous Gladiator informs us, "It should take 30 minutes to an hour. We have three different scenarios. After we remove any died, obstructed or scared bowel we could retie or leave it outside the body. We could also find nothing in the best case. I will come and talk to you after the surgery." Dr. Glamorous Gladiator does ask if I have any other questions. I do not. I trust and believe our surgeon. She is a remarkable woman and doctor.

Ruby, my mom and I are in the waiting room. We will be in the quiet room shortly. It is peaceful and serene to me. I have my pillowcase that is quite colorful and a bright, fuzzy, green blanket. Time to be present. Initially I am not looking at the clock. I do not want to see the time. Ruby, my mom and I have a long talk. Miscommunications, trials, tribulations, aspirations, dreams. Ruby asks, "What do you think Cailin will want to do or be?"

"Ruby I am not sure what she will want to be. I believe it will be something magnificent. I envision her as a rainbow. A rainbow or bridge of bringing others to another place. A healer like me. I will have to guide her into not trying to save everyone. As I have learned that you have to save and evolve yourself to really transform to your fullest potential. When you are there that is when you will really do his work. God's work that is."

Ruby has a meeting. She thinks that they are boring. I agree. Talking about what is going to happen. I am an action person. I believe action speaks louder than words. I give her a hug and head to the restroom. Today is an action packed day. No meeting for me. Just respectful and sincere visits, medical updates and major surgery for my daughter, Cailin Jane.

I await the process and I am present. My mom and I spend the day in the "quiet room." The quiet room is a very tiny room. I like it though. I find serenity there for some reason. I peaceful quiet room on the outskirts of this wild, wild west. Jem, the nurse, knocks. I see her and welcome her in. There is a saying on the unit. "There is only one Jem." Well, the statement holds true. Cailin and I have a special bond and pleasure to have her in our lives. She was there the first meltdown I had; she was there for the Radiologist upper GI and now awaiting her surgery. Jem bought Cailin her first doll. It is a Russian stackable doll. It is pretty cool. I am so happy. How thoughtful. Jem was at Brookfield Zoo yesterday and couldn't find anything. She also said there were like no animals there. There were only two monkeys in the huge monkey display. She finds out that they lost some monkeys due to old age. She also has a fear of birds. Most people have been traumatized by some animal. So, she is at the zoo and her husband tells her to stay to right and walk rapidly. She turns her head to only see a pissed off peacock. Well, there you have it. She always makes me laugh and happy. I am glad she stopped by to visit.

January 19

Jem is pulled down to the newborn unit to "play" all day she says. Lucky her, oh no! Lucky them. She is a so very special!

My mom is really enjoying the company. I believe it is having time go by quickly too. Dr. Wise is the next to stop in. He describes the bedside as calm. They have been working for about 45 minutes. He can't eye the vent settings though. That was my only question. He briefly discusses how he believes the surgery is going well. My mother and I believe he received the memo. The memo from downstairs that is.

Now the very next visitor is brief. It is a tall woman that looks similar to Dr. Glamorous Gladiator. I say, "You look like Dr. Glamorous Gladiator. You could be sisters. You are the taller version of her."

She smiles, the lean counterpart of our surgeon. "We still have not found the source." That is the feedback.

More healing to come out of this situation. I should say more healing needs to happen. I am a huge part of the healing. Cailin is healing her physical body. Mine is mental and emotional. We both are shedding skin of the past and past lives. Our current lifetime together is sure going to be pure and special.

Katie, our nurse angel, comes to visit. She talks of Cailin, family and work. She shows me her badge holder. She has amazing pins. She gives me a pin with the tiniest feet in gold. It is an anti-abortion pin. Nana would be proud. The pin reminds me of the fear I carried to disclose my pregnancy with Nana.

I could not tell her in person. I asked myself, why do I have to be the perfect one? Back in July, I told Nana that I was expecting and I would be a single mother. She thinks my child is the luckiest to have a smart, stable and established mom. Nana makes me feel so good about myself. There is nothing like the bond between a grandma and her grandchild. I will need to remember that when my mom drives me crazy. Cailin needs her grandma. Katie talked to me about that before as well. Katie's visit ends shortly after a few stories due to her shift beginning in about a minute.

Dr. Vague entered the quiet room hesitantly. She shook my mother's hand and I reached for hers. I was laying on the loveseat for Cailin's surgery. I was trying to stay calm as possible. All the visitors, not looking at the clock and breathing made it possible. Dr. Vague explains that there was one piece removed from Cailin. Priscilla had shown it to Dr. Vague. Dr. Vague explained the post-surgery plan and how it was going to go medically. Her main focus is pain control so Cailin does not have any recollection of this surgery. She will come up with a plan regarding her fluid retention, output and anything to help Cailin. "She is very sick," Dr. Vague states. She will keep us posted on any other developments.

My mom and I look at each other thinking. Did she get a memo regarding my complaint? I assume this due to my past experiences with her. We chat and reflect and do not look at the clock. We hear a knock and a slow entry. It is Princess Aurora, our nurse. She says ever so softly, "Hi. How are you?" We chat about how long Cailin's surgery is taking. I also tell her that we are avoiding looking at the clock. She is sympathetic and frightened as well.

January 19

Nearly three hours later, the procedure is finished. There is a knock on the door. Dr. Glamorous Gladiator enters and sits down. She states to us, "I do not envy either of you. Cailin is a trouble, troublemaker. She is a very strong baby. We removed two sections of her intestines. The amount was ten centimeters. The obstructed pieces of bowel were very compacted." I breathe. I have no questions for her. I am told I will be able to see her shortly, not yet though.

I wait until Dr. Wise knocks and enters the quiet room. "You can go see her."

Upon entering Cailin's bedside, there is still a lot of action. I see the Animal Tamer by her breathing vent. "She can hear you, Carrie."

Priscilla says, "It's not a pretty sight." I am not amazed that she said this, although it is not what I want to hear. I will make my own impression on the aftermath of Cailin's surgery. I attempt to put the heartbeat sound on Cailin's sound machine for her. Priscilla does not agree with this approach. As a mother, the only familiar peaceful sound would be a heartbeat. Not Priscilla coming down anxiously after the surgery, her loud voice and her continuously snapping the doors. I am very grateful for her hard work during Cailin's surgery. The power struggle is not good for her, me or the most important person, Cailin.

This is the beginning of another very, very critical point in Cailin's life. She is struggling to manage in her fragile, sick preemie body. I am struggling with the thoughts of pushing her too hard, losing her and getting through the recovery. It always gets worse before it gets better.

Manifest – January 20

I enter with a cougar with a magnificent orange cape complete with amazing markings. I see a sunset upon the unit coming from Bed 34. I arrive desiring privacy. There is privacy with curtains. I visualize the setting. The environment has a warm breezy climate. We are in the jungle and isolated due to the need of healing Cailin. I sit at the beside while my courageous cougar is to the left. The tail whips the ground showing power and seeking comfort. The intentions of others are taken in by the cougar. If the intention is not good, the entry will not be allowed. Teeth, claws and the growl are our defense mechanisms.

Streaming around the curtains are wind chimes, mirrors of all sorts and shapes, crystals and crosses. Upon entering there is a waterfall with playful mermaids and brightly colored fish. The statue at the waterfall is Mother Mary. She is the protector and provider of our love. God has plans. We will leave in wholeness of good health. I speak to my daughter, I provide her with praise, uplifting communication and updates of messages. Cailin you are puffy and so very cute. You are beautiful with all your strength. God has light and love all over you and me. God is using you as an instrument for the medical staff. You are making Him proud and He will carry you through this journey. I have you in my heart always and forever. I am on the outside of the journey at times. He has plans of truth and change for this unit. I am suffering to voice our journey and our needs to help other families. It is not an easy road, but it is ours.

He has promised to guide, aid, strengthen and light our road. I promise to be your hand, shoulder, voice and mother forever. I place Cailin Jane in my heart with pure unconditional love. This love we all share is immeasurable and unbreakable. Surgery, snares, miscommunication, lies, avoidance and disregard cannot or will not stop our work as his servants. He has placed us here. We are not alone.

For when I am low, he carries me and same for you. I have my mind to paint and visualize our place. I hear cries of pain around me. Our place does not have cries just clear and good intentions. I visualize your curly blonde hair smelling fresh and feeling lovely. I see your bright blue eyes filled with happiness and joy. Your smile is contagious. We dive into the water. I pick you up under your shoulders and twirl you around in the water. We are mermaids with beauty, joy and fresh water. We have a remarkable bond as mother and daughter. I hear splashing, laughter and the calm sounds of the waterfall. "Play," you say to me, Cailin.

I play a part. I am a warrior for you as I navigate this jungle. You are my young. I will fight any measure to keep you safe and protect you at any cost, my love. Before my glorious entrance as a mother, I had an exit. A memorable exit of my "old self."

Manifest – January 20

I am a warrior. Bang, bang you're dead. Egos... bye, bye. The nurse, Snake, the one that was swearing and cussing at a sick child due to her bowel movements. I stored it in my memory bank. A large bank. A calculated bank. Emotions are present. Yes, of disguise and disappointment for this creature, Snake. The lean build and angry movements and gestures. Bad juju. She was only present due to a break Cailin's nurse was taking. I was your warrior. She was told not to move you. You were in very critical condition due to your recent surgery. I refuse to allow miscommunication be at your mercy. I am your mother. I will help and provide comfort for you. Snake hovers over me and snares, "I could not open the bottom x-ray drawer due to her heplock and bicarb. You will not tell me how to do my job."

I reply anxiously, "I don't appreciate your tone, I do not read your mind, you should have verbalized yourself. You don't even need to talk to me. I know and heard how you talk to these babies, you are horrible!"

I leave to fight for your safety with Laine.

She is the gatekeeper of the floor of nurses. We see the list of the fools that will not care for you go up. I am sorry that there is even a need of such a filter. The jungle. Only the strong survive here. I will protect my young. I am done. Shape up and ship out. Out with the nonsense. We are on the up-and-up. Healing and recovery. Roadblocks, not allowed. We are moving forward, not down or to the side. See the light, Cailin? I know you do. Keep holding mommy's hand as we are being guided. Let's stay centered in our faith and keep moving forward. We are strong and have the right instruments to help us.

Cup of Joe – January 22

I am not talking about my sweet friend, JoAnne. Although I enjoy the cups she serves me. She will serve compassion, humor, reflections and pure connection. I connect my finger to the down button in the South Elevators. You have to go down before you go up. It gets worse before it gets better. It all comes to a head. The strides I take to the cafe in Human Spirit Hospital are to have a cup of coffee. I am exhausted. I see my friend, Jade, the cashier. She has spirit well beyond limits. She has the soul that soars. Resilience. She and Cailin both have that trait. Cailin is still paralyzed upstairs and I'm on the hunt for a cup of Joe. The cup of Joe and I meet up. In the café, I am asked about my baby. Two women that work there know my reason for my steady presence.

Jade calls me "pretty lady," not "young lady." I have arrived at a new, higher level with her. She knows about Cailin through a few brief questions. She says she believes in God and Cailin. I agree. She shows me the three pins she finds on the ground. She does not throw them away. She passes them into her inner circle of faith. Jade shows me the angel on her nametag. "This one is for Cailin." She winks and says, "I believe."

I do too, Jade. My smile responds for me.

I feel as if my cup of Joe has replaced my usual glass of red wine, Blue Moon, Martini. I am a mother of a NICU amazing lil' girl, Cailin Jane. I head to the waiting area to watch people and reflect. My iPod is already playing. It was mysteriously playing Eric Clapton. My dad looks like this guy. I love Eric Clapton. I will not change it. In my new book, *How to Hear God*, it describes this ebb and flow of life. Go with the flow. Most of the time it is God's way of providing what you need.

I had been dipping in my energy level and needed a break. I am trying to write, but no inspiration. I usually have a passion about an experience to write. I start to feel the tunes. Yep, my foot is tapping. Tears of joy and harmony are in my eyes.

I wave. I say "Hello, Cat!" She is one of the hundred nurses in the NICU. She is petite and just a wholesome lady.

She asks, "Who is that?"

"It's Baby Kacen's mom," I state with a smile.

Cat walks over. I speak from my heart. Cat is a mother of an Aries. Lilac is her Aries. Cat describes her past parenting approaches of many attempts to tame, smother and change her child's Aries ways. She tells about Lilac's mysterious personality. She correlates her daughter with me.

Cat asks, "How's Cailin?"

I describe Cailin's journey to this point and how she is an instrument of God's will. She is making us all be better. When I think of her intentions I see challenge, change, truth-seeker, leader, extremist and an amazing soul. I feel her soul when I put my head in her incubator. I describe it as busting out of the incubator. I thought I was powerful. Shit. I have nothing on her. Evolution they say. Damn straight. Cailin is going to give me a run for my money. God's plan is something of great magnitude for Cailin. She signed up and he trusts her entirely. I describe my perspective to Cat.

Cat asks, "Have you always been so introspective?"

"Yes, ever since I was a little girl." I have always known certain things. I have always had a gift. I am now really tapping into something that is going to bring Cailin and I to a wonderful place.

I have inspiration when I talk briefly and deeply with Cat. Write. Write it. That is what I hear when I ask God, "What do you want me to do?"

Here I am writing. When I write it is from the heart. Do you feel it? Sharing is what writing is. Yes! God wants me to share. What? Me, my journey and the struggle of life. The twist, turns and the sweet blessings he provides. For it is not what you take, but what you give. I give you all a view, gander and a long glare into my soul, our journey and God's work.

This cup of Joe ends. As all ends in life, there is another beginning. I begin to see Cailin during her 8 p.m. handlings doing much better. Why? I have many reasons, Joe! First, I was really holding her various small body parts more since her surgery. Healing her through my motherly touch. I speak to her through my soul right to hers. I bless her with the holy water. It gives me the idea of what I would want. Move all the possible valves, wires and medical nonsense off any possible area of her body. Placing a cool soft washcloth on her neck, ear, head and hand. I hold her tiny hands with both of my hands. I visualize God's white light from his Scared Heart through her body. 100, 100, 100. Her oxygen demands go from 97% to 90%.

Yoyo, her nurse says, "I don't want to push her."

I reply, "Let Cailin lead you, and don't put limits on her."

I have the enjoyment of The Animal Tamer, come up from the right. She pretends to swim through our bedside. I tell her of Cailin's new vent developments. How we cleaned out some webs at the bedside. Only our web is here. We do invite, but only one web. Ours.

I reflect on what I am doing. Balance is how I feel I need to keep close to my heart. Balance the amount of work I do. Work, meaning relationship work, spiritual work with some people in my life. Family. Friends. Medical Staff. I feel confident. I am independent. I believe. I believe in my inner-self, Cailin and the most of all, God. We are going to get through Cailin's recovery. I just feel it!

Eyes of Faith – January 23

We all have faith. Some sort of faith. Good. Bad. Indifferent. I feel glued together by my faith. I have many questions, glares and stares to see how and why I am holding it all together. For I have faith. My faith is my glue. I see my daughter wanting this life so dearly. Most adults complain and give up all the time. *I started working out, but I just can't. I don't have time.* Cailin has faith. She is not lazy, ignorant, naive, ungrateful or weak. She has great faith in God. I have all my pieces of my mind, body and soul glued together by faith. Yes, to all my family members that try to dissect and rearrange my glued pieces. All my pieces are working just fine. Actually, working grand for that matter. They are arranged, hung and glued where and why they all should be. Just so. I am strong. I am confident. I have faith. I am not so independent. I am dependent.

I depend on Cailin to lead the way. Tell us, my child, what do you need? More medicine. Tweet medicine. Vibes. When? Vent adjustments? What calculations? I depend on my inner-self to guide me. I depend on God to keep my inner-self informed and comforted on where to go. I depend on technology. I depend on communication. I depend on medical staff. I depend on the fan to work and cool us off under these hot capes. I depend on the gliding rocking chair. I depend on my laptop and my hands. I depend on guidance. Spiritual guidance.

I am selective on whom I tell, and how much I am dependent on all of this. I distract many with all my void fillers. Books, laptops, CDs playing, reading to Cailin, asking questions. For a very independent woman if you dance enough the dependence, it is a fun dance. Smooth and sometimes downright, a dance off. My last real dance off was with Dr. Wise and Dr. Vague. It all came to a head. I needed them. I kept demanding and desiring the approaches to provide medical communication.

They saw a ferocious, aggressive mama tiger. Everyone says "mama bear." I am not any kind of mama bear. I am a mama tiger. Low and calculated. I will watch and attack or defend when needed. I am not big. I am not the largest animal to frighten them. Oh, no! I am the shiny coat of a tiger with all my makeup and hair. I move with direction and draw viewers in to watch. I am viewed slowly by many eyes and minds as if I am a tiger on *National Geographic*. The narrator is all wrong though. I do not prey on the weak. The weak don't even want anything to do with me. It is the strong, smart ones. I want to make sure they know what I need and desire. I will bite with my approach and words. You ask, why?

Well, here you all have it. Miss Carrie Kacen is perceived as a petite, young, new single NICU mom. People will pity me. Pity the cards I have. Cards I hold in my hands. I am playing them. I know the game. People, places and things. We have people. All sorts of people. Each to their own right? Each, background, pride, ego, personality, issues, disorders, demeanor, intentions, practices, coping skills, problem solving skills, faith, family, friends, life perspective. So many people here at this NICU. Places of each. Where they live, where they grew up, where they wished they did both, where they like working, where they don't like working, where they are emotionally, where they are consciously, where they are mentally, where they are spiritually. Things, heights, weights, outer shell, inner-selves, voices, gestures, preferences, willingness. I baffle many.

What do people do to me, poor lil' Miss Carrie Kacen when they are baffled by me? Comfort, to a point of controlling. Embrace if there is a true pure connection. Rebel my spirit. Disregard or ignore, hoping I will go away or give up. Walk on eggshells. Confront to attempt to change me. Watch and observe me. Gossip. Question and wonder why I do and say as I do. Well, to everyone but God and Cailin, because I am me.

I am a person of great faith. I have amazing strength and joy during such a dicey game of life. I believe that God has big plans in store for Cailin and me. Guess what? They have already started. I reflect back on my life. I see how the poor Carrie moments and tribulations have been character builders. You cannot build an empire in one year, one day, one month. Oh, no! It takes years, dimensions, lifetimes. Here I am. He has prepared and granted me this. All of this.

Cailin knows the game. She was granted a spectacular entrance into this life. Her mother was the only parent to believe and have faith in her. I was the only one to provide love and nourishment from day one. Joy. Not pain.

When she came 22 minutes before Thanksgiving, yes, it was confusion. I knew something of great magnitude was occurring. The magnitude was of such greatness it was very challenging to wrap my head around it all. I wasn't supposed to. Daily bread. Daily grace. One day at a time. That was one minor lesson to cover great lengths in our journey.

Mystified - January 24

Cailin is up to 1500 grams. Her working weight is 900 grams. She is in recovery from premature delivery, but most of all her GI surgery. What surgery? When? How? Blah, blah, blah.. Cailin Jane resides at Bed 34 in the corner of the NICU. It is a widow seat. Her ventilator is next to the end wall, then her bed to the left of it and finally her nurses' station. She has two IV racks. She is working with two medicines on one rack and the other has all her IVs. Most importantly her TPN, which is her main source of nutrition. Cailin Jane is requiring a head shift right now. She has desated three times and brought herself back to good stats.

It has been a rainy day. The weather reminds me of Ireland. A place I dream of taking Cailin Jane to one day. The fog, rain and smell of spring are wondrous. A misty outside calls for a slower pace especially driving. I was moving slower today. My horoscope prescribed it. I surrender to a slower pace. Cailin teaches me each day how to just be. I enjoy being with her, even with all the medical attention she needs. I love being with her. She mystifies me.

Mystical is how I describe Cailin, God and our journey. The weather represents all the fog and fluff in the journey. Miscommunication, conflict, resolutions and joy. I do not jog around or back down with all the fog. I search from within. My inner-self contains the feelings that are present and navigate me through the mist. Cailin is clear. She cuts through all the fluff. The truth is always there. It may be covered up by rain, fog and feelings. The truth always prevails.

What are some of my truths? I am single. I am confident. I am independent. I am working through each day. I am discovering a lot of truths. Truths that are not what I hope for nor want. It is what it is. Sometimes "it" is just disappointing. I work through disappointment. I am doing a great job with it. When you become more and more aware it becomes easier.

When you drive in the fog you can only see a few feet in front of you. That is how the truth is. You can only bite off and chew a bit at a time. The truths that I have recently been mystified by are of great magnitudes. Cailin is in the Grace of God. Cailin is God's chosen child. I am her chosen mother. Egos fog and cloud necessary work. Work, not of a paycheck, but your life purpose work. I have to continually remind myself to operate out of my inner-self and live in the now. There is no time like the present. In the fog you can only see a little. The little is the now. Working with that makes this all possible to handle. Using my inner-self through prayer and meditation that is not the ego. The focus is working with and for my life purpose. My purpose has changed and transformed. This transformation process is mystical to me.

I am now on the brink of a whole new wide wondrous world. Cailin has brought me here. I am honored and anxiously working through all our hurdles. I speak to my dear friend, Kiki, today about all my trials and tribulations. Christine, Chrissy, or Kiki are her names. I tell her how I think of her children, Flynn and Fiona, often. "I think of your family, us Kacens and the Johnsens (Nina and Jake) going to Brookfield Zoo and having a wonderful time."

"Really?! Wow. Yeah, we are going to have a fun summer, Car," Kiki says.

She tells me how I make sense of all the confusion. I believe I have, and I am willing to cut through the fluff. Fluff, nonsense or really just bullshit. Who needs it? The people that can't handle the truth… what a waste, right?

Christine wraps up our conversation. I head around my condo to finish laundry, wash the facial mask off and pop in the shower. I am rested and moving slowly, as my horoscope recommended. Cailin is slowly making her health stronger each hour. I am thinking of how fast I can get to her. I live close, but it feels far away a lot of the time. It took about two hours after waking up to get back up to her. I brought some letters to paint. I will hang them for her over the changing table area. I am envisioning the transformation of my home to embrace her and all her needs. Her spirit is so very present at home already. I feel her all the time.

I arrive back to see Princess Aurora, her nurse, having a pink receiving blanket on her shoulder. "Oh, I see you trying to wear pink," I say loudly with a smile and laugh.

"I know. I am just gonna pretend to do some burping for Cailin," Princess Aurora responds.

Auntie Jem is peering down the row and smiles with our commentary. We are all having fun on a peaceful Sunday. I was unable to make it to church today. I did go to the Chapel and pray.

I am peaceful. I am mystified. I am strong. I have faith. I am a mother. I have a sick daughter. I am a truth seeker. I will fight for Cailin and myself through any fluff we are tossed. Bye, bye fog. Hello, sunshine!

Strength, Balance and Flexibility – January 27

I haven't been to yoga consistently since Cailin was born. I left my girl to utilize the "rounds" time to get yoga in, shower and eat. I need yoga. Yoga brings a lot of my internal stuff to the surface and I breathe it out. I am an aggressive person, so it helps to be physical. I have the drive and need a release. Yoga is a practice just like prayer. It is a way to honor your body, mind and soul with the universe.

What I like about yoga is the concept. For an overachiever and competitive person, it challenges me to let go. Give it up to the universe and God and breathe. There is no typical day of yoga. How your body is feeling is the measurement or boundary to work with in that moment or position. You have to connect with your inner-self. How many of us really connect daily with our inner-self? Well, there would be a lot less confusion in this world if we did.

Strength is a strength of mine. I am strong. In yoga, my muscles and mindset allow me to hold a position and alter the alignment to perfection due to my strength. I am always proud looking through the mirror at my strength. It is a sign and action of confidence. I am confident. I love that I have this aspect going for me in yoga. Yoga positions and the flow of them challenge my levels of strength.

I seek them as an opportunity to shine, to deliver and to be strong with an inner smile at myself.

Balance is another aspect I excel at in yoga. Tree, Warrior 3 and Triangle are only some of my favorite balance positions. Balance is key in holding a position. You must breathe, concentrate and continue to do both simultaneously. There are distractions. Other yogis shaking, falling and the mirrors. This is life. Distractions will always be present, though it is what you choose to concentrate on.

Flexibility is my weakness. I am independent. I am strong. I am confident. I have horrible flexibility. My instructor, Fabulous Fran, explains and reminds in class how we all are made differently. Indeed we are, Francis. I am strong and I have balance, but entirely lack in my flexibility. Why? I believe it is a symbol of handling life. My flexibility hurts as I work on it. You are not to do anything that makes you feel pain. I back off often on using my flexibility. I look in the mirror and see stiffness. I am reminded of my father and my mother. My mom can't put her neck down well, nor can my dad. Every time I cut their hair I am reminded of their stubbornness and inflexibility. The aspect of flexibility is being able to see other's point of view. Ha!

Cailin Jane has amazing strength, balance and flexibility. Dr. Glamorous Gladiator, the surgeon, describes her as a "strong baby" who tolerated three long hours of surgery. Most premature babies can only handle 30 minutes. Cailin was able to give Dr. Glamorous Gladiator the time she needed to explore, discover, solve and fix her GI issues. I smile and think, that's my girl. She is strong with her

Strength, Balance and Flexibility – January 27

20-week measurements and only 23 weeks, 1 day of gestational growth at birth. She survived and proved to the doctors; where there is a will, there is a way. God's way. Balance is not a weakness for her. She is handling her premature, damaged, collapsed lungs while her intestines are outside her body. A balance act not many could imagine. Although she is living it. Flexibility is in her hand. Cailin has already made yoga hands to the heavens. She has been paralyzed for several days twice in her short-lived life. After she comes off being paralyzed, she is strongly moving her limbs and demonstrates her flexibility. Cailin has put her hands with her preemie pink blessed rosary in prayer formation. Meanwhile, her breathing stats come up. I do require her to say her rosary once a day.

As I describe strength, balance and flexibility I imagine our journey with others here at the NICU. I can think of the slow-moving, procrastinating Libras in my life teaching me balance. Gitta Marie, my dear friend, who has made me scratch my head many times. She has taught me a bit about life. Balance. Libras do have the scales as their sign to show balance. So it is very fitting. My strength is always cheered on and brought back with my dad. *Car, I know you have that fighting spirit. You don't get down.* Well, I have not received that from him much in this life experience. Weird, but true. I have the memories of many other times he has said this. My flexibility is my major lesson.

How am I being served this lesson of flexibility? Many ways. When you run, hide, stay blind and fear that very lesson, it will hit you harder. It will always catch up with you. I have to be flexible. Many people care for Cailin. My baby is a gift. A gift I have no choice but to be flexible with. Her care requires many hands, hearts and heads. You have to be flexible and trust that God will keep her safe. My gift has many lessons to serve to and for many of her caretakers. Not always do I want to be flexible. I will voice our needs and concerns. Then you have to sit back and see how the cards fall. The flexibility piece is my hardest. At times, you see the cards falling in the wrong way. A way that I am concerned for Cailin. Cailin is protected and will have mistakes at her expense. I believe this is her deal with God for me to learn flexibility. Ouch. Growing is painful.

Painful like the shoes that just don't come in your exact size, but they're so cute you buy them anyway. You know when you are dressing in those very wrong-sized shoes they're not right, but you're gonna try them anyway. Ouch. Such a cute and nice appearance, but content is no good. Well, lesson learned. I hear the babies crying. I know those shoes do hurt but it's all for the greater good. I am happy Cailin is making me learn to be more flexible. I think it's about time. I could learn to do the splits without those one size too small shoes though.

Oasis – January 28

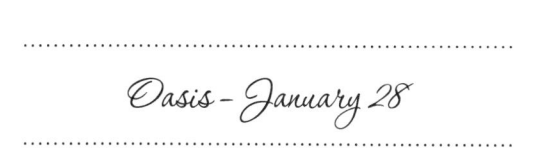

She rolls herself as a Flintstone in her wheelchair. She is blonde and has a mask to cover her mouth. The nurse turns to the patient. "There you are. I was wondering were you went," the nurse says nicely.

"You have to take a look at the skyline with the full moon on the bridge," the recovering patient says.

I listen to her and stop and see the wonder. An oasis through this castle of sickness, death, life and healing. The oasis.

As my busy little mind and vibrant voice is active each moment throughout our days here, I seek an oasis. I have the pleasure to be present in the now by myself often for an oasis. I embrace my oasis when I feel it. Sometimes I smile, I cry, I exhale deeply when I feel it. My shoulders are depleted for a few moments. I believe an oasis is the grace of God. Cailin is an oasis to my search for my life purpose. I never knew I was lost until I became her mother. I was found.

The Animal Tamer is an oasis on this wicked, dark and mysterious unit. We have a whip sound we do to connect. Our connection always follows with a smile or a true emotion. There are no mistakes with our communication. She finds me and I find her. I seek her often. Even hearing her voice makes me calm and centered. She is an angel and an oasis to Cailin and I. Cailin adores her. The Animal Tamer has named Cailin, "The Challenger," on the floor. She describes how Cailin challenges us all to be better and present. The Animal Tamer and I will have light, deep, imaginative, silly and serious conversations. Cailin will communicate with us through her machines in a positive way. She reads the energy of a higher connection on our spiritual journey. Some of the nurses give us stares and glares by our connections. Dynamic Duos always are admired and feared. It is the numbers game. What is better than an Aries? Two Aries!

I see light and orange with The Animal Tamer. Abundance and comfort. Stories she tells me to discover more of her and unravel my own mystery. We connect. We are refreshed and our thirst is quenched. I am blessed to have her in our lives. I vision classes and self-discovery trips we will take. We love Cailin. Cailin is loved by one amazing oasis.

I glance over; she walks and places her bag down on the ledge. "Hi, Carrie," says. She has big blue eyes, large lips, dark hair and a nice friendly demeanor. She is interested in Cailin, healing energy and the larger picture in life. She loves our CD. She is in the inner circle. She is our oasis of comfort in this deep forest. She is Snow White to us. A joy. I tell her of my challenges, fears, feelings, routines, schedules, conflicts, resolutions and thoughts. She takes them in. She truly engages to see my point of view and gives me guidance. Guidance of focusing on Cailin. There are many babies, many cases, many windows to view. *Carrie, don't compare, just focus on Cailin getting better.* She has a giggle I love. Cailin and her talk all night. She will encourage Cailin to do better numbers and praise her improvements. I can sleep well when Snow White is on a shift with my love, Cailin. Now that is an oasis for us. Peace she provides me.

My personal pleasures are an oasis to me. I enjoy my $18 basic facial over on Harlem Avenue. I schedule my appointments after work and before I head to see Cailin again. The Beauty School has a variety of students. Today I had a girl that was a Libra. I like Libra for their gentleness I lack. It is a compliment. She had two weird piercings in her face though. I kinda thought it looked vampire-ish. Well Twilight is pretty popular these days. Fashionable? Regardless, the student did an amazing job. I was able to get to that restful, deep relaxation place. I was dozing off and was just melted butter by the end. Job well done. My manicures and pedicures are well loved. I am upset that my oasis had a hand in my cookie jar though. Apparently, I was charged $104.44 for a $32.00 manicure and pedicure. Thanks, Ben. You really gave yourself quite a tip. Then you or your coworker decided to use my debit card number to take me for a ride financially. Although you guys really took a ride in the rental car charge of $1,751.86. Shame on you. I will return this next week. I will ask for you to deliver an oasis. I will glare and stare to let you know, I know! Although you won't be getting a tip anytime soon. We have makeup. Oh, Ben, you do hell of job on the nails and toes, just a tad bit greedy. My last relaxation is my Mindy. She is a massage therapist that has seen and felt a lot of Carrie Kacen. She has seen me broken down. I mean really, really lost and sad up on her table. My Libra Mindy will tell me, "It's not too bad." She means my tension in my muscles. Yeah, right! But she keeps my mind focused on healing and relaxing. Thank you, my Mindy. I love and appreciate your work, kindness and your giggle. "What?!" Mindy replies to me when I fill her in on the week long comments, actions and behaviors that I need to work through. She encourages me to let go of it all through my massages.

I rock thinking of my Sunday massages. I need them dearly. I remember in Jamaica I had one on the beach. In Mexico, one by a man that relaxed me completely. I am going to think of those beaches, waves, sun and the feeling of being away from it all on Sundays. *All right, Carrie,* I can hear Mindy say. Yep, visualization. Katie, our angel, talks to me about positive thinking, mindset, life purpose and what a great job I am doing. I have known Katie since November 24, 2009. I feel like I have known her forever. A connection, right? A soul of equal capacity and guidance. An oasis for sure! She leaves notes for Cailin and me. Trinkets. Texts. Voicemails. We are grateful for an oasis. Right, Miss Cailin?

Oasis – January 28

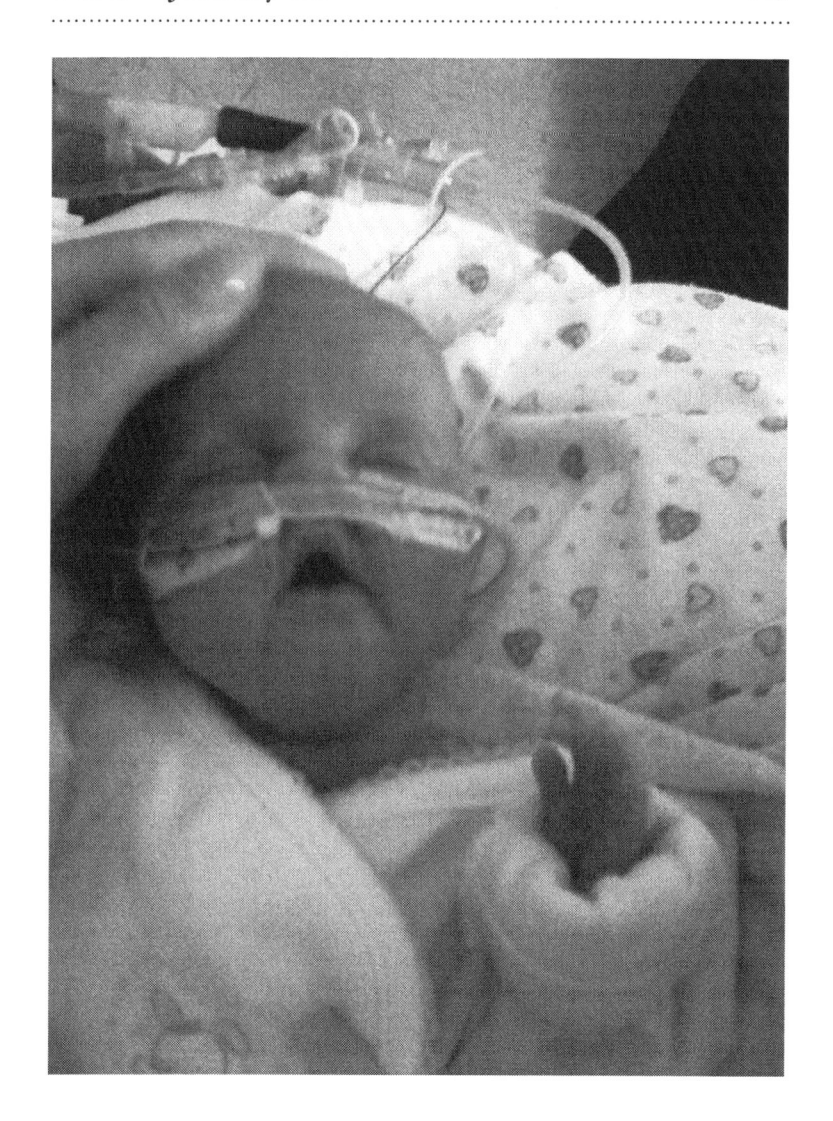

Blossom – January 28

Magenta with shades of pink on a green lily type pad. Around is mud and moisture. I hear nature's beautiful sounds of life and activity. I feel the comfort of a stable, kind presence. I sit on the side of the swamp area. I have my baby in my arms. She is about eight months. Sitting peacefully and drooling on me. We watch the sun peek through the clouds. The sky is a bright blue hue. The trees make the sunlight only peak through strongly in certain blessed areas. I rock from side to side. Cailin is cooing and drooling. I feel grateful and amazed at the amount of presence we have at this moment.

There is the one we focus on. It is in the center of many others. It is a lotus flower. The flower that is most beautiful and blooms in mud. Similar to my life and Cailin's short-lived action packed life. Sagittarius' love action as does her Aries mother. This flower is magnificent and amazing. I am starting to have my heart race from the excitement of it blooming. Wow! I whisper to Cailin, "There is a story behind a flower of such caliber. Just as the butterfly. Let me explain and you keep your eyes focused on the flower and all the wonders around us. Keep an open mind. Beauty will always blossom."

Yes, it slowly opens and is amazing. What does this action do for us? It shows us the beauty of the icky mud and the setbacks we face can only encourage a full bloom. When the full bloom occurs everyone stops and wonders how and why. Well, God takes care of the hows and whys. Faith is what allows the flower to flourish. Nature flourishes only in nature's time. Nature always wins and has miracles happen before our eyes. Gradual is the key. The key is to be still and present to witness the beauty of nature.

I recall reading Goldie Hawn's biography and the cover has a Lotus flower. The book has some of the major aspects of her life's journey and much of the spiritual side of her life. I have always had a special place in my heart for Goldie. My dad loves her character as well. We loved, *Overboard!* Gitta Marie, waited on her at the Peninsula. Gitta stated, "She is so nice; just as she is on the screen. Pleasant, nice and a bit silly." The impression she has on me impacts many aspects and I grew reading her book. I purchased it on clearance and enjoyed it immensely.

The story of the Lotus flower had such a great impact on me. The tattoo I will eventually get will be a nice-sized Lotus flower. This will represent my life coming into full blossom. The new tattoo will be done at a local shop in Oak Park, Illinois. I will have Fran, my friend, hook me up and watch the creation blossom. The new tattoo will cover a peace sign with a butterfly I currently have. My dad purchased this old tattoo and let me pick out any piece of artwork. I had two conditions. First, think about where you want the tattoo permanently for life. I had to think about it for a year. Secondly, keep the artwork your boyfriend drew in your pocket and look around as long as you want. My dad, my yoda. He guided me in the right direction. I will instill some of his ways to my parenting style. Love you, Daddy! The old tattoo represented my own inner peace I wanted to achieve. I believe I have and it is worn into an old icky tattoo. I will have a magnificent butterfly. This butterfly is my Cailin Jane. I will have her name and birthdate tattooed on my back. Tramp stamp? No, no. A mark of a major moment of my life, our life.

Think it, see it, feel it and receive it. Right, Jack Canfield? Heck, yeah. I see this tattoo. I see my daughter home, safe and sound. Cailin Jane is a troublemaker. She has a great sense of humor, sweet smile, blonde curly hair to die for and simply, a pistol. I think it. I see it. I feel it. I receive it. Full blossom.

God's Unfolding and Planting – January 30

Our seed was planted in June. I found out I was pregnant in July. Excitement and joy! The bud grew from cells to a tiny baby doll with transparent skin, fetal eyes and a ton of development to go. The flower was delivered November 24, 2009. I should say my flower is God's flower first then mine. I am a second child so I used to the one before. Cailin was the chosen name which means "girl" in Gaelic. She arrived despite all the drugs and elevation of my pelvis. Yep, she's mine. All mine. "Yes, mommy. All the plans you made I destroyed. I am here this way for many reasons. Sit back and let's play." I can hear in my heart and head from Cailin. God serves you what you need in conviction. Right? Yes.

God's garden does not always appear as flowers in a garden. Although love can make scary, alarming and frightful flowers feel like a weeping willow. Cailin's flower was planted in an isolette. First Bed 18, then Bed 20 and now Bed 34. Third time is a charm! I seek threes and eights now. Why? Father, Son and the Holy Spirit. The three souls that guided my garden to deliver our flower safely at the Human Spirit Hospital. Eight, because Cailin said, "The eighth day will make more sense, Mommy. Please don't be scared." Cailin's birthday, 11.24 equals 8. The number eight is auspicious and the structure of an 8 is infinity. Her soul is timeless and represents the infinite of eight. My flower is planted.

God is unfolding her flower His way with will and grace. Healing is required for the two of us, "Dynamic Duo." C squared. CK squared. Us. Love. I am learning about life God's way through prayer and peace. Cailin is His instrument to the medical staff, our family and my support system. She is doing a very good job. I am very proud of my flower. I hear the wind blow gently on my flower. Her petals get wet, dry, peal, open and are repaired through God's healing light. Light is necessary for a flower. Light protects us from the darkness. Light shows us our way.

Cailin is a flower that needs to be watered too. She is a social flower, so talk to her. Not at her or about her, to her, please. Respiratory Therapists know how she likes her treatments. Cover the flower's chest with a small soft washcloth and talk to her. She responds well. Cailin Jane, what are we going to do with you? Oh, yes. You are the leader and will tell us. We need to listen and respond well. Just as a flower will show if it is dry or needs more sunlight, Cailin displays her needs well. A two pound baby and a mighty strong communicator. Yep, she's mine. She's a people person, feisty, strong-willed, pretty, active, flexible, expressive and sweet. I am crazy about my little flower.

She has some fans of her petals as well. Snow White loves Cailin and talks about her breathing/vent numbers, she talks to her about not dreaming of big bad bears and giggles at Cailin's ways. Pocahontas loves her and does not want to push her too hard, files her nails, cleans her ears and every little crease. Pocahontas treats her as her own. Princess Aurora is always talking about Cailin's own plans. "Nope, the PDA surgery is not gonna work for me. No, the GI surgery won't be that day or that day. It is gonna be this Tuesday, people!" Cailin's mindset displays. Princess Aurora giggles and laughs at how she behaves. My lil' baby is bad to the bone. There were four fans close at her bedside. Then there were three. I watched it unfold. I spoke quietly, I stared, I shouted, I spoke anxiously. I wanted the fourth fan to stay on board. The rocking of the boat tipped Priscilla right off. Sorry, only one Captain and Co-Captain. Mother and daughter. By the way, Cailin is the Captain, and I am her Co-Captain.

I never said I wanted her off of Cailin's medical case. I am not sure if she decided or if Laine or her family and friends guided her. Whatever her cards became I saw the result. She is not on Cailin's care any longer. I know she is still a fan. Of Cailin, not me that is. She will ask the other nurses how she is. She will come to the beside when I am not here. I know she loves Cailin. But, do not tell me whom to respect, do not play the political game or share how you feel I am. I am the one fighting for Cailin's life. You are one of her many, many medical staff members. I am her mother and will have the song sound the way Cailin and I need it to sound. Too much emotion always takes away intelligence. It was lost when she became overly involved emotionally. I wonder if she ever thought that her high school girlfriend's niece would buck her. Spider webs, mud puddles and rain never distract a mother's intention or action.

I bucked for us. I am sure she took it all hard and personal. It was not. It was business. My business. Her business. God's business.

When I felt anxious of her arriving back on Cailin after her hard-ass day of surgery, I knew to pray. God will take care of it. He brought both of us to this breaking point for many reasons. Yes, you love my daughter. Yes, there is a huge gray area in this area of medicine. There is always a silver lining. Priscilla missed that line a long time ago. Her intentions were never coming from a heartless place. In fact, she reminds me of myself in some ways. I was dealing with a strong-willed person, emotional and controlling. A mirror. It cracked.

Priscilla will always have a special place in our hearts. Things come and go. She is gone though. Next watering session. More new faces. Some have a connection with her. Lee, Priscilla's buddy, is one nurse I would like to punch in the face. I would like all of her petals to be plucked. Why? She rubs me the wrong way. She wants no contact after I said something about the breathing tube on Bed 18. Her ego got in the way of her petals. Good for you. You have been a nurse for so long. Cailin is my daughter. Take your petal and shove it up your big doopa. She is always leaning and whispering on our isolation counters. Get to work. You have plenty of other beds to gossip at. Leave. It will come to a head real soon. She will stare at me. Watching me like a TV. The station is on Lee. I will give it to you when I am told to do so. The watering she seeks is other people's business. For a masculine looking woman she sure gossips a lot. Birds of a feather flock together. That is what I should

God's Unfolding and Planting – January 30

have seen a long time ago. Your bird is no longer here so go… bye, bye.

Cailin will sense God's work unfolding in her quiet isolette. She will ding her stats differently depending on the energy outside her isolette and the conversations occurring. She knows what time of water her flower needs and wants. That's my girl. Don't lose sight of that Cailin! The doctors are told to communicate with her. Dr. Sensible does. Follow her lead. She is amazing. Cailin always responds to her. Their statements, praise and requests are sunlight and rain drops to her delicate flower.

I spoke to Public Relations regarding the lack of communication the doctors have offered to me and Priscilla's communication of obtaining updates off duty. The gray area was all ass backwards. I kicked, I screamed and sat back for a bit. Yes, for only a bit. For a premature life, a bit is a long time. Fix it or it will be legal counsel next. I am not playing. Well, yes, I am playing hardball. You want me to play a game? You will not enjoy receiving the ball. I expect a certain level of care, respect and communication. I believe God has me with Cailin as a very critical, complicated premature baby to have his work unfold on this unit. An employee stated to me she felt a lot of things she has never felt. Yep, we have rocked the boat. The sail was not proper. Premature care includes a parent or two, communication of medical updates and compassion with a boundary. God wanted me to voice this and change the memo for it to read properly. Do I believe they received it? Yes. Each member in their own way, shape and form in their own level of awareness. Consciousness and awareness really vary. Snake, the nurse that tried to move Cailin after her surgery for an x-ray, only received a "scant" they say. A little bit. She lives in Negativeland where she resides as a victim and verbalizes it all the time. Go away. No, her lessons will unfold harshly for her. Like me giving it right back to her. I was able to tell her I know how she talks to the babies and staff. She is a miserable person. Misery likes company. We ripped up that flower invitation knowing that the cover doesn't match the inner meaning in Cailin's case.

Pruning is essential for a proper blossom. People are placed in our lives during this journey for many reasons. Some of the reasons are more for "them" while some are for "Cailin and me." Trusting in the ways of God is what keeps us progressing in Cailin's uphill battle for life. Cailin has beaten many of the odds for a 23-weeker here in her watering garden. Unfortunately, there is no crystal ball for life and its unfolding. There are choices, consequences and options for life. Cailin and I choose to have faith in God and his wondrous ways. I will continue to believe in my daughter, embrace the proper supportive medical staff, verbalize unprofessional encounters, make requests on Cailin's behalf and pray everyday. Through my prayers, I will continue to learn more about Cailin, life, God's word and myself. I need to try to have some fun in the garden though. There is always a lot of work in a garden, but fun is not wrong. Joy and fun is what any blossomed flower brings.

Bits and Pieces - January 31

I park in the hospital garage. I pull my purple purse that is more of a bag. The purple purse has some shine to it, which allows for more wear and tear than usual. I joke around about how the items in my purple purse are Nana's table, just in a bag. Although I have more makeup and she has more pills. I shut the driver's door to open the passenger door behind my driver's seat. There is the gray bag with my laptop and other essentials. I place both bags on my shoulders. I am a petite 5-foot woman. My bags and what I carry describe me and my ways.

We all carry our "stuff" around. Sometimes we shed some when ready and the time is right. I carry a lot through out my journey. A middle-child syndrome, a child of a divorce, Catholic school girl until I was ten years old, a move, adapting to the suburbs, new friends, new faces, public school, CCD, soccer, cheerleading, evil companion to my mother, weekend visits to my dad's, abuse physically and emotionally, college, drugs and drinking, rape, nervous breakdown, depression, recovery through faith, isolation of emotions, college degree, social worker on the Westside of Chicago, cycle of abuse seen in horrible ways, career change, independently purchase a condo, sales, management, success, emotionally-unavailable intimate relationships, travels, gathering of adult friends, back to Beauty School, hustling of two jobs for five years, two condos, failed relationships, miscarriage in the second to last relationship (before Cailin), successful leadership at new position, running a salon, reunite with first love, pregnancy, breakup, alone during pregnancy, preparation of my child, premature delivery, old-self crashing to bits and pieces.

Here we are now, Miss Cailin. Mommies interesting life of many puzzle pieces. Bits of lessons learned along the way. Pieces of strength, courage and wisdom through coping with life. Enjoyment, regardless of my situation. The ability to get back up on my horse and ride. Cailin is a Sagittarius, so she is half-horse and half-human. Her animal instincts have a great positive impact on her healing process. Our puzzle is bright in color.

I just went to Border's after yoga today. I headed to the journal and notepad selection. I found an amazingly detailed journal with a lock and key. The journal is for Aubrey, my niece. She is turning seven on February 6. She shares the same birthday of my dear friend, JoAnne Douglas. Both are Aquarius. They are such similar characters, just generations apart. The details of the journal draw me in closer. Unicorns, butterflies, fairies, symbols with a beautiful array of vibrant colors. I imagine this as the places all three us will be together this summer. Magical time together. Aubrey, Cailin and me. I envision the time spent together as a piece of our puzzle.

Bits and Pieces – January 31

The journal is for Aubrey to write to Cailin about her daily and weekly happenings. If Cailin were in my belly then Aubrey would be telling Cailin and me about her life. Her fun times, aggravations, school lessons, friends, parties, about Jackson and his ways and of course, her parents. Aubrey always tells me about her parents. Good and bad. I agree with her. How can't you? A child is raw and real. There is no filter and there should not be. As adults, our bits and pieces are placed under rugs, in closets and left at home in a dark safe places. Children expose our bits and pieces out of pure honesty. When children start to use defense mechanisms in their relationships... bingo... mom and dad, shame on you!

I look at my puzzle pieces. They will not go away. Just placed where I need them to be. I will not hide them from my daughter. For they are lessons I learned to help myself and others in life. A mother's job is to help her child the most. I will help her see my puzzle pieces. Nana Kacen exposes her bits and pieces to me. I enjoy our visits. I am so very real to her. She sees me. My guide. My grandmother. There is something so easy about puzzles of a granddaughter and grandmother. The pieces are placed gracefully together. The puzzle of a mother and daughter are a little more complicated. That piece will look like it belongs there, but nope. Try again. The nature of bits and pieces is what always wins.

Cailin and I have a puzzle. Our pieces include a donor of poor quality, co-dependent loving family, low capacity of many surrounding people, handful of folks that get this situation, get us. I have put some pieces of my puzzle together through many completion and reconciliation conversations. Loves. Loves of my life. I have had bits of dating and a few pieces. Pieces of love. I have fallen a number of times. Each has a place in my puzzle.

Michael, a man-child, a heart of gold. A bald, Harley dude, stage-hand with 12 brothers and sisters. A mother that is amazing, Jerre. A sister that is a jem, Susie. The family loves me. I love them. Michael was the black sheep in the family. Attractive to me, due to his wild spirit of a Sagittarius. Really he is lost and a scared man. He complains too much. He will work out his ways in the long run, but it will be a long run. He loved me. He loves me. I know him and he knows me.

Patrick, a man-child, a marshmallow just like his daddy, "Big Mike," baby of three. He is a sweet, tattooed guy. Silly, scared and sweet. A person that seeks balance as his zodiac of a Libra is. Aries and Libra are great for short term. We were just that. Connection was deep, but short-term interactions. Paramedic long to rescue. You can't rescue an ice princess with such a soft, sweet and vague way. Emotionally unavailable.

The donor is a co-dependent person, addiction issues, lying to the point of mental illness and the oldest of three. My first love and last mistake.

I have approached and been approached by all my loves during this journey. I embraced all of them. It allowed me to be real and raw. Ways that are helpful for me to clear my relationship space for a prince I have in mind. I will always speak to Michael and Patrick. They genuinely care and love me, although they have a hard time expressing it. I know them both well enough to know their Irish ways. Care, concern and good humor. I will always have a special place in my heart for them. I know there is much more to experience with my prince though. They were just a mark. Not the real deal. Cailin knows and brings my walls down to have the real deal crash into our new home.

The puzzle displays a new home. Home is where the heart is. What is in our heart, Cailin Jane? Love, life, light, adventure, respect, trust, medicine, friends, family, boundaries, expectations, standards, rules, honesty, care, compassion and adventures. Life. Life in a real wholesome way.

Cailin and I will depend on the Human Spirit Hospital, medicine, faith, family, friends, nurses, doctors, front desk divas, fellows, residents, surgeons, the surgical team and respiratory therapists… just to identify some of our bits and pieces. We started our puzzle once I discovered I was pregnant. As I stated before, it is colorful. Pierre, RT, says, "Live your life like today is your best day." Our gathered bits and pieces will be our best regardless of the hurdles. Our best. Colorful bits and pieces.

Butterflies for our transformation. Flowers for our blossoming ways. Grass for our growth. Blue skies for our lungs and breath. Fairies for our helpful angels in human bodies and spirit. Sun for our light of God. Unicorns for our way. A different path a different way, but ours. All the shapes and symbols of "stuff." Our stuff.

Fallen Flakes – February 2

I came and went. Worked and left. I arrive back to clean Cailin's mouth and settle in the glider chair. There is not enough OPI lotion to take away the smell of this chair. Many hours and many people rocked in this chair. I will buy this unit new, improved chairs. The chairs will be easily cleaned and sanitized. I look to the right and see the flakes and they are falling. I breathe in the OPI smell and breath deeply. I am waiting for Dr. Balance to come to the bedside.

Cailin Jane's lungs opened up yesterday. Dr. Bolt swiftly walked up to Princess Aurora and I at the bedside with this news. "I just looked at her x-rays and her lungs completely opened up! I expected to see the same as yesterday, but they are completely open." Dr. Bolt nods with pleasure while delivering such great news. Doctors rarely get to deliver great news! They typically are problem seekers and solvers. They are investigators and experimenters. They love to solve the issue. What a ride?

I continue to breathe and see the vent numbers. Pressure was at 37 and then she weaned down to 31 yesterday. Last night she weaned down to 26 in pressure. I am so happy. Cailin is getting a break and hearing some good news. Dr. Balance arrives to the bedside. He describes her lung as closing today a bit on the lower right. "You know the game of push and pull with these babies. I want to know if and when this month we will feed her. Do we feed when closed? When open? This month? Next month. I have not cornered surgery to discover. I am hopeful, but I prepare for the worst only to be surprised then when it goes well." Dr Balance delivers this with his long shaggy hair and kind face.

"I know. It makes sense how you have to push and pull with each baby, because they are different and have different complications," I reply.

"You know the roller coaster is not over. I have been in this business a long time. I know we have a long way to go."

"I know, but I hope it doesn't get as dark as post-op. Those were some dark moments. Almost worse than when she was first born. Well, I was naive and really did not know how bad it was. God has a way of protecting you," I add.

Dr. Balance responds, "Yep, he does. To keep you focused. Just as parents. If your parents knew what you were going to go through, do you think they would be in?"

I smile and giggle. Well are they "in." My mother is doing her very best. We are trying to work at our relationship. My dad is trying his best and is not "in." They are fallen flakes though.

There is not one snowflake that is identical to another, just as people. A fallen flake has graced to fall. Unique in its size and shape. Fallen is good, bad and indifferent. It is what it is. My parents are doing the best they can. They

Fallen Flakes – February 2

have fallen though. I am working toward a higher purpose. A different flake, in size and shape. I have always been the child and family member that is a bit different. I am the free spirit. The spiritual one. "You and your Grandma Irwin have that connection, almost an Indian thing, a spiritual thing," my dad reminds me often. I believe him. For I know my grandmother's presence during my darkest moments throughout my life. I have not felt her much this time. She is an angel. I believe she watches over me often. I do have a connection with her on the same level. During Cailin's surgery and the chaos of professionalism here, my mother was saying I reminded her of her mother, Grandma Irwin. My mother was burned very badly when she was only seven years old. She spent three months in the hospital and two weeks for three summers there after. My mother had some nurse experiences just as Cailin. "You are ferocious!" she mumbles to seek a word. I smile. Job done. Protect my young. Those claws Priscilla described do indeed hurt. Don't mess with my girl, or me for that matter.

The fallen flakes are peacefully dropping through the air. The sight is helping me breathe. I look again outside in my glider. I process the words, thoughts and statements Dr. Balance shared with me. I know it is not over. Cailin's bowels are still outside her body. We have to get her fed, off the ventilator and in control of her temperature. It seems a long way away, but I think of how far we have come. We have fought, we have conquered and we still have a fight in us. I have fallen to become more humbled and aware. I am aware of the medical severity of Cailin, capacity of my friends and family and life. I compare this experience of twenty-five years of life in ten weeks. Cailin is up to 10 weeks today and 33 weeks gestational. She is my favorite fallen flake.

Her flake is planned on her execution of delivery date with God. I certainly did not know about all that! Her delicacy and beauty come from the gene pool. God did some great diving on the selection of Cailin's creation. Her form was a work of art during my short six months and one day of carrying my angel. Her personality, which is fun, feisty as all get out, sweet and strong like a bull mentally and physically, is all I displayed during my pregnancy journey to her. When you carry a child, you discover their ways and they emulate your demeanor. Nana told me to be happy during my pregnancy to help Cailin have a positive demeanor. She had six children and reflects on her emotional ways during each pregnancy and each child has a demeanor similar to her ways at that time. I stayed happy, restful, positive and focused. I believe Cailin displays this each and every day of her fallen flake life.

I will sit, cry, sleep, stay long hours, run off to work, stand up for us, eliminate nonsense and drama and focus each day for Cailin. Her fallen flake dance is as no other. Graceful in her own way. My daughter can twirl and confuse us all only to flip and drop slowly to stability. It is her flake and she will do with it as she chooses. We will respond to her medically. I will support her anyway and anywhere. Always and forever.

Healing Light – February 4

She has a badly bruised head. She weighs in at 1 pound, .02 ounces. She looks as if she has black hair. She appears dark on her entrance which is nothing of the sort. She is my healing light. Cailin Jane chose to enter as she did. What a major choice for a soul. She is a daredevil and ready to conquer her past, my past and God's requests. This is my daughter. It hits me to pieces only to be put back brighter, better, clearer, lighter, wiser, kinder and more humble. Thank you. Is that enough? Oh, no. I will work through my gratitude each moment, each shift, each sunrise, each sunset. Tears. Oh, yes, I do cry of joy. My glass, our glass is half-full. Don't you dare tell me anything otherwise or less. It is not yours to judge, smudge or analyze. I have no fear. The light will shine you away or transform you upon entry.

My terms have changed. Ten weeks and two days today. My space was created. Forced to change. I search and reach for my healing light. She arrived. I will embrace other healing lights to complete our inner circle. Circle of trust. Circle of life. Our life. Scared life. I head home after conversing and smiling at my daughter to do hair. I am the provider for her. I must make money to provide shelter and a life for Cailin. Angie is waiting for me. We discuss my coping skills. "Carrie, I believe you are doing better than most. You do better than me. You know what to do for yourself," Angie discloses. I am walking the clean clothes to my dresser. I smile in my serene bedroom. I believe her. I know this, but to hear another speak of it. It is a healing light that hits me gently. Angie has no clue what a healing source she is for me. Our friendship blossoms only to know she is moving on in many wondrous ways. These moments and our experiences, she will always have a piece of. From day one, when I was in labor. She is calm, sincere, intelligent and real. Real and kind. Can you ask for more? No.

My search for various healing lights has been interesting to say the least. The family members and friends that I expected to be there do not have the capacity always to be a healing light. I had to have conversations of confrontations. Confrontations of intolerance in ways I would tolerate before. Spider webs I was trapped in before. When Cailin entered as my main healing source of life, my space shifted. My residence will never be the same. For it was not meant to be the same. I build and arrange our new house. The lights that I search for now are very different. I will let go of expectations. Expectations can be very disappointing. I must focus on the path. Our path of healing, recovery and a new life.

Magenta is running late for our trade. She is a healing source for me. A great listener, a medium, a healer. She does a clearing of my energy. I am lighter. She assists me in understanding how to protect my aura. My head and shoulders are killing me. Why? I was whacked through my aura by family member's behaviors and words. Really? Oh no, I know for sure, yes. My true spiritual guiding light is Nana. Nana Kacen. Jane Kacen. She is amazing. She listens

Healing Light – February 4

to my qualms, complaints and challenges. She encourages me. Eighty-seven years of life. She can guide. Nana also steps back and sees. She expresses how she never has had this magnitude I do. Wow! Honesty is her specialty. Fresh breeze, safety, oasis and my true healing light. I am grateful for her being. She is amazing!

I have been interested in a light of a male form. Dr. Eyes is his name. His game is true. I feel safe and something very special about him. I have for the last year of servicing his salt and pepper hair. He acts close to forty. For a man, that is not too shabby. He isn't even thirty. Cougar? Heck, yeah. I can be. I ask for his assistance in Cailin's medical condition. Specifically, her eyes. He is an eye doctor. I confide in him regarding Cailin's condition, medical communication problems, friends and family. My life is complicated, Dr. Eyes. Although it has never been more clear. I see rainy skies at times during this process, but Dr. Eyes always appears as a source of shelter. Too soon to tell what will happen. As it should be for Cailin's recovery and our relationship. Friends or more? Regardless he is a healing light and completely unaware as I write of this. He and I spoke for about thirty minutes today. He was clear, concerned, informative and real. Fresh air and light. A healing light.

As the walls are closing in and follow the tracks that lead me, I seek, reach and will find healing lights. I see no reason to be around black, dead ends, spider webs, old dysfunctional ways. I visualize tears of joy, Cailin's baby cries loud and clear, a light on both of us, bright and sunny. A healing light will shed and bring new fresh things. Fresh is an important thing in life and our development in it. Bring it on!

Capacity – February 5

The air fills it up. I blow and blow the purple balloon. I see her bright blue eyes and blonde curly hair. She is four today. Cailin has come such a long way. I use my lungs. She had such a hard time growing. I abused mine for a bit, but learned the sacredness of my body, my lungs. The balloons are filling up my dining room. As I prepare for a birthday celebration, I experience the capacity of the balloons. A few just popped, some cannot get as much air in as others. There is no size or shape the same in these purple balloons. The few that popped, hurt and disappointed me. Now I had to start over by stretching a new one out and blowing. I wonder how the few tiny ones could call themselves balloons. I feel the smile beaming out on the few that are nice and perfectly shaped. These good suitors are gonna be great for the celebration!

I feel myself be pulled back to the bedside of 34 where my daughter is today. She is waiting on the surgical team. Dr. Glamorous Gladiator and her team are going to change Cailin's dressing on her wound. Her wound is her intestines outside her body healing after her three hour surgery. What is Cailin's capacity? Amazing for a soul to choose this path. Dr. Glamorous Gladiator is pretty amazing with her "super human" stamina. I have yet to see this woman deflated as the low-capacity, purple balloons I daydream about.

I take a step away from myself and our crisis situation, Cailin's life. I think about the comment Mrs. Resolution, Public Relations, stated to me, "You have to pick each person for their capacity. Some are great at getting groceries, others can laugh, others cry and vent." I pondered on this commentary during the peak of clearing another layer of unneeded stress. I can honestly say that for the heartaches, disappointments and frustrating confrontations with nurses, family, friends and doctors there were never "ill intentions," just capacity. I can work with this concept. A major life lesson I must understand and apply right, Cailin? I believe she had a buffet for me to taste and discover before I made my ideal meal.

My capacity is a large magnitude. I have been through a lot of character building life struggles and always get up on my horse and ride. I may cry, scream and fight but I ride. I ride for the better of my life and now for our life. I will not settle when my soul feels restless. My inner-self is the compass I must attune to, for family expectations and old ways do not fit anymore. I have a new skin on as well as a blindfold off. I have flown to my daughter to meet the way we should live. I often wonder the whys and hows. I must let those go and give over to God and just go. The way will be shown.

Easy? Hell, no! As any good healthy growing pain, it hurts like hell to move forward and be disappointed by my sister, my brother, my dad and a few friends. How could they say

Capacity – February 5

and do during this time of my life? It doesn't get any bigger than this? Here is the plate. If you can't step up now, then when? How do I handle all of this? How do I move forward? I just do. I let my balloon fill up, move around and glow.

It is not easy, but it is a celebration each and everyday. Cailin deserves purple, pink and aqua balloons everyday! She is amazing with her capacity. I believe our capacity is similar on many levels. I need to keep focusing on the balloons that have the capacity to float along in our journey. The balloons that burst are part of the journey and celebration. Journeys are not a quick arrival to your destination. The journey is the work of discovering each person's capacity. We have had nurses that are great for awhile and then their capacity is no longer "good" and "helpful" for our journey. Although along the stretch that they were good, was needed. The discovery of capacity is draining and frustrating because there are more without the capacity to help me than they are. I am grateful for those with the true capacity to help me. God is really the only one dependent I have that is truly there for the whole, entire journey.

I did a lot of legwork on this area of life, capacity when I took over the Park Ridge salon. You have to get to know the players of the game. Once you do you can have the game played at another level. I have high standards and expectations. I have learned to keep my bar and standards high, but let the expectations go. Capacity will determine where relations will go. The cool thing about capacity is that it can change and grow! If people do their "work," it can transform. Work meaning blowing their balloon to greater heights through self-actualization. Be real.

As I transformed and continue to do, I must be true to Cailin and myself. This will cause stress for relationships that will not fit the capacity we need. I have quite a few great relationships through this process. Such as Angie, my mom, Nana, our Chaplain Ruby, my soul sista, "Animal Tamer", my favorite nurses, Ockto, Jem, Pocahontas, Princess Aurora and Snow White, my coworker Annie, Marge, Fran, Chrissy, Courtney, Ami and my niece Aubrey. These are to name quite a few cherished relationships that bring so much to me. They listen, digest and help me process this crazy painful and joyous journey of Cailin's health. I envision them entering the door of my condo and hitting, holding and sticking those purple balloons on the wall merrily saying, "Happy Birthday, Cailin."

Cheese – February 6

So, I am sure your have read the who moved the cheese book? I am a dairy, well a cheese lover. I have all sorts of cheese around me. Our cheese moves daily. New babies, heaven, home, new doctors and nurses. I am different and that is really, really hard for a stale piece of cheese, my sister. I had plans for tomorrow with my niece, Aubrey. Her birthday is today February 6, 2010. I planned to meet her at noon in Schaumburg for the Tooth Fairy movie. Well, my sabotage sister can't find that possible. Marie and her family chose not to attend the mass in honor of Cailin. Marie is "triple-booked" on the date of my baby shower. The same date we had planned for months. We put it on hold until I was ready to have it. She tippy-toed around the subject of the shower. She isn't coming on my voicemail. She is such a bitch on the phone, voicemail and text but never to my face. That's her game for years and years. It hurts and I am disappointed. I relay that I am disappointed on her voicemail, but I can live with it. Although I state that it is very important to have Aubrey at the shower. No response. For a verbal bitchy person she sure is passive aggressive at this point in time. The cheese has moved for her. She will contact me to try to manipulate the date I have with Aubrey. Sabotage Sister. Marie's name in my heart and head. She proceeds to start my day with another piece of sabotage.

Aubrey's gonna see the movie with one of her very, very best friends. Let's reschedule. "Well Marie I'm really busy with work, Cailin at the hospital, getting my home ready for her arrival and my baby shower," I say.

"I know you have a sick baby in the hospital, but you're not the only one with things going on in their life. Why are you so aggressive?" Sabotage Sister responds.

The conversation continues with her telling me I'm sick and a bully. She's the only one that really loves me and is honest enough to stand up to me. Well, I respond how horrible she is as a sister, aunt and godmother. It was her choice not to come to church and my shower. Now, she's messing with my relationship with Aubrey. Psychoanalysis is Marie's cheese of a reliable nurturing sister has moved. I am no longer the Band-Aid to her marriage on weekends so they can drink and socialize with neighbors. Also, I am not there to be the emotional piece she lacks in her parenting. Yep! She is pissed and pouting. Beat it! Sabotage your family over there. Mine is safe without all your mental abuse. Bye, bye. No drama for this mama!

So, I post something on my Facebook status update saying, "Another goal is to pray my sister gets her head out of her ass this lifetime." It is true and funny. Well, my beloved family and her neighbor decide to be "flies on shit" and stick up for her crazy ass. I am not fighting with Marie. I released myself from her wicked maze. Toodles! I have new cheese and no longer need your traps. I am free of the former bullshit.

Cheese – February 6

I am laughing on my iPhone with my friend, Cyn. She is so cynical and really makes me take an emotional step back and laugh my ass off! She is hilarious! Cyn is like, tell Marie there is wait staff to boss around at the baby shower. I am dying of laughter. Cyn has a way with the ways of people. It is called humor. I need it these days. Right when I am venting to her she is already looking at the funny side of things. My friends are the great-aged cheese I reach for with my glass of Pinot Noir. I love Cyn and her silly ways. A bit cynical, but real. Real and raw. Princess Aurora is on Cailin today. She is gonna get a laugh at all the drama of Sabotage Sister. Is this a Gemini or what? No more Jekel and Hyde. I am nice, no I am mean. Yep, you are both. I will continue to keep an arms length, cause you are cruel!

How do you add more stress to someone with a sick infant in the NICU? Well, my sister has showed and proved that she can serve bullshit and nonsense at any time. Especially the time when you need love and care. Wow! This is real, no joking. I love my friends that I can laugh with and have other techniques of handling her hurtful ways. I feel better I told that stinky piece of cheese just how stinky she really is. If your sister can't tell you, who will?

The baffling part is how my family members will support her nonsense. Well, that just isn't gonna work for Cailin and me. My daughter is a truth seeker. Any confrontation or skeletons that were stored is out in the open and being addressed. It makes people feel really uncomfortable. Who is more uncomfortable though? A first-time single mother of a 23-weeker in the NICU and a beautiful Cailin that is surviving with only 20 weeks of development in utero, collapsed lungs, intestines outside her body, eyes requiring laser surgery or healthy family members with too much damn time on their hands to want to pry and support an unsupportive sister, Sabotage Sister? It makes absolutely no logical sense. When emotions are high, logic is low. Exhibit A. Facebook and family.

I take my piece of goat cheese and savor the taste. My favorite cheese just as my favorite person, Cailin Jane. She is the tiniest piece of cheese. She is amazing. She smiles at me now. Her mental development is normal. She only had grade two on her left ventricle. She has the opportunity to develop normally. That is my girl! My mom anxiously awaits the updates. My mother and Cailin have a great picnic with their cheese all the time. Cailin is crazy for her Grandma Irwin's pure love. Grandma Irwin seeks nothing of her, just gives pure love. I am happy to have delivered my confrontation to both my parents. Let's face it. My cheese moved. I had another piece of cheese to incorporate. Shit has hit the fan.

My mother and I had a heart wrenching conversation. We yelled, we cried, we sat in silence, but we worked to find a middle ground. Our cheese is different, but better. She respects me and I respect her. We communicate and disagree, but respect one another. My dad and I had a hard conversation where he actually walked out on me in the restaurant. I was crushed, but not surprised the truth hurts. He has met me halfway and hugs me when he sees me now. He respects me and I respect him. I want texts messages everyday. He will do it for Cailin and me on a weekly basis.

Cheese – February 6

Middle ground. My brother doesn't even acknowledge my child or me. My sister is twisted in her non-supportive and disruptive ways. She is overwhelmed and doesn't have control. When you're a control freak, middle ground isn't even possible. Life goes on.

Life is moving in great directions for me. I look around and have the support system I need. A few family members, my staff, my great girlfriends and a few nurses. A new piece of cheese is a helpful hand and mind of Dr. Eyes. He is so helpful with the preparations for her eye surgery. He reached out and printed a ton of paperwork to help me. Now that is support. Help. Not information seeking to satisfy your wondering mind. I enjoy speaking to Dr. Eyes. He is a fresh perspective on getting help.

I recall reading this book, *Who Moved My Cheese,* at a work retreat. It describes all the different ways people process changes. There are seekers of new ways, hoarders, quitters, savers and all sorts of ways. I am thinking of the various approaches and laugh. I see them all trying to mess with our crisis. It is intense stuff. Everyone has a plan about what they think I should do, shouldn't do, how I need to share more, lean more. Who is to say I am not doing all of this, just not with the talkers? I am sticking to the selection of cheese that makes me feel safe, happier, humble, good and peaceful. For the rest, good luck finding your cheese.

Faith After Betrayal – February 7

I am still upset with the way my sister is treating me, Cailin and our life situation. I am upset that certain family members are going to give me "shoulds" and "should nots" and how out of line Marie's neighbor is. I know my life situation right now, I know my daughter, I know the NICU and it is our experience. I am validated that I am doing the right thing by being private. Too many intentions, energy and monkeys on my back. I shake it off. I am in need of more cleansing and self-acceptance. I do not need the chaos, drama and nonsense. I am betrayed once again by Sabotage Sister. Why? She is judging my decisions and me. She does not agree with them and wants me to see that and change. I believe she has a family of her own, a struggling marriage and demands at work. This is not her place to interfere. Shut up and support. She replies that all she has is love for Cailin and me. Bullshit is what she is displaying if that's your love. You are messed up. Marie does not need to agree with me nor any other family member. I don't agree with all the ways they lead their lives with eating issues, anxiety, backstabbing, gossiping, drinking and so on. We are human. I respect them and do not approach them on how they should raise their children or when, where and how they should celebrate their child's life because I respect them. Agreeing and respect are two different things.

I decide that it is best to keep Marie out of our life. She is only bringing nonsense, drama and verbal battles which is a waste of energy. Today I rejoice knowing that she is not coming to my baby shower. She is not celebrating Cailin and I. She is sabatoging anywhere I allow her to. Game over. Oh Marie, take care of yourself, God Bless. This is my mental and verbal response at this point. She loves to battle. I do not. Playing with a pig will only get you dirty. I am out of the pig pen.

Today is Sunday, a day of reflection of your faith. How you served God this week and how you will this upcoming week. I get up nice and early at 4:50 a.m. I rise after 5 a.m. to start laundry, write out bills, make breakfast and wash up for the day. I arrive to Cailin by 7 a.m. I am agitated and need to recenter from all the nonsense. I talk to Cailin. She looks like a little burrito in her swaddle. She loves her swaddle action. All the rest the doctors and I hope for this weekend is happening! I love my kid! She is so very cute and precious. We are going to have a good day. I delete all the nonsense from my Facebook wall while she sleeps soundly. I talk to Princess Aurora, her nurse, and we laugh a bit. I discover her plan is minimal handling and a quiet day. Great news!

I am off to Mass. I pick up my iPhone and call my mom. We talk a bit and laugh and check in. My next call is to my dad. We catch up and I tell him that I will not be spending anytime with Marie anytime soon. She is not very helpful or positive these days. I need to focus on my Cailin and myself without any additional unneeded stress and aggravation.

He agrees and understands. I am sure she is burning up his ear over there. I told my dad when I had my baby there would be grief. I was so right! I share how this week is a big week for Cailin. She has a lot of excitement. Antibiotics will end, eye surgery, dressing change and she will be extubated. "I knew she would be on another ball game by the time I had my shower, Dad. I have so much to do before she comes home. I called my handyman for the new hallway lighting, removal of the winterized plastic on the windows and new blinds. I spoke to the cleaning lady regarding a major deep clean. I got my money back from the identity theft. So, there is a lot of work and positive things happening." I share with him. He is happy to hear all this. I hear it in his voice. He is going to cheer for the Saints in the Superbowl game tonight. I am too! I believe the team needs to bring that to their city! I hang up and head to Mass.

The sermon is about your strengths and weaknesses. I believe my weakness has been to allow my sister to assault me as long as I have allowed it. She was one of my abusers in my childhood. I have forgiven her. She is continuing her emotional and mental abuse again. The long texts stating nothing positive, nothing on seeing "how" I am. Oh no, Marie has all the answers. Well, she is reading the wrong damn book. It is not mine. She is not the author and it is pissing her off so badly that she keeps lashing out like a teenager. I am praying on it. I am stepping back and laughing too! This is so baffling. Whatever her core issue is with me, I don't care anymore. I am done with that space and place with her. The door keeps slamming. I see the exit sign and the way out. I am out.

I am out. I am sitting in Ascension church thinking of my weaknesses regarding our sisterhood. I am forgiving myself and her, but not her actions. The wonderful thing about forgiveness and faith is that you are letting go of the pain. It does not mean you tolerate or need to validate the abuse any longer. It is so freeing. I breathe in and out deeply and pray. I ask my angels to take the mental bucket and take care of it. My shoulders relax. I think of the nonsense everyone stated to me about how I should be and shouldn't be. Take that too, please. God please provide peace for me and take away all my anxiety. Help me think of how to handle this cynical sister of mine. I hear the response of… oh, Marie, take care of yourself, God Bless. Thank you, Lord. I will do it. I will do it. Thank you, thank you. I needed this so much to focus on my sweet Cailin Jane. She is the one that needs all my energy. I am sorry I was distracted and upset, Cailin. Marie has her place now. I closed that door. If she chooses to come around it will be on our terms. The old ways are over. Bye, bye. Oh, do I feel free, happy and joyful.

Betraying me during a life crisis. How can you be there for Cailin and me if you can't be now? It doesn't get bigger than this. Right? Yes, Carrie, yes. I choose to stick to my faith. My prayers, mass and meditation bring so many grand serene feelings to me. I will find all the answers when I let it go. Let it go is a theme in this journey. Time heals all wounds. Time apart is so very needed and healthy. I have no regrets. Marie disrespected us and was very abusive with her actions and words. I forgave and let her in again. She did the same thing. I gave her the benefit of the doubt. She betrayed me again. Past behavior predicts future behavior. Lesson is solidified.

Old Navy is calling my name, Carrie Kacen! I hit the store in 15 minutes. I purchase a spring bag, three tanks, four to-die-for Cailin-sized outfits at 75 dollars. Retail therapy is wondrous. I head to yoga to work it all out physically, mentally and in my soul. I love the new technique I learned on cleansing your charkas. I breathe and center myself. I have a wonderful class. Sunshine is beaming in, I am working up a sweat and my endurance is at a higher level since being pregnant. Whooo! This is a great way to have faith in each hour, day and week of healing. We have a really big week this week. Fabulous Francis is conducting a challenging class and we go over time. I text Chris Feeney, "I just got out of class. I will be there soon."

She replies, "I just pulled up to your house."

I hit Chipotle for two hard shell tacos and head home.

Chris Feeney is limping from her voluntary foot surgery on Thursday. We lug my many bags of bags upstairs. I hit the washer with Cailin's bedding. I eat my tacos and her talk about Chris' hair. She brought her Angel Healing Cards and is letting me borrow them. How wonderful! I color her hair. It is processing. We do three quick readings on the Angel Card. Divine Timing, Forgiveness and Meditation are the main cards. Right on! I talk it all out with Chris. I read two entries of my book. She only thinks of one word. Conquer. Conquer as in accomplishment of struggles, not overpowering. I agree. I am conquering all the obstacles. This is a transforming journey. It is of great magnitude. We finish, reschedule and hug. We will see each other on Valentine's Day at my shower!

I take a quick nap. I leave with all my bags and Cailin's clean linens. I head to the mall. I speak to my mom about all the precious outfits I found for Cailin. I head into the mall to pick out my outfit for the shower. I find it quickly at Forever 21. I have a red dress with a purple cardigan, which I was building off of my retro Mary Jane purple and red heels. I grab a pair of earrings, as well. The total is $34. I hit Children's Place to seek out any other potential outfits for Cailin. I find a tiny cap she can wear at the NICU. I find a magenta and white polka dot bathing suit with a matching sun hat. Love it! I call my mom again. "You stop shopping Missy! You don't know what you are gonna get at the shower," she says. I don't think I am gonna get a lot of outfits. I think I will get a lot from my registry. I hightail it to the hospital to see my bugaboo!

Cailin is still snug as a bug. I show Princess Aurora her new cap and bathing suit/hat combo. She is smiling so much. There is a Valentine from Cailin to me signed with her footprint! Oh, so cute and so special.

Princess Aurora wrote a long note from Cailin to me reading: *To My Mommy, Thank you for being my mom =)! You are the best mommy in the world! Thank you for all my kisses and talking to me, cleaning my mouth, changing my diaper, and always knowing when I need something. Thank you for always being here when I need you. I always hear your voice and your heartbeat even when I don't see your face or smell your sweet mommy scent by me. Thank you mommy for all the wonderful things you do for me =). I know you love me and I want you to know I also love you too =)!! Hugs and Kisses, Mommy. I can't wait to be in your arms again! Happy Valentine's Day. Love you, (stamp of Cailin's footprint).*

Now there's faith working for me. I believe in angels on Earth for Princess Aurora is truly one of them. She gave me so much with this note. I am so honored and melt from the warmth in my heart. She proceeds to say, "I have something for you to do." I am thinking what (medically) can I do? She looks closely at me. "I am going to have you hold Cailin once the doctor is finished looking at her." She grabs my shoulders and looks and say, "Don't get all worked up."

I reply, "I am not. I just should pee first. Oh, my Princess Aurora, this day is such a good day!"

We smile, laugh and move about the necessary preparations to get Cailin Jane in my arms for the third time in our relationship. She is 33 weeks gestational and 11 weeks old. I am honored, and didn't believe this would happen until after her belly issues. Oh, thank you, thank you.

I sit and write this an hour after having her in my arms. It was magical to see her suck on her tube close up, her little button nose and just her. Faith is always present even when betrayed. Betrayal is only a roadmap or sign that it is no longer worth it. Not to say I will never have a relationship with my sister, but it will not be in this manner. I have strong faith in how we, Cailin and I, will lead our lives. If I show her to take that kind of aggravation just because of the title/role in your life, then I am not doing my job for her. I am a servant of God. I will suffer. I am suffering great depths and at the same time I am rejoicing in my transformation to a better me. I love it! Take that step back. Look. Listen. Pray. Hear. Move forward. Amen.

Mindset - February 10

"Go back on that Facebook stuff," Dr. Balance says.

"I am writing," I quickly reply.

"Ok, writing then," Dr. Balance responds. He keeps talking about not being out of the woods. He expresses how he doesn't want to say anything about bad vibes. I have a clear understanding about how we are not out of the woods. I understand that when she is extubated she very well could be intubated again due to relapse, procedures or just needing the oxygen support. I know I see the other parents arrive, cry a little bit, head to row one and then go home. I sit praying, talking, writing, meditating, processing, reading to Cailin and cry a hell of a lot more than the others. I hear all the stories of others with premature babies. The only common ground is a struggle. Each situation is worlds apart. Cailin is much more critical, unique and truly has a plan of her own. I know this with my superb mindset. The doctors and nurses have caught on to Cailin's mindset. Her way in God's guiding light. No one can make, do or rearrange the plan for it is not theirs to unfold. I am the one closest to it being her mother. Others are outsiders, helping hands of God, Earth Angels, spectators, nosy information-seekers, faithful friends too. I know my mindset.

I am set on keeping a daily focus. Prayers, Cailin, work, home duties and caring for myself. I have a handful of folks knowing my mindset a bit. God sees my mindset. I hand it over to him knowing I can only handle one day at a time. I am not to see and know all of the outcomes. Cailin's life is not a present to rip open and just take for granted once the next present arrives shiner and newer. Oh, no. Cailin is a precious gift that is unwrapped each moment she decides to show me more. I am asked by Ruby, the Chaplain, "Do you miss holding her?"

"Well, I can't say I have been doing a lot of holding, Ruby. I have held her three times." I glare and wonder where she is trying to get me to go.

"I know you haven't done it much. How can you hold her with her belly and dressing?" Ruby replies.

"I hold her when she is swaddled. We can't do skin-to-skin," I explain. I know my mindset. I will be holding my daughter once she is extubated very often. Once she is reintubated I will have to patiently wait again. This is my mindset of a greater understanding than many. I am asked bazaar questions, told who I am and how sick I am throughout this experience. I know my mindset. If you are not bringing joy and support, then beat it!

My mindset is to be sure to eat, sleep, meditate and connect with family and friends. Try to laugh, listen to your inner voice and go away if you do not find or feel peace. My mindset is set on being a great mother. Finding patience, investigating questions of care, medical research, second opinions, pooling questions to gather a direction, sit back and watch characters, trust my gut instincts, stay true to our progress for Cailin. I am set on taking my daughter home safely and do what is best for us and no one else. Ignorance baffles me daily, weekly and monthly. You would think that the advice givers, opinionated folks, judges and jury of my life, Cailin's life and our life to do a little research on premature babies. I don't recall asking people about the last time they slept with their spouse? Do you have violence in your home? What is your biggest fear? Then responding with a rebuttal with what you "should" do. Crisis brings a lot of minds that are lost. I set my mind on the minds that are glued together and provide me a damn good laugh at the abuse I have received. Ignorance is bliss. Well, I am not blissful these days!

I am set on creating the web of our lives. I know that spiritually evolved friends old and new are coming along on this journey. I see vacations, picnics and zoo visits. I have my mind set on discovering more of this life with them and my beauty, Cailin. I struggle knowing how she works so hard each day to get better. I am going to be available emotionally, spiritually and financially for my daughter. I will spin our web of goodness. Our web is tangle free. I will ensure that it will be better than my childhood. I will keep my decisions for the best options for Cailin. I am dedicated to her, knowing we will have many medical appointments on one end and oooodles of fun on the other. Balance will be my mindset for my Miss Cailin.

My mindset will be to teach my daughter how to follow her heart and faith when she is unsure about how to handle certain situations in life. Many people will give opinions, but ultimately you are the deciding factor. It is very important to pray on it. Be quiet and reflect on what your heart is telling you to do. People will always judge, give unsolicited advice and influence, but God is the leader you want to follow. He is the one that brings you where, how and why through life. Logic is not always seen in his ways. I am set that he is in my heart and mind. He will guide us through all of the struggles to do His work. His work in his ways. He shapes those that are intended for.

I have a mindset that is a determined one. I will not allow people that are not supportive and judgmental into my mindset. There is no room for the nonsense, distractions and drama. No need for it. I have come to learn that my mindset is puzzling to some. For those, Nana says, "Let them fall to the curbside and continue on your path with the folks that are reading the same page as you." I find comfort in the analogs she provides and it only solidifies my mindset. God Bless.

Do You? - February 13

Do you smell what I smell? Of course not. It is some masculine oil Martin from the Spa placed on my neck. He placed it on me during my chair massage. Well, he was very aggressive and helpful to loosen me up in his way. I keep getting whiffs of this oil on me. I think he was training for the Olympics! I was asked earlier today if I watched the Olympics by Pierre, the Respiratory Therapist. Nope, I haven't. I don't watch TV anymore. I cannot come to putting the TV on. I am overstimulated and don't need anymore stimulation. We have our very own series we are living. I have an Olympic champion named Cailin Jane. She is enough for me to cheer on. Do you have any idea how my life is going?

Do you know about premature babies? Do you know the stats of premature babies? Do you know about a NICU? Do you know how much support I need in my life right now? Do you know how many medicines, hands, minds, IVs and pieces of equipment are needed for Cailin Jane? Do you know I am working, caring for Cailin, advocating, setting boundaries, working on relationships and preparing for Cailin's arrival home? Do you know how many people have sent us beautiful cards? Do you know how many nasty texts I received from my sister? Do you know my mother has surprised me with her love and support? Do you know my dad and I have worked on our relationship? Do you know I am proud of myself? Do you know I have a big crush on someone right now? Do you know I love my girlfriends like family? Do you know I am super-duper excited for my shower?

I do know that each day I feel very tired and frustrated. Then I will tell myself I am one day closer to taking my daughter home. Home is where the heart is. Cailin's home is here at the Human Spirit Hospital. I will visit her day in and day out. She does know I am here. Even when she sleeps, she knows my presence. I am in love with my daughter. She is conquering so many physical obstacles. She is on a Vaportherm oxygen device. It keeps her lungs open slightly to produce an easier flow for breathing. She has had a few difficult hours with it. She has been "behaving" since last night, February 12, 2010.

"Behaving" is an interesting term the medical staff uses. How would you "behave" if you were her? Do you have your intestines outside your body? Did you have a surgery at 8 weeks old to remove 14 centimeters of your intestines? Do you know Cailin has a wound vac that has never been used on preemies here at The Human Spirit Hospital? Do you know how many questions I have asked during Cailin's stay? I know a lot of things these days.

I am wise beyond my years. I am a reflective thinker before I act. I have been quite reflective on the chain of events. I visualize an old house that had comfy broken-in chairs. Things you just didn't fix even if they were broken. You

Do You? – February 13

learned to manage with the brokenness. My old house was demolished, and I am building a new one. My new house has ground rules. The guests from our old house have come to view. Some are invited in on a whole new level. Some are trying to move in their favorite, usual broken pieces. I am not allowing old broken patterns. Oh, no. Home is where the heart is, right? So, I have been ointed and accepted God into my heart. God wants me to forgive the old guests that have hurt me. He also wants me to keep building this healthy, happy new home. Cailin is being healed by him. I am being healed by him. I have my relationships and home to change. Cailin has her body to change and function. We are two girls hard at work. So, let us keep working. For the few that have tripped us, we can dust off our wounds, forgive and move right along. I do know this is the way to lead my life.

I think of our home. I helped change her diaper, wash her mouth and hold her hand for her vibes. I know my girl is getting her "hands on" even without a bolus of pain management. She is just amazing. She is so sweet. I have held her Thumbie, the smallest little pacifier ever! Cailin becomes very aware for a solid 10 minutes with me. She is grasping my hand very tight and going to town on her Thumbie! I am so very happy with her progress today. I heard my daughter sneeze for the very first time tonight. I heard her, not the breathing tube herself. Wow! The little things in life are amazing. She is so sweet. She has really gotten bigger. Master Pickliner and Nurse Practitioner are going over her nutrition to help beef my baby up!

I am happy. I am relieved we had such a good day. Pierre, RT, got some laughs about Martin, the Massage Therapist, beating me up. I know that Cailin got a kick out of the story also. She appreciates when I am chatty and laughing. That is how I was carrying her. Times can get very difficult. I do try my very best to keep my glass half-full and my mind peaceful. I need some more laughs though. I know I will get them tomorrow at my shower. I can't wait. I am letting a lot of "stuff" go. I am going to have fun! I will, I will. Then I know I will rush over to the hospital to tell Cailin all about it! She will enjoy all the information. I know she will. I just do. Do you?

Shower Me with Love and a 'Lil' Understanding – February 14

I rise knowing it is my special day. It is the day of my shower. I will need to wax my eyebrows, mask my face, shave my legs and put a little more effort into my appearance. Lots of pictures and people to greet! I roll over and grab my iPhone to call for Cailin Jane. She had a good night and Caring will be her nurse for the 7 to 7 shift. We love Caring. She is really nice and so very understanding. I proceed to have something to eat, a cup of coffee, read an angel card and shower. I am getting ready it is 7:26 a.m. I call my mom. We are meeting at 8 a.m. at the hospital. I want her to come to my house and help me with my dress. I should not carry my outfit to the hospital. I can ask for help. So I did. She was running late. Late is better then never. She is always late. I am concerned with making it to see our precious Cailin and then Mass. Mass is at 9 a.m. My mom says, "Stop talking to me so I can leave. I'm just getting my purse together." We giggle. Me, shut up? A chatty Aries is never very quiet unless livid. I hang up to only call her back with a better plan. "Mom, let's go to the Chapel and pray instead of 9 a.m. Mass. But, you have to be here by 8:15 a.m."

"Sounds good. I am leaving in a minute," my mom replies.

I take a breath. Flexibility, Carrie, don't get mad. God will make this day what it should be. Follow His lead. Well, I will! Also, I will pray for peace. I want a peaceful day!

My mom is at my house on time. I have been taking my time. I have my robe on. I ask her to iron my dress with many specific instructions. She helps me. I remind her to check out the price tags on this cute dress and sweater from Forever 21, because I got a steal! We finish up. My mom makes me feel special, "Ohhh, Carrie how cute is this!" She is referring to my dress. I am on my way to a great day!

My mom and I head to see our little angel. Cailin is eating up my mom as she reads to her. She loves every minute of it! I am so thrilled that my mom provides this love and support to Cailin as well as me. I have really wanted my mom for years. I feel like I have a mom. I do. I do.

We stop and talk to Jem about the shower and then off to the Chapel. The outside of the Chapel is all decorated for Valentine's Day. It is beautiful! All the quotes. Whoever does this, just makes me happy! I love each month and what is done with it. I can tell there is a lot of thought put into it. I head to write in the book at the chapel. I grab a few medallions and head to the Mother Mary benches. I pray. I breathe. I pray. I breathe and talk to God a bit. I ask for peace within myself. I know some of my guests are bringing a lot of anxiety and wonder as well as worry. I want peace. I want peace during and throughout my shower. I proceed to leave and wait for my mom who is sitting on the far right side of the pews.

We head out. We arrive and run right in with Chrissy. Chrissy looks so pretty. "Hi, Car," she greets me. Chrissy is a friend of a lifetime. She has really been there for me. Even when I strayed from fear of it all, she never questioned me. She cried to me saying she really wants to be there for me. She is such a true friend. Chrissy is part of our family and will always be. She has more than a little understanding. She gets me, this, people and how to process peacefully. I have shown myself to her. I slept at her house the one night after Cailin was first born. Chrissy is my Irish girl. She is hilarious and has a "heart of gold." She is a friend in spirit form as well. We have traveled many times before. She has been ahead of me often. Now she is helping me along side-by-side. I feel like I have matured emotionally enough to meet up with her. Chrissy is the sweet breeze on a summer day, the long warm laugh that keeps going when we depart and the fabulous comforting glass of red wine you savor.

My mom and I proceed in. We receive help with some of our items. Chrissy is minutes behind. We are ohhing and aaahing about the room, the light, the space. The space is perfect! It's warm and cozy, with plenty of space above with the windows on the ceiling and sunshine pouring in on Valentine's Day. We are claiming the table by the fireplace. I am always cold. Well, not today! My mom and Chrissy will be sitting next to me. We are seeking an outlet and table for my stereo with my iPod. Control of music equals setting the tone of the experience. Music is half of the experience. Marge shows up slender and pretty as usual. She is one hot mama!

Marge is another BFF I have. She is my Polish counterpart. We have built our relationship a lot this past few years. We lost contact and reunited through Kelly. Small world, will allow roadways to reconnect with impeccable timing. She is a guide for me. Margie is solid, sincere and just simply strong. I love her and her family immensely. Jake has had some major conversations with me while I was emotionally overwhelmed. I was a mess and slept at their house. They did not look scared at me. Josh, her husband, couldn't wait for me to get to their house to hug me like a bear. He is such an amazing person. He will be one of those awesome male figures in Cailin's life. Marge brought quite a few presents from her and Chrissy. Chrissy was the bridge to bringing us all together. I meet Marge through Chrissy. We are a terrific trifecta! Marge has always been such a warm friend. Never has she turned me away or been too busy. She broke me down a bit to help me let Chrissy in during this journey. She cried with me. Held me and spooned me for God's sake. I needed a body; someone to hold me that loved me, and it was Margaret.

We all mingle to only have Miss Cynthia arrive with her plans of organization. Cyn is hilarious, optimistic and cynical. She hugs me, and starts talking about my boobies. She states, "I now know how men feel when they look at boobs like yours." We all laugh. They, my boobs, are out of control. The sisters are out saying, hello! Cyn has plans of pure organization on the gift writing, getting the guests to fill out their thank you envelopes. She is simplifying a complex thank you process with personalized stationery and return labels. Cyn is so thoughtful and nurturing. She is a friend that is always referring to me as, "Carrie Kacen" and cheering me on. Always. Lots of sarcasm, but lots of love. We have been through a lot. Cyn is a friend that is reliable and going through a major life change herself. Our journey just gives her some strength and added perspective.

The next sprinkle of pure love, peace and joy was my sweet friend, JoAnne. I love my Jo! She comes in to say she is bringing in the cake. The cake is simply amazing. A white cake with pink designs and a pink ribbon reading, "Welcome Baby Cailin." When you think it can't get better, there are two pink feet. "I love my cake!!" I shout with a smile. I love getting hugs from Jo. She will hug you and give you a soft but solid rub on my back. Love it! Jo has a long history with me. She is such a loyal, sweet and reflective friend. She really is great to share with. I never feel a lack of understanding or compassion.

The games begin with family, friends and neighbor friends. I give a speech to everyone to describe me, what the intention is for my shower and what I will be doing before we open presents. Nana is introduced to say grace. She stands up with her bright red blazer to announce, "I am Catholic so that is the only grace I will say." She says grace and we begin to head to the buffet area and eat. We enjoy our meal! Grilled chicken, penne pasta with grilled vegetables in oil, bruschetta and a number of dips. Bean dip was Margaret and Christine's favorite! We had a wonderful time finding more. Nana, my mom, JoAnne, Chrissy, Marge, Cyn and I sat at the same table. Cyn had a seat saved, but disregarded my informing her of this until she asked to sit with us. Hello! I have been saving your seat, silly goose. You are in the inner circle lady!

The conversation was amazing. Chrissy told a "cornbread story" about her feisty 2-year old, Miss Fiona. Marge and I understand Miss Fiona's presence. Hit the decks! She is in charge of that household. Nana spoke. Cynthia talked about how we meet. My stupid fake blonde ponytail, Tarzan shirt and the aggressive way to be a successful cocktail waitress. JoAnne smiles with her big lips and teeth. It was so very special and pleasant. My mom looked great! Everyone took notice of how good she looks and how "nice" she was. Well, she is happy. I am happy to help with her happiness. I looked at my mom, "I think we should start."

I got up and Chrissy helped me put to tall bar stools together. I asked Marge and Chrissy to be there for me. I imagined crying and needing a hand or a hug. They were there for me, all right. Enough to not have either happen.

I read three of my chapters: God I'm In, Viva Las Vegas NICU and Eyes of Faith. They were in the order of me writing them. I started off with a description of my journey and how I pray and hear God tell me, "Write, Write It." This is my purpose to get through all of the experiences to move forward with my life. There is not much talking except of course, Auntie Rose, "Louder Carrie." She wanted to hear. I was going to sit in front of them, although that turned into a production. Chrissy got me out of real quick. Needless to say, there she was interrupting loudly for me to speak louder. A few people made comments of "Who was that?" I know she wanted to hear as my voice trailed off. I spoke a little in between the chapters. I showed myself through my writing and my emotions. I really opened up. Right when I finished, guess who was loud again? Although Big Jerre's spirit knocked it to the floor.

Big Jerre rose to announce how she was inspired to sing her favorite song, *Smile*. She mentioned how we would all be familiar with the song. I knew this was her favorite song. I've heard her sing it many times up at Mars Piano Bar in the summer. She proceeded to sing the song. Many others started to hum and sing. Oh no, she is a soloist. She bellowed it out. I went over to her to hug her. She embraced me. Then Big Jerre announced, "I have been to a lot of baby showers, probably over 40. This by far was the best shower ever." That was the feedback.

Presents started and we had fun. I spoke about many of the gift givers and who they were. Various stories. It helps to show the giver how they are in my life and to others what stage I acquired the giver. It was very pleasant and wonderful. I had an extraordinary day! There was mingling, pictures and then an intimate round table discussion. It all went back to the core friends of the planning. We talked about our favorite parts of the day. My readings, my speech and Big Jerre singing. Marge shared, "This is right now talking."

JoAnne added, "When you told stories or about the gift giver as you were opening up." It was just all-in-all a smashing event!

Everyone helped to place my gifts in my Pilot. Cyn, Gitta and my mom helped get me in my house. It was wonderful. Everything I imagined and more! I was showered. I received a little bit of understanding as well. I know some guests got the picture. Some only moderately, and others very little. It is all about understanding. Not everyone has the same capacity. Now do they?

Elevator – February 17

The south elevators had one go bad. I saw a very, very large man a few days ago fixing it. I remember my Aunt Besty's second husband worked for Dover. Jim worked his way up to the top of the company. I thought of Michigan and the memories of the pig roasts and good times. All the while I was thinking how I certainly would not want to get stuck in the elevator. I tried to change that thought thinking that is not a good thought to put out into the universe. I have been using the "good" one on the right side. I took it up today. Today is Thursday. I do not work on Thursdays. I am happy about having an easy going day. I can organize a bit at home during rounds. I head up. I see Dealer, the nurse, in the isolette.

Dealer welcomes me with, "She is a bit fussy and I am not sure why?"

"Well, she is a baby and will be fussy from time to time," I reply.

"I guess. I am glad you are here. You can read to her," Dealer replies.

I put my hands in the isolette and start talking to Cailin. She is a bit fussy. Dealer is going to go on break, but just can't. Cailin is having a few bradycardias. She gets the oxygen up a bit and heads off. During her break, I am tending to Cailin's bradys. She is not breathing often. She is dipping down to the 50s, 60s, 70s. She needs to be shaken often to wake up. Cailin is so sound asleep that she can't remember to breathe. She is very tired as well. It goes on and on. I am talking to her, "Cailin, take a breath baby girl. Good job." This happens over and over. Dealer returns for a couple more dramatic dips. She calls over the doctors.

We have a stage of doctors coming. Dr. Vague and Dr. Sneakers come over. "There they are," I say.

Dr. Vague welcomes her, "Hi, Peanut."

Residents flock. Dr. Bolt comes through the crowd. It is too loud over here. They leave with Dr. Bolt coming over to take care of the situation. They are thinking to go up to five liters on her vaportherm or reintubate her on the ventilator. I am not sure what is going to happen. I do know that seeing your baby girl not breathing and changing colors is quite frightening. I am dealing and coping with something of great tragedy. This is hard as a parent to watch, but for Cailin Jane this is very hard for her.

Dr. Bolt comes back over before rounds to talk to me, "She will be reintubated today. This may allow her to gain some weight." He was mild-mannered and very pleasant delivering our side step. I need to leave. It's rounds for the doctors. So I head home. I know that Christine is available to talk to me this morning. I call Christine and talk to her about this morning and the trial for Cailin. My poor girl had such a hard time breathing. Christine talks to me quite awhile today. I was able to process everything that is going on. I was able to talk to her from the heart. I am very thankful that we had this time planned to talk. We are planning on going to eat to celebrate my book and my birthday on April 8th.

I think about April 8th and know this is a time I look forward to. I am anxious to see where Cailin is with her healing health. I can't wait to see how she is doing when I get back up to the hospital. I keep visualizing Cailin in the summer being healthy and happy. I think about being with Marge, Christine and my mom's backyards. I am really anxious for us to have her get healthy and get the heck out of here. I know I have to be flexible and patient. I am struggling with this. Cailin is busy with the medical staff. I am eating, talking and napping. I head back up to the hospital to only find a parking space on the fifth floor. I believe that the hospital is a very busy place today. Something is in the air?

I come in to see Cailin in a much better state. Dealer, the nurse, was really great with me. I was happy to have her be so supportive and helpful to Cailin and me. She was very warm to me. I know she truly cared and had a hard shift too. I was thinking on the way in about having a Chaplain come in and give a blessing. Dealer told me, "You know you can have an anointing of the sick at any time, Carrie."

I reply, "That's funny that you would say that. I was just thinking about having you call. I wasn't sure if I was being dramatic. Would you?"

She does. Ruby, the Chaplain, takes awhile to get here. I ask her if she feels like her day is busier? "A bit," is the response. She asks if I want a blessing or a sacrament of anointing.

"A sacrament," I reply. I want the whole kit and kaboodle. I want Cailin to be in the good hands of the Lord.

Blessed, the Priest, arrives. He is the Scottish Priest and is quite funny. He makes me laugh a lot. I am happy to have him come and bless my baby girl. We join in. Dealer, Ruby, Pierre (RT), Blessed and myself. I place my hand on Cailin in the isolette. I smile knowing this is the support every person needs and loves. I am happy this is happening for Cailin to receive this support.

As the elevator is broken, I feel stuck. I hope Cailin starts making more progress so we can leave this place. I feel the tension again here on the unit from the nurses. I try not to pay attention. It does baffle me that I am here to support my very sick daughter and they can't believe I am here all the time. Get your head out of your ass and realize if she was your child you would be a lot different than your nurse role. Oh well. I will not feed their energy at all. Shame on them for being so small-minded. I am fortunate that our elevator is being worked on and leaving someday. I fear being stuck. I am stuck due to Cailin being very ill and needing a lot of support to grow and heal. Our elevator is viewed and rode by many. The cart itself can be very heavy. Some days we have speed to glide up and down. Other days we break down and need another direction. It is our elevator. It is called Kacen. Kacen is a solid name. We back up our name with our efforts, our strength, our courage, our wisdom and our girl power!

Stepping Out with a Glide – February 18

Cailin is reintubated. A side step. We are gliding. She has a big day today. Back on Que 6 and receiving her very first feeding of 1 cc of my "gold" breast milk. The "gold" is before the milk. The good stuff. I am recovering from yesterday. I need to visualize the glide. Chill, Car, chill.

Gliding is easy when the day before you are shaking your baby to wake up and breathe. It is common for a 35-weeker to have bradycardias. It's not common for a mother to see their child not breathe. Pretty darn scary stuff! I wanna keep gliding. I open my Law of Attraction book to retrain my brain. I need to get on track with our side step. Two steps forward then one step to the side. I know it is a side step because Dr. Bolt shows me the x-ray this morning. Cailin's right lung was collapsed yesterday and now is looking a lot better. I know it is a side step due to her starting the feeds today as well as the lung improvement.

The issue is I deal with is the crisis the day after. My head is really hurting me. I have a horrible headache. Why? I carry all my stress in my neck, head and shoulders. Ouch! I take care of all of this with a cup of coffee, laughter with my coworkers (SimpleSophia, Redhot Roxy and Animated Annie), a big lunch, a face and back facial and the smiles

Cailin left me with. Before I venture in my daily glides, I hold the thought of Cailin smiling at me. Not just little smiles. No, no, really big smiles. Embracing smiles from my lovebug. She has one of Brilliant Brett's aqua bows! We are looking good and smiling during our glides.

Is this a tango dance? Yes, the dips scare me a bit, but the turns feel great. I can't wait to literally glide, jump and dance with my daughter. If she is anything like me, then she will pick up my love of dance too! I had glides throughout the day. I always miss her so much. I have to say my glides each day have a larger purpose for Cailin. She is the reason for me to dance. I love to be with her. I feel complete with my glides knowing they are purely for her life. Cailin's glides, twists and turns. She steps forward and back quite often for a 2 pound, 16 ounce premature baby. She always has a good recovery. She will squirm often with a wet diaper. I require her to say her preemie pink rosary daily. Cailin wears bows to accessorize for her daily battle for life.

I sit back and take in the glides. I wonder why I have a few folks that can't make it for me when asked. Those same very folks need so much of my time to make themselves feel better. I battle it all out on the dance floor in my heart. I am going through some major growing pains. I am no longer pacifying and making others feel good when they make their mistakes. You ask, why? Well, I am here to live for Cailin to fight this medical journey out. I have very, very long winded voicemails of justifying why they can't make my shower or why they missed. I do not feel joyful to call them back. Let go and let God.

Stepping Out with a Glide – February 18

Usually, I will listen and comfort them. I just don't have the time or energy for their inner child. I am baffled that they can't be apart of our shower day, but want me to call and talk, go to dinner, come to the hospital. I feel a lot of wants. When it is time to give and show up, they are not present. I am not mad, sad or surprised. The shock is that they keep calling and dragging a mistake or inability out. I feel they need to leave it alone and let it go. What do you want from me? Acceptance of the behavior or lack of presence? I don't have room for it, folks. For I am gliding. Gliding with my Conquering Cailin.

Work - February 20

What is work? Oh, I know what work is. I have hustled my whole life. I have earned a lot, a little and tons of personal development. I felt discouraged with my first 100% commission sales job until I completed a Chicago marathon in 1999. I need to think of the training and that race again. My completion and efforts to get there is a road of conquering a major mountain. The trail runs on the lakefront were long. Some were more painful than others. Today is one of those days that I have to sweat it out or yell. I get into my Pilot after work to call my mom. She is at AT&T to get her blackberry phone fixed with plastic around it. I am venting to her and stop to yell at her. "What are you doing with all that noise?" I say very aggressively. Now most would not handle me. This is why she is my mother. My mom embraces me. I scream about work, about my sister, about one of my friends. I express to her how I can't handle all this pull on me. How many pieces are there of me? I only have so much.

My coworker, Redhot Roxy, tells me, "Car, this might sound mean but just don't talk to the people that are dragging you down. Surround yourself with the people that make you feel good." She has a strong point. Breaking out of the habit of being an enabler and pacifying others is my work. Work to personally develop into a healthier person. Who needs the cards from someone trying to say, "I Miss You" or "What family means…" Who needs five contacts from one friend that missed my shower? Let it go, Carrie. Well, I want to scream! I am about to tell someone off. I don't want to hurt my sister, my friend, my coworker or my boss. I wanted to tell them this: I almost lost my life, I have almost lost my daughter multiple times, our fight is an uphill battle, I am in a Neonatal Intensive Care Unit for Cailin's health, I am working, I am managing my household, handling my finances alone, I don't have time to pacify your regrets, I will not be dissected or controlled. How about leaving me alone if you are just gonna put pressure on me, bring me down and distract me? Go away. Thank you very much. I understand not everyone has compassion. Some people are selfish, controlling and self-consumed. I get all that. I just really, really don't have time or energy for it.

My work I do have time for is to support, advocate, hold, read and soothe my daughter. Cailin is working so hard for her life. We have complications and one hell of a fight behind us and in front of us. I want to work on being at peace by letting go and ignoring all the drama I am getting from different angles. I must recommit myself to our fight, have less distractions, more peace, more joy. I need to recenter myself after a hard week. I had to shake my daughter alive a few days ago. Yet, I have my sister telling me what family is through a card! Yikes!

Our work will be continuing a good fight with pure genuine love, not fear. I will remain committed to loving my daughter and believing in her recovery. Music, laughs, uplifting folks and having our hearts warmed is where we will be found. For the others that do not provide such things and are continuously selfish, bye, bye. I do give them credit for their persistence of their selfish behavior. The answer for them is NO. This answer baffles them to being dumbfounded, which turns into anger and lashing. Continuously attempting me to comfort them. My comfort is God's work to focus on Cailin. She is a fighting Irish lil' wee one of 2 pounds, 11 ounces. She needs me more than the selfish adult beings.

I will refocus on God and his ways. I hear him knocking, I trust him and I follow. I see the footprints in the sand. I work to make out the moment as there is only one set. For I know, yes, He is carrying me. I thank you, God. I am not afraid to give it up to you. God works mysterious ways. I see his mystery everyday unfold with my dealing and Cailin's tribulations with her health. Gotta get to work. Work that does not have policy. It has no paycheck. It has no numeric measurements. It is the love I have for Cailin, God and myself. It is our journey. In the marathon there is a reward, a medal. Our reward is life!

3 – February 21

Three is a crowd they say. A triangle has three points. It is half of an eight, our favorite number. Half in the shape, not the number of course. Three heads are better than one. Three keeps coming up for me, for us. I went to sleep on November 23, 2009 and felt the presence of three souls. Long, lean souls. Strong, yet gentle souls. In my mind, they were for Cailin. Now I know for certain they were for us and our journey. Father, Son and Holy Spirit. Exhibit B represents our nurses. Pocahontas, Princess Aurora, Snow White and Priscilla. There were four, but four is not our number. Only three. Twists, turns, songs and a break came, which turned it into three nurses. Pocahontas, Princess Aurora and Snow White. Our family here of primary and associates is totaling three. Three very different types of female fellows. The fellows are White Angel, Vague and Jasmine. Three that is.

I think about the number today when I was one of three. Beth, Susie Q and I. We did hair, cleaned, hugged, talked and rescheduled. Three people putting their hearts into my home to help me. I began to think of the importance of three. Being a single NICU mommy, there is my daughter, me and a nurse for each shift. Three people at bedside 34. A triangle. A trifecta. Christine, Margaret and I all have a daughter. Close friends with a daughter to offer love to each of our families. I am a number type person. As Pocahontas, the primary nurse, will say, she likes even numbers. Three is a nice number. It creates a need for our balance, but is an odd number.

Each angle of a triangle needs one another to create such an important shape. The nurse depends on the baby to have a job to do. I depend on my daughter to be a mommy. My daughter depends on me to be a mommy and a nurse to be a nurse. I see the triangle in this dynamic. I see it all day long with hair color. The primary colors are the corners of the triangle. Along the line to the next corner are various colors. Red-orange, red-yellow, blue-green, green-blue, violet, yellow and so on. All of the colors are essential to make the wheels. Three corners to make a wheel. A wheel goes round and round.

I watch the wheel go in its circular formation and I see pieces, people fall into place. I thought the more associate nurses would be great for Cailin's consistence in care. I was wrong. I let go and watch, fight for the proper care, and watch everything fall away to be left with three. I saw a nurse fall in love with my daughter, rebel my role and purpose, get carried away with her emotions and then fall away to have three nurses left. I wonder what was that all about? I analyze and see God has his purposes. I had to fight for the lead seat. Cailin's voice is her mother, not a nurse and not doctors turning away from me. I watch the pieces fall to create a dynamic shape. A shape of a triangle. I embrace the shape. This is the formation we need around us.

3 – February 21

Cailin gets better and stronger after the shape of triangle took place. I keep learning more and more through each experience. The experiences are not easy. They are painful, emotional and quite draining. I have to keep recharging my batteries. Sometimes, I just yell at a friend or my mom to get rid of all the pain. I get rid of it to go back. I have to keep fighting. Fighting means to face the hurdle and conquer it. I spoke to my friend, Angie who is a Neonatal Nurse Practitioner, regarding how I am in a corner. "Do you want to go for a drink?" Angie suggests.

"Yes, I do! I am in a track suit, so let's stay near the hospital," I anxiously reply.

"I am in sweats. So, do you want me to come like that?" Angie says.

"Of course, I do. There is a local place in on Cermak we can go to for a beer. Just text me when you are near," I say.

Angie, me and Blue Moon. This is a great combo of three. I had enough from every layer, aspect and angle of my life struggles today. I texted Angie, "I am down today. I really need a friend." Now for a strong, confident, independent single NICU mom this is great healing progress. Good job, good work, Carrie. Angie responds by a text to call when I have a chance. I find it odd and neat that my most difficult conversations from the hospital to a helpful hand are on the bridge of the fifth floor. The bridge of the past tribulations to the future of handling the trial and moving forward. Do the work and move on.

We arrive in our lounging clothes. We agree to pick an appetizer of Calamari and two Blue Moons. That is a delicious threesome. We talked about Cailin. Cailin's amazing medical journey, defying the odds, how pretty she is and how my motherly love had made this all possible. Love conquers all! I truly believe this statement. For I witness this daily, each shift, each week, each month. Love defies the odds. God's love, my love and Cailin's love for life have conquered it all!

Angie and I have an amazing and well-needed conversation. She asks me, "Carrie, what was your scariest moment?" I reply with an answer of three. There was not one. One is the loneliest number. There have been three. First, after I had Cailin, I had her baptized then I feel asleep for 20-30 minutes. The first moment was waking up in my hospital room to find out it was all real. I felt like someone ripped my baby out of my stomach. I missed her kicking me where she was safe within my body. I screamed and cried hysterically. I pulled it all in after 10-15 minutes to get my ass up to the NICU to see my daughter. I wasn't positive she would make it. Apparently, the first 72 hours were extremely critical. The whispers of the staff were that of death. Poor mother is gonna lose her baby girl. I was wheeled by my Philippino nurse that said Our Fathers with me the whole time to the fifth floor to see Cailin. She left me with Pocahontas and Cailin. A loving threesome. That, by far, was one of my scariest moments. My second moment was when she started having major belly issues. She was not doing well at all. I had to talk to her about living for her, not me. A mother's love can drag someone around. I want her to live for her and God, not just for me to be a mom. I am

3 – February 21

second. She will decide if she needs and wants to stay in this life and then God will take care of me after. I verbalize this to her at the bedside of Bed 20. Princess Aurora, Jasmine and a resident are there. Jasmine tells me to stop being negative. For she was in the very beginning and I believed in Cailin. No one else on the staff did besides her. Jasmine said if she has made it this far, don't let go of your faith and positive loving force. I had them in tears. Cailin and I have had many, many medical intelligent folks cry. Cry and really feel this journey in their core for moments. My third scary moment was after her three hour GI surgery when they couldn't get a read on any of her vitals. I know for certain that there were only one set of footprints. For God carried Cailin and I through this impossible medical recovery. This is one of the many medical miracles he showered us with. I can tell you this for certain because I am on the other side of it all. I weeped without moving my chest. I weeped with tears falling into a large pond of a mother's love. I had the nurse in tears, my mother and the fellow, Dr. Sneakers, a deer in headlights. This was our turning point this dark moment. I was so exhausted I had to get an anointing from the Chaplain for Cailin and me. I dragged myself to the quiet room where I told Cailin and God this: "I am not sure. Do want you want to do, Cailin. But it is important that you do what you need to do for yourself. God will take care of me after you baby girl." I took a deep breath to keep it together before I curled up on a stiff loveseat to crash. I said in my head, "I am not sure what will be when I awake, but God is with us Cailin." I heard clear as day, Cailin's laugh at about 8 months old. I smiled and laughed. I said to her in my head, "Let's play in our dreams, kid!"

I cry and can bring myself back to the work that has happened. I choose to move forward, pray, meditate and visualize my child healthy and home. I have to tend to her daily medical needs through questions and medical discussions. I grip to Dr. Bolt regarding the last dressing change on Cailin that was not good at all. He listens and replies, "We use this wound vac every three years." There you have it. Three, I hear again. This is what true medicine is, a learning experience. My daughter, Cailin, is nothing less than amazing by challenging the Neonatologists, Nurses, Respiratory Therapist and many other minds on the fifth floor. I can hear Cailin's thoughts... one, two three! She is always bringing a triangle together.

Trickster, The One and Only – February 22

I hear the pounce of the huff on the ground before looking up to see the stallion. The coat of the horse is shiny and striking. The horse is amazingly beautiful although that is not the core of the horse. The outer beauty shows just how amazing the soul, the root of the stallion, is. The tail whips back and forth. The motions are loud, yet the horse is peaceful for being active. The horse was not anticipated to make such sounds since its beginning was rough. Although the horse acquired the nickname, Trickster. The name is suiting for the black active horse that beats the odds.

Trickster knows how to pull stunts of all sorts especially on Tuesdays. When you gamble on this horse, try to do it on a Tuesday. November 24, 2009 was Tuesday that this Trickster only weighed one pound. The weight was not heavy, but Trickster's will outweighed all our wills. All the medicine and the tilting of my pelvis didn't stop or hinder that. Trickster was coming to join this race on November 24th. She pushed for over 15 hours on my cervix and came out very tiny and very black. Black and blue. Well, not even blue, because she was just black. She had a head full of hair that appeared black for the bad bruises. The gamble was the first 24 hours with a 10% chance of survival. Then came the next 72 hours. Trickster defied all the hours, all the days and was there on the following Tuesday pouncing on her isolette.

Trickster was lying and being nursed to good health. Trickster was stomping her little huffs over and over. She had the medical staff running to her bedside over and over. Her trainer, Dr. Sensible, would tell her what she wanted. "Cailin, I look forward to the day we are not all at your bedside." Then Trickster will eventually provide the request of her trainer at the time. Dr. Sensible approached her with a request of an entire week of a quiet bedside. Trickster came around the corner eventually to provide an entire week without needing as much critical care. Dr. Sensible always described Trickster, as a tiny baby with her strong accent. Not a 23-weeker, a tiny baby. Sure there are odds and numbers, but the being is more important than the metrics. Not all of the folks understand that until Trickster defies the metrics and evolves into her nickname. She is fragile and looks frightening in her tiny shape with translucent skin. She is the size of a little frog and her bones are so delicate. The outer shell is all of this although Trickster has a being, a soul, that outmeasures a healthy strapping male. Trickster can do circles around all the spectators. She is told that she will have a PDA heart surgery by the doctors. Trickster will have nothing to do with this. She decides that MRSA is her better bet. For Trickster is all about sidetracks, hurdle jumping and finishing the race in first place despite all the doubts.

Her biggest fan is a woman that considers herself strong, independent and confident. Although when Trickster came along all the illusions and old ways of this woman changed. The change has been an easy win and doubts in placing

Trickster, The One and Only — February 22

her bet everyday. Multiple times a day this woman comes to her stable and places her bet on Trickster. Rain, shine, snow, clouds, conflicts, confrontations, uplifting conversations or hugs will not change this woman's determination to place her bet on Trickster. Trickster is a risk for many, but for Trickster's biggest fan she is the safest. There is something about her will and wit. Each day Trickster comes out smelling like a rose. Scares, lack of breathing, loss of blood or infections are only part of the journey for this horse.

Everyday she seals up another heart on her seating area. They come by with their eyes big wondering, "How does she do it?" Trickster knows each race is a challenge. She will defeat all her obstacles without reserves by pure heart and soul. Her race is won daily, weekly and monthly as she grows shiner and stronger. Trickster knows "this woman" is her biggest fan and will not leave her side. There are many purposes to fill for Trickster. So she asks, did you read my chart? Do you know what I have been through? Do you know how to handle things under pressure? Trickster will frighten you if you don't have the stamina to tend to her needs. She is not typical. She is 12 weeks old and has more fans than any other horse. She is the underestimated underdog that surprises the audience daily!

Trickster is my own flesh and blood. I am her biggest fan, her mother. I am served daily with plans and goals. Although Trickster is the boss of the applesauce, folks. Take your seat, keep reading and grab a tissue or two. Her story is nothing less than that of a shiny stunning child!

A Familiar Place – March 1

I wanted to hug her. I wanted to talk to her. I wanted to sit with her. I knew the look in her eyes. I knew the pain. I knew the uncertainty. I understand motherly love. I am not sure when we starting talking. Talking to Silvia is what I need. What I wanted. I talked briefly to her regarding her child and her need of a heart surgery. Cailin dodged that bullet twice. The PDA surgery is a "typical," almost routine surgery for a preemie. Of course, Cailin would not be typical and did not have this procedure. She had to have the three hour process from start to finish. The exploratory, yet with some idea of where the "issue" was. Regardless of the difference, we have a common ground. Mothers with preemies with surgical needs. I see in her eyes all of this. I feel her heart, her fears, her hopes and her dreams, which is all too much at times. A familiar place.

Silvia is wrapping up her night. I give her words of encouragement. I pray for her and her daughter. I have prayed for others. Parents that lost their babies and parents that are in this petting zoo along with us. I stay later than most. I am different. Different we all are. Not better, just different.

I head home to rest and think of my daughter and Silvia's. I rise at 6:30 a.m. to have Pocahontas provide an update on Cailin's night. I hear hesitation and an unusual tone in her voice. She proceeds, "I am not sure if you know that there is a surgery across the way. So for visitation, it probably doesn't look good."

I reply, "Well, I have no problem working with you guys and leaving for 15-20 minutes during the surgery."

Pocahontas replies, "I didn't know if they told you. I am just giving you a heads up."

I anxiously and sternly reply, "Well, I am coming up to visit my girl. Goodbye."

I am pissed and not happy at all. I try to let my emotions flow out and then breathe. In and out. I am telling myself that everyday is just another adventure. I am told by my mom not to expect a fight. Well, in a premature, actually a micropreemie world, everyday is a fight. Fight for life, proper care, respect, compassion and healthy relationships. Nice try, mom, but no cigar. I jump in the shower and disregard washing my hair. I put a cute hat on, dress, toss my two makeup cases in my purse and fly out the door. So much for a routine today. I am not waiting until 5 p.m. to see Cailin. We need to have sometime this morning. I am praying for just 15 minutes at this point.

I have my Pilot in gear and down Roosevelt we go. I arrive up to the fifth floor. Sonica says, "I can't let you back there because there is a surgery."

I reply, "Okay. Is Laine here?"

She replies, "Yes."

I say, "I want to talk to her." I pace three times and then say, "Tell her I will be in the waiting area." I proceed to breathe and sit on the couch I have laid on, cried on and watched others sit many times.

Silvia is on the couch. "Hi. How are you doing?" I say to her.

"I'm all right," Silvia says.

"Do you have anyone to sit with during your baby's surgery?" I ask.

She says, "No."

I reply, "I can sit with you during the surgery if you want. I know how scary this is. Don't feel obligated to say yes just because I am offering."

Silvia says, "I really want you to."

I look up to see Laine arrive in the room. Laine says with her arm waving us up, "Let's go ladies. Let's go see your babies." I am so very relieved. We enter to wash our hands.

I turn to Laine, "I was just told this morning that I couldn't come see Cailin at 6:30 a.m. I would have scheduled my day differently if I was told sooner."

Laine says, "We should have told you."

We all walked in our usual way down Row 1 and then we are at a dead end because of the surgery set up. Laine looks at me, "Can you walk around?"

"Of course, let me just drop my stuff here," I reply.

I turn and walk with Laine up Row 2. I run into Delightful PT. She just finished PT with Cailin. Cailin gets a fabulous report. She is going to go see Cailin later this week with me. She apologizes for doing it without my presence. I say, "It is most important that you do this with Cailin whether I am there or not. I appreciate it. I hope to be there next time." I hustle down Row 3 to my baby girl. Southside Irish Chickie is with Cailin today. I take a breath and I am relieved. Southside Irish Chickie is a solid nurse. She does complain a bit, but really is quite peppy. I find that she complains to let the other complainers feel more comfortable. I truly don't think she is a half-empty complainer just peer pressure. She has bright blue eyes and is moving around Cailin's needs to comfort her. I am happy. I am here and didn't stay home. I came with my head high and determined to see my child.

Silvia is across the way with the white curtain. The fishbowl has curtain options. Lots of privacy? No, people, not much at all. I read. I talk. I change her diaper. I finish up to the last minute before her neighbor's surgery. I head to the bathroom to put my face on. I go into the waiting room and Silvia is crying.

I rub Silvia's shoulder. I tell her I am an affectionate person. I will hug you, hold your hand or rub your shoulder. You let

A Familiar Place – March 1

me know if you need any of this. She tells me about her history, her faith, her hopes and dreams. I disclose a lot of myself. My challenges, Cailin's challenges, my disappointments, hurts, fears and my faith. We talk a lot about God. Now I am in a familiar place. A place of uncertainty with surgery on a baby. A place of complete familiarity. Not a place I want to be. A place with a new beginning. A friend. A friend that I could be open to. Cry and smile to. A familiar place with a NICU friend.

Glamorous Gladiator – March 3

When you envision a Gladiator, you may see a large, husky smelly man. Almost like a caveman. Right? Well, let me paint a very different picture for you. I was at bedside 20 with Cailin Jane with a swelling belly that was not at all a good sign. The GI surgeon and her team were on the case. The case was Baby Girl Kacen to them. The case for me was my daughter. This was the beginning of their medical work and my family work. GI issues are family issues. I find it interesting that my niece had GI issues until the day I delivered Cailin. Marie assumed the worse, Crones. Of course, that was not the case. Her mindset is always the worst. Surgery and possibly death. I am happy that I am different. Cailin starts signs of an "issue" of what, where and how bad, we are uncertain. As she displays symptoms of issues, my father and I have a dispute. I had disclosed myself, my feelings, my needs and my questions to him as a father. Of course, it didn't go over well. My intention was to be true to myself. He wasn't drinking, so he really felt my words. He fought back and left me. Abandonment, a feeling all too familiar. This time I turned to a friend, Christine. She embraced me and helped me as Glamorous Gladiator helps Cailin Jane. During Cailin's GI journey, my dad is admitted, released, readmitted and released with medical issues. What kind you ask. GI issues. Ummm, I think. Interesting very interesting. I am on to something.

Glamorous Gladiator is onto something and her medical challenge, the belly. Before I get into the trials and the tribulations of Cailin's belly, let me shed a stage, some lights and a diva. The character is short, feisty and beyond human capacity. Glamorous Gladiator arrives in the morning with heels. Not just heels. Killer shoes. I always look at the shoes a person is wearing. A huge decision on decorating your feet. Where and how you are getting places and how it all looks, sounds and feels. Glamorous Gladiator was very confident, certain and strong with her explanations. I recall stating some feedback on Cailin. She was sharp and worked very hard to point out her knowledge. I took a step back. Actually, I sat up straighter and cocked my head to the right. Right on! Someone like me. I like her immediately. What do I like about her? Her wit and knowledge. Not ego. Knowledge.

I liked her for awhile. She is pushed around and pressured to conduct surgery by the Neonatologists. Dr. Wise, Attendee, at the time is brilliant. He knows this will fix Cailin. Although it is all about Godspeed. God will shed light and show Glamorous Gladiator when, where and how. She is fully aware of the pressure and her own intuition. This is the timeframe that my strong "like" grows and expands into pure love. She is the angle on earth every mother prays for in a surgeon. She is not anxious to slice and dice. She is calculated and conducts an upper GI that takes 48 hours.

Glamorous Gladiator does not want to conduct a complete 100% "exploratory" surgery on her patient. My daughter grows to love her. I know Cailin can hear her clicking of the heels down the row, her peppy voice and her certain touch. Cailin gives her high fives and micropreemie waves. Glamorous Gladiator compliments her bows. She also describes Cailin as such: she is trouble, a troublemaker, but a very strong baby. Glamorous Gladiator takes a liking to my daughter, but we fall in love with her.

Glamorous Gladiator has the stamina of a troop of men. She is determined, calculated, friendly, kind and very competent. I see the teams change with her all the time. I know that they are blessed and lucky to be able to study under her. She is a mighty, mighty surgeon. She offers families, like us, a chance at a happy and healthy life. I see her walking through the Human Spirit Hospital and campus knowing exactly what she is made of. Pure love, passion for life, expertise and a woman larger than life. I am still looking for the cape with a large G to peek out of her Attendee lab coat! I know it is there, Glamorous Gladiator. We love you and feel very blessed to have had you in our life.

The Village – March 4

I just got off the phone with a villager. Her name is Brett. She listened, sympathized and was a breath of fresh air. The Village has all sorts of folks, seasons and current events. It takes a village they say. Our village is one that I am creating. When you become a parent, you buy the home. The home is your heart, mind and soul. You want to create a good, stable and healthy home for your baby in "the village." The Village has its idiots too. So you gotta be careful with who you give your address to. Some may seem fine and then you see that they are not respecting your home. I am learning more and more about this Village. I am making mistakes here and there, but learning from all of them.

My home is a warm home. I don't care to be cold. I am cold too often, so I need to keep warm. I warm my home up with consciousness. I am attracted to the folks in the Village that recognize and enhance my consciousness. I have a really pretty structure to my home. With beauty comes some jealousy, ignorance and a desire. I do answer the door at times that I shouldn't. The great lesson is that I have friends in our Village that keep our home safe and blessed. Just like the friend, Brett. She twisted her fingers to make the smallest bows ever! I always get her emails and Facebook posts delivered that end in a warm heart and a smile. She makes me smile and warms my home.

The Village offers lots of avenues, courtyards, buildings and grasslands. You know of the Village. Just look around. There it is! My home was purchased and built with the purpose of Cailin Jane. We depend on the avenue of Respiratory Therapists. This close-knit subculture here at the Village is a positive force. I have many of the RTs that have a special place in our heart. The Animal Tamer is the leader of this group. There has not been one member of this subculture that has rubbed me the wrong way. Good energy through and through. I recall watching Cailin's boyfriend be the very first person to calm her down in the unit. She took her vibes well and was able to feel his calming energy. He is an informative, calm and very kind man. He will always be Cailin's first boyfriend. Tim is a long lanky man that has a gentle soul. He complimented me on my parental involvement one night. A night that I needed to hear such a positive opinion. Liz, a fellow Aries, with a strong demeanor. She chews her gum, wears a jade bracelet and always has good hair! Pierre is a gentle, adventurous, story-telling man that brightens my day each day he is here. I enjoy his face and smile. Cherry named Cailin, "a tiny doll," in the beginning of our journey in the Village. Cherry is sensitive, kind, warm-hearted and very easy to talk to. I enjoy her voice and demeanor. She brings me to a quiet calm place when I see her. This group of folks in the Village makes it a much kinder, real and calm place. I am glad that they value the breath of life in the Village.

The Residents are a revolving door. Some get caught in the door and come back a time or two. They rotate around the door. Every Village needs fresh blood and new greenery to groom. The Fellows are seeking out their passion with the babies here. They each have tremendous amount of knowledge and passion for their job. Each are very different. White Angel is hands-on, a force that is happy and present at all time. When I say present, not just physically, but consciously. Vague has a serious look about her. She dresses the diva part. Don't let it fool you. I wasn't fooled by it. Her heart is big and her knowledge is present. Bolt is tall in physical size that is filled up by his big heart and mind. He works with everything; he has to be great. Bolt has a calm demeanor and a good sense of humor. He is a fast talker with compassion. His blue-collar work ethic and his lab coat make him one hell of a doctor! Sneakers is short in build. It's always him moving about with his quick mental capacity within the Village. He has a smile. He shows himself as the days in our home builds. The first impression was not a warm fuzzy one. The hill was high for him to climb, but he changed gears and is warm. I always liked his shoes. Jasmine has a very special carpet we jumped on when we moved in on November 24, 2009. She was very informing in Neonatology about Cailin and my options. She has informed us of our new home and warmed it up. Jasmine is someone very special to me. She honestly has fought for Cailin and shown me x-rays of Cailin's body to allow me to understand. She is never bothered by my questions, concerns and comments of the Village. The Attendees have been here a long time. This is a staple in the Village. Each of their knowledge base is tremendous. This small tribe of leaders is full of character to say the least. Dr. Sensible has a larger-than-life aura about her. Although she is caring and very down to earth, her presence is always known and feels warm. Dr. Wise is goofy with his humor to cover his nervousness. His very own brilliance frightens him at times. Dr. Balance has a "chill" persona about him. He is always weighing and balancing each medical step. For each step has many other avenues. Dr. Tour Guide is smart and allows walking around. He spreads his commentary as well as his demeanor. He is always showing the unit to a new set of eyes. They are glamorized about the "guts and glory" while Dr. Tour Guide sees a whole different unit. The tour is always together physically but very different emotionally. There are a few others that I see in the halls of the Village, but never at the bedside. They are Kings of the Kingdom viewing from afar.

The Nurses are prevalent on the Village lands. There are many different types of nurses. We have the core group that waters our garden and helps it grow. We have had a few that went through the motions of a daily watering and were not doing anything of the such. I smell those little rabbits in the garden trying to eat up our food. I glare and stare first so they know, I know! It doesn't seem to stop their intentions and behaviors. I confront them and attempt to get them where we need them. Eventually, I need to go to Laine. I think it through always before I say what I need to say. I will always express their side as well. They're just hungry little rabbits that are misbehaving. Every dirty little rabbit needs to be scared a bit to get back on track. Unfortunately, I have had my garden messed with a number of times. Once I built the white picked fence, there were only a few more attempts to get in the garden. I caught the dirty rabbit. I know that each garden needs their oxygen to thrive. The oxygen should be in the nose and nowhere else. I understand that the dirty rabbit didn't like me, but

The Village – March 4

too bad! That dirty rabbit made my sweet pea of only two pounds suffer close to two hours after extubation. The dirty rabbit got hers! I shield our garden in the Village.

The Village is not a place that I would wish upon anyone. I am blessed that the Village has advanced over the years. It is a Village that has many, many hands in your garden. Presence, questions and gut instincts are the proper equipment to build a foundation within the Village. I learn about the different Villagers, streets, avenues and courtyards while we live here. I know this is only the beginning of our story. I must pray, meditate and dedicate my heart and soul to my sweet pea. For I know she is growing properly with all of it.

Awakening – March 9

I arrive to the parking garage here at The Human Spirit Hospital. Again, I am behind a vehicle that passes the ticket dispenser and is staring at the gate. The gate does not lift due to the driver not hitting the ticket dispenser. Today I am patiently waiting for the driver to realize how this process works. I watch the man eventually pull his door open and then step out. He hits the large green button to get the ticket. The ticket comes out although the driver still does not figure out that you have to pull the ticket out to engage the gate to go up. I am sitting there correlating this with my conversation with a friend today. How consciously aware are some people? We go about our days and wonder why the gate is not going up. How come we can get past the gate? Cailin has jumped and pushed many of her gates up and right off the hinges. I reflect on our life together, which is being awakened.

Yes, we are all awake when we get up and go about our days, weeks, and months. Our lives unfold with the various structures and routines we have. I know I have been a very aware and sensitive person throughout my life. I am considered a sensitive soul. Cailin is not falling far from the sensitive tree. She has reacted to nurses when they speak in an aggressive agitated voice to me. Then I hear, "I haven't even touched her!" I smile in my heart, knowing just how protective my daughter is to me as I am to her. It hasn't been easy to been shaken from my core. I am an awakened individual. My new journey is to connect with folks that are the same. I can see, feel and smell them. I try to connect with friends at times although my heart is not completely warmed. The awkward moments from my heart are a signal that they are not here. Here being really awakened. I can dedicate my evolution to myself, God and definitely, Cailin. My answers are in my hand, heart and head. I need to watch folks that just don't get why the gate is not opening up for them. I will be watching and waiting for them to figure it out.

Now that I am awakened, I have released my old patterns. My mother and grandmother have encouraged me to continue on the path that I have recently paved. I need to not explain myself. I need to keep moving forward. Cailin is doing a lot of work to enjoy her life. It is my role to create better patterns for our future. While I was holding her today, Dr. Sensible and I were discussing her future. We have to wait on Dr. Glamorous Gladiator to disclose her plan for her patient, Cailin. I am present and feel grateful that we are having talks of such things. The last rotation my discussions with Dr. Sensible were very critical discussions. I am hopeful and realize how far we have come. Cailin has been working to develop and function each of her systems. I have been working on educating myself, advocating, being true to my feelings and changing. I viewed all the pictures I have of Cailin from my pregnancy until yesterday. I was awakened again. I was able to see how healthy and mature she is becoming. Pictures tell a story. Our story is the gift of life!

Shortly after, our favorite Chaplain, Ruby, comes for a visit. She and I talk for a long time. We always can talk for a long time. She is pure, understanding, compassionate and very supportive. We talk of the joy of Cailin's life. How these are the times to enjoy. I am holding Cailin. She is sound asleep. She is peaceful in my arms. Ruby and I talk briefly about the medications and the weans for Cailin's care. She is going to go home. It is only a matter of when. I disclose all of myself. Work, family, homefront and my realizations. I am awake and going to lead my life consciously. Ruby expresses, "I wish more NICU parents would express their feelings like you do." I was taken back for a moment. I have not been holding anything back. I have confronted and made sure I have had a "heard voice." The heard voice is for professional, compassion and appropriate care and service for Cailin and me. The heard voice from a lot of my pacified relationships don't hear me or my voice. That is where the letting go needs to be sprinkled. I look around and know who in my life leads theirs in a sort of presence. The ones that are not hearing me say what I need, what I am not tolerating and so on just "don't get it." They are living their lives differently. Not worse, just different. It is okay for them to lead them anyway they choose. Just don't come pointing, knocking, pounding, gossiping and disrespecting me, because you are not going to get anywhere with me. I am here. I am present.

Many folks will never understand what I am going through. How I have to support my daughter through many medical struggles. That is fine. I don't wish this experience upon anyone. It has not been easy. I am blessed to have gone through the lifetime crisis. It has changed me forever. Forever for the better. I know it is better. I imagine myself wearing a great pair of striking heels. Killer heels for that matter. They have been worn in and look great, but I just don't like them anymore. I don't like how they feel. Of course, I get myself a new pair of shoes being a "shoe person." These new pair of shoes are amazing! They are not quite broken in yet, but where have they been my whole life?. They were just waiting for me to figure out where the green button was. I hit the green button, grab my ticket and the gate is up. Here I am. I am on the other side with my new pair of shoes. Different, but so much better!

I love being awakened. It makes me understand what life is really about. My life is centered around Cailin. Everything else we need comes from God. I pray continuously for his guidance. I receive it through my heart and feelings. I charge ahead with the "work" I need to do. This work with keep me conscious on developing the life of love, peace and happiness we both deserve. I will continue to stay awake and present. There is just too much to look forward to!

The Due Date – March 22

"Just wait 'til your feet are all swollen, you are waddling around and you can't sleep," everyone would tell me. The last bit of your pregnancy is supposed to be very uncomfortable and make you mentally ready to have your baby. Well, I have experienced many situations in the last 17 weeks that are a lot more uncomfortable. For example, seeing your child looking like a fetus with transparent skin and hair all over the badly bruised body. Another example, being told how sick and critical your child is on a "row" of the NICU. No privacy during your life being unraveled. Exposed, examined and judged during my most difficult life experience. I am equipped with the last 17 weeks of life lessons to weave, duck and bob through the last stretch here at the NICU. Our challenge is not over after our discharge. Oh no, we have a rough road, us Kacen chicks.

I reflect throughout the day that I was due today. I am only a few inches away from my size 6 pants. I could possibly get into my bikini by this summer. I am healthy, just thoroughly exhausted everyday. For a "high-energy" person, I am struggling everyday. Cailin has had such an intense struggle for the last 17 weeks. Miracles have occurred for Cailin and I. I am at the best hospital in Chicago and close to my home. I have learned so much about life in the last

17 weeks. The teachers of life are around my "everyday" life and I am aware. Once awakened and on a self-revolution, there is no stopping, turning away or hiding. I am aware that Cailin has an intense surgery to tackle and recover from yet. I pray for our rest and our quality time until the surgery.

The weird thoughts are how would my life be if Cailin was born full-term? It would be challenging as a single-mother, middle-child of my immediate family and an available enabler. I would not wish this journey on anyone. This is a very hard road to cross. I honestly wouldn't want it any different though. Of course, you don't want your child to suffer. I believe that this was the plan for this lifetime between us. Her early arrival has uprooted me. "You have never been more emotionally stable and aware in your life, Carrie," my mother discloses to me. I am pure as an infant. I will raise my voice when I am in a conversation that calls for it. I will cry from the bottom of my soul when I am suffering and not hold back my thoughts. I have become the better person I was supposed to be.

I think of how far Cailin and I have come through her medical struggle. We are amazing, courageous, pure, real, raw, sweet Kacens. Cailin was staring at me today with her big eyes, heart-shaped lips, almost invisible eyebrows, new vellus hair on her perfectly shaped head. I know what my daughter is made of on my due date, March 22, 2010. You always have an idea of your child's personality before birth, but I have seen her grow before my eyes. She was a tiny doll, just a fetus. Now she is a full-term beautiful, brave

The Due Date – March 22

and truth-seeking newborn weighing in at 3 pounds, 12.3 ounces. She is nothing less than utterly amazing!

I started my day with four missions. Missions were speaking to Laine, speaking with Glamorous Gladiator, holding Cailin and sealing my book deal process. I accomplished all of the missions. Laughter fills my soul in a sarcastic sense about "due dates." We all have our ways of life. Some plan, some watch others and some just can't get either. I am a planner. I am person that is determined and tries to do things properly. This is where the laughter comes in. I have learned that being quiet, listening and praying are more important than planning. So, to all you planners (which I attract a lot of planners being one myself), try to just "be" each day. When I say, "be," I mean slow down and listen. We hustle around too much for our own good and the people we are meant to serve.

I am meant to serve God and Cailin. Through raising Cailin, I will continue to evolve spiritually. Cailin's life will help me guide, protect and continue to have my new tree groomed by Cailin.

Fine Line – April 9

Life is full of the "gray area" although there is always a fine line. For many, life is black and white. Until they endure a life experience to throw them right out of the Garden of Eden. I was thrown out. I never realized how nice the garden was until I was out of it.

Cailin has had 10 centimeters of her bowl removed due to NEC. Two pieces were removed including a sacred valve. This resulted in about 20% of her bowel not being present. Unlike the lungs, the bowel does not rejuvenate. She has experienced the last 11 1/2 weeks with a majority of her remaining bowel outside her body.

As I write today, Cailin is being operated on to reconnect all of her bowel possible. The bright side of things include her weight (4 pounds, 4 ounces), her recovery time from the last GI surgery and her stability of the other systems functioning. She is living in the "fine line." I am not certain the outcome of my child's fatality, nutrition and functioning.

I know that I have accepted that my child will have special needs. She will not have "normal" bowel functions. I will have to be at doctor offices to keep a close watch on her progress. I write and think hopeful thoughts. I know that her procedure is crucial to her life and our lifestyle. I am waiting outside the waiting room in an area set back with my mother. I notice, Dr. Tour Guide, from the NICU, and say hello. He asks me about the valve being present. "I have seen some kids go home without the valve with only 27 centimeters of the bowel remaining. Without the valve they need about 50 centimeters." Dr. Tour Guide informs us. Cailin has already lost 10 centimeters, which frightens me.

My head bows to pray and my chin rises. I look fear in the eyes and smile doubt out of my mind. I believe in miracles. I really do! The fine line has created quite the balancing act for many of our caretakers, friends and family members.

Cailin's surgery procedure started at 4:14 p.m. It should take close to four hours. Dr. Glamorous Gladiator has quite the job ahead of her to reconnect most of the bowel together. Although when I get a call from the nurse in surgery a little after 6 p.m., I have a bad feeling. My mom comes walking up from the bathroom. I look at her and say, "They just called me."

My mom gasps, taking a breath, opens her mouth and with a look of concern, "What did they say?"

I reply to her, "The nurse said that Dr. Glamorous Gladiator wants her to tell me that Cailin is doing fine and she will be finishing up in 45 minutes."

I look at my mom. She asks me, "What are you feeling?"

I say, "I do not have a good feeling. If they were reconnecting her bowel it would be more complicated. They are

Fine Line – April 9

finishing up sooner than they wanted. I believe she has removed more than anticipated."

My mom looks at me, "Don't go there if we don't have to. Don't go there." I listen to her and try to remain optimistic though I can't shake this feeling.

The next feeling I have is I have to go to the bathroom. My nerves are shot and my stomach is very upset. Not a fun combination. I have the Operating Waiting Room host come out of the door to grab me. She says, " The doctor is ready to talk with you in Room 4."

My mom and I grab all our stuff and walk through the Operating Waiting Room, which has a lot of televisions and screens stating the progress of each case number. This reminds me of the airport. You are given a case number and then the number appears on the updated television screen with either PreOp, OR or Post OR.

We drop off our stuff in Room 4. I turn to my mom, "I have to go to the bathroom. I will be right back." I head to the restroom to find a large cleaning cart blocking the entrance. I have to go so badly. I wait and turn to go to the other bathroom. I start walking and see Dr. Glamorous Gladiator. "Hi, I was just heading to the bathroom. They have us set up in Room 4."

Dr. Glamorous Gladiator proceeds with, "Let's use this door."

I say, "It's nice that they have these rooms for the debrief."

She replies, "It is good to have some privacy."

We all sit. I am on a small couch next to my mother. Dr. Glamorous Gladiator is across the room in a chair. The distance seems so far apart for a "close talker" like me. I proceed to hear most of what she says. "Cailin did very well during her surgery. I have some bad news that I was unable to preserve most of her bowel from being outside her body as long as it has been. She has a remaining of 20 centimeters of her small intestine. She has a colon in great condition that only absorbs water, not nutrition. Her liver is enlarged and has some green tone."

I cry here and there while asking questions. How long will she live, 2-4 years? I am told up to one year. One year. One year is all I keep hearing in my head. All this fight and she is going to pass from her lack of bowel. Can I take her home by June to spend some time with her out of the hospital? This is a possibility. I am so happy and so very deeply saddened.

Dr. Glamorous Gladiator did not want to say Cailin had Short Gut Syndrome until after she was in there. Cailin has severe Short Gut Syndrome. The way this would make sense to anyone is being giving the prognosis of Stage 4 Cancer of a loved one. I receive a death sentence for an innocent child with a fight of a Gladiator herself. The outcome of her surgery is quite the fine line.

Hurt – April 10

I have described my trials and tribulations while Cailin fights for her life each day. I sit here during the doctors "rounds" to write of the pain and hurt I am enduring. I have spoken to my mother, my grandmother and my father regarding Cailin's condition. I foresee being able to take Cailin home. I hurt knowing that our lives together have a large black cloud over us. I am deeply suffering knowing she is fighting to recover from her surgery. She fights so hard to get past her surgery. Meanwhile, her fabulous nurses are preparing for skin care procedures and staff contacts to help Cailin. I am researching and asking questions to learn how and where I can help.

Knowledge is so very important to be able to help Cailin. I gather knowledge and then crack. I need to know as much about Short Gut Syndrome. My emotions as her mother are so fragile. I actually have had to sit down on three occasions regarding Short Gut Syndrome and Cailin's reality. I have been knocked right off my feet.

I am feeling hurt from the bottom of my gut. I have had the wind knock right out of me. I am grasping for air. I am trying to wrap my head around knowing that my daughter is going to come home, yet has a low-life expectancy. When you think of children and babies you think of a thriving long life. Our reality is all new to me.

I was so happy to have a baby, then shocked to have a micropreemie. I am deeply saddened that she has severe Short Gut Syndrome. I feel that a dark cloud keeps following us and trying to scare me. Well, listen "black cloud," I have been petrified and lost my breath enough. I am not angry with God. I am sad. I do not want my daughter to suffer. I want her to have some good memories. I want to hold her. I want to see her crawl, walk and go to Kindergarten. I want to share the rest of my life with Cailin. I do not know if I will be granted such "wants." I do know I have to change my mindset again.

I need to treat everyday as a gift. I need to choice wisely what I spend my time and energy on and whom I do it with. Cailin is my purpose, my reason and my all. I am sad and happy at the same time. She and I have had heck of a fight and still do. The uphill battle continues with many odds already overcome. The mountain that we are up against is a very steep one. I have been hurt many times in life. Nothing compares to this hurt though. My prayers continue. What are my prayers now you ask for? Guidance, is what I pray for now. Guidance.

Next Step - April 19

Cailin is up to five pounds. She is recovering from her reconnection GI surgery. She has passed two stools. I was so happy to wipe the smear of stool off of her. On April 15, Cailin Jane decided to pull out her breathing tube. She was handling breathing with the VaporTherm device for a few days. Her right upper lung was collapsed. As the days proceeded, her x-rays showed that her right lung was completely collapsed. We hoped she would cough up the debris in her lung. It didn't happen.

My child had to be reintubated on the breathing tube this morning. I am having a hard time with it all. I want her to get better to go home. I am sad that she has to suffer, not only from the GI surgery, but from her lungs. Our next step was the upper GI exam next Monday and my meeting with the Short Gut Clinic. My next step is not the same as God's will.

The next step is for me to surrender. Surrender and pray. What to surrender to you ask? To God's will. He is the one to determine what is best for me, Cailin and our life together. Easily said and I wrestle with the action. I read my new book of Miracles. I read of greatness, angels, God and human life. I am reminded of the need to surrender.

I don't go to work today. I decide to be gentle with myself and support Cailin. I am having a hard time knowing of her struggle. She is extremely exhausted. Princess Aurora, Liz and I are doing her breathing treatments and suctioning out plugs and mucus. I see Cailin's vent dependency decrease throughout the day.

I assumed she would be fine with her lungs after this surgery. I keep getting reminded that assumptions, expectations and wants are quite foolish and such the "human way of life." I have to pray and accept the guidance I am shown.

Receiving guidance is daily through God. Princess Aurora's sarcasm, Ockto's silliness, Pocahontas' warmth, Snow White's bright eyes and giggle. They all celebrate my birthday with wishes and precious gifts. I sit back and observe who and what is being said to me. I know God is working through the people in my life. I listen and I am comforted each day. Just enough to get up tomorrow and fight for Cailin.

Ducks - April 21

When I arrived to help, visit and connect with Cailin I noticed she had a bit of throw up on her shoulder and blanket. Ockto, her nurse, was getting Cailin handled for her 8 a.m. jazz. I was able to help and eventually get her settled. She is a newborn on a breathing tube that wants it out. She is fighting it and would like to have it gone to the wind. I keep telling her to let the staff help her clear the mucus and old blood plugs out of her lungs first. She is my daughter, so she is alert and aware and rebellious. I see it in her eyes. She will be pulling it out shortly. We have tried our best to put her on house arrest. She has little hand mitts and a tight swaddle to try to keep her feisty pulls to a minimum. Her head is mobile and she really wants to squirm right out of the tube. I am curious when and who will extubate her this time. Odds are on Cailin.

I head home to tidy up and get a walk in the fresh air. I am such a thinker and my little mind is never resting these days. I attempt to focus on the trees and keep my head up. When I am thinking and processing my tribulations I tend to put my head down. Chin up, Carrie, and take time to smell the roses! Well, I am smelling the trees in Barrie Park during my mile walk.

Throughout my walk I am mentally and emotionally putting my ducks in a row. I think of the rows in the NICU. Most new babies, new parents and new tribulations. I will see most of them endure a surgery, a recovery and feeding to be sent home. They will be sent home before we are. Home for us is coming around the bend. I will be talking with the Social Worker and the Home Nurse Program Coordinator. I will be finding out options and resources. This is one of many ducks to get in a row. My home front duck is looking pretty clean and organized. A few more cleaning projects as well as a steam clean of the furniture. This duck is dander and dust free. The other duck is work. I am having trouble with the manner my boss is talking with me. This is the second time she has been extremely aggressive with me. I know that I am a terrific leader and have a great team. My team respects me because I respect them. Unfortunately, I am not the "old" Carrie. I spoke to her directly for a clearing of the air. I feel she threatened my job due to having a bad week of numbers. I contemplated to going to Human Resources. I thought it all through and decided to give the Regional Leader a shot at a solution.

I discussed the work duck to my mom. "Go big, or go home," we say. I have not caught a break once during this life experience. I took a step back and look for spiritual guidance and speak to my angels. God's will is more important than mine. He knows my life purpose better than me. Although I still have a mortgage to pay. It's a rough balance of human reality and your soul's purpose.

My last little duckie is Cailin's medical condition (SBS) and her care at home. I have a meeting at the Kiddo Hospital

Ducks – April 21

to help with her nutrition, care and lifestyle. I have a good feeling about the two meetings. I am eager to make our next step to home. Cailin is my favorite little duckie! I continue to dedicate, focus and love her daily. I feel that my life is changing drastically for the better. It is darn painful though. I have to be true to myself. Being so true causes a lot of confrontation though. I am mulling through each day trying to make a better tomorrow with each of my ducks getting in a row.

Walk It Out - April 22

Cailin is one month "corrected age" today. I arrive to the hospital to find her sleeping on her side and pass the Surgical Team. The glares and stares from them are of awe and concern. They all know the stats on Cailin. The question is do they know Cailin? Cailin is not the typical micropreemie who spent the last five months in the NICU. Her demeanor is often calm as well as feisty when needed. I read the last few chapters to her in the Miracle book Ockto, her nurse, gave us.

I am amazed how Cailin can barely wear her preemie clothes anymore. She is up to five pounds! She has recovered from her last GI surgery and her right lung collapsing. I am so proud of her! I tell her as she wakes up and stares at me with her big eyes how her breathing tube will be taken out today. I am anxiously waiting to arrive back up to the hospital. My Pilot is getting back brakes. I sit in my living room with a beautiful breeze on my face, the scent and beauty of all my birthday bouquets and knowing that soon Cailin is homebound.

My walk today was the typical mile I walk. I keep reminding myself the importance of looking up at the trees and flowers rather than my head down thinking. I can't turn my little mind off might as well concentrate on the trees, flowers, wind and the great outdoors. As I do glance up, I am reminded of life's beauty. There will always be plenty of things to worry about. Turning worry into wonder is a challenge I believe will help me be Cailin's mother.

As I turn the corners of the sidewalk briskly, I think of the last time I was walking in Barrie Park. I was pregnant grieving the betrayal and hurt going into parenthood alone. I would never imagine walking this spring without my child, let alone her being in the NICU. I wonder when will I be able to take Cailin for a walk in the park? I think of her cute little face and how all the great outdoor sounds will be much different than the controlled chaos of the NICU.

I have choices in life as anyone does. My choices are turning worry into wonder and truly surrendering to God. I just recently have become to understand what surrendering actually is. Surrendering is accepting what is. What your reality is. Not fighting, complaining, playing the why game, taking on the victim role, the poor me pity party. Oh, no! Surrendering is owning your kingdom and making the best of it. It is a choice to "change the story." You tell yourself, as the Animal Tamer would say.

Our kingdom is a single-mother running a business, spending every possible minute comforting Cailin and educating myself on her conditions. I believe that you can make better choices for your child when it is about them not you. I see the parents that complain or find pleasure in the drama of a sick child. This is repelling to me, but to each their own.

Walk It Out – April 22

My walks around Barrie Park are just a mile. A mile of many thoughts, feeling and prayers. I breathe, I glance up and take pleasure for the opportunity to clear my head. The hospital is a draining place although required for Cailin to come home safely to me. I walk it out. I choose to consciously make good choices each day for Cailin and I. I head home to get back up to the hospital before work. Today is another day full of opportunities to make tomorrow better for my Miss Cailin.

One Side Down – April 25

Cailin's recovery from her April 9th GI surgery has been a hard on her lungs. Before her second major surgery, her lungs were looking fantastic. White Angel couldn't believe that they were the lungs of a 23-weeker! Cailin self-extubated herself from the breathing tube. The doctors decided to see how she would handle it even though her right upper lung was down. She managed for a number of days until her whole lung collapsed. She was reintubated for a few more days and given breathing treatments as well.

The Respiratory Therapists were taking good care of my baby girl once again. Both of her lungs were not looking so great. She eventually opened up and was extubated off of the ventilator. I was able to enjoy holding her for two days. She does so well when I am snuggling with her, reading to her, talking, humming and just gazing with amazement at how beautiful she is. I always tell her how strong she is and how great she is. I believe in positive affirmations and the law of attraction. I focus on what I want. I put it out in the universe. I talk to our angels all the time and pray my heart out to God.

Unfortunately, Cailin had to be reintubated last night after her bath. She was kicking her feet right off of the plastic tub. Snow White and I were giggling and cleaning up our beauty. The photo shoot began with her wonderful blue onesie with flowers on it. I asked Snow White to take a picture of me kissing Cailin. No response. I looked and Cailin was not looking so hot. Snow White was holding her in a sitting position while her breathing stats were declining continuously. Snow White needed to take a parent call and still feed her other baby. I help Cailin and pressed the silence button over and over. I asked Snow White, "Is White Angel on call tonight?" Snow White confirmed she was and agreed to call her over.

White Angel came and talked to Cailin. She was being proactive with Cailin's VapoTherm settings during the day when the x-ray disclosed her right upper lung not functioning. Cailin had a ton of secretions saturating her lungs and just can't cough them up. White Angel ordered a chest x-ray stat. Radiology was taking so long and Cailin was just looking at us saying help. She was working so hard to just breathe. White Angel looked across the crib at me and stated that she would have to reintubate her. I understood and am surprised her lungs have been taking a turn for the worse during this recovery.

I say to Cailin as I do every night, "Now I lay me down to sleep. I pray the Lord my soul to keep and if I die before I wake. I pray my Lord my soul to take. Amen." I add that White Angel and the staff are going to help her feel better. They are scrambling to get her drugs to make her paralyzed and less traumatic for her. I head home not wanting to see them paralyze her. I will call Snow White in the middle of the night to see how she is doing. I pray for her lungs to recover. I visualize her lungs getting stronger and growing to help her sustain her body. I hope for two up. Two functioning lungs on my daughter.

Inspired – May 4

The eyes widen, the eyes have clarity and my soul is warmed. I am inspired. I ask myself how did I come to this point of having a sense of inspiration? I have had to process Cailin's prognosis of Short Gut Syndrome. I read, asked questions, meditated, cried, turned to my mother and still the answer was Short Gut Syndrome. Statistics, risks, liver disease and sepsis are all on the hillside. I climb. I sit. I sleep. I cry. I am not independent. I am human. I am a spiritually aware human. I am not confident.

Cailin is struggling with her breathing with the right lung. They have to perform a scope procedure and put her under for a bit. I go to the hospital. I pray. I talk to her. I wait. I am given the results. I then come home to shower, eat, pray, wonder and pull an Angel Healing Card. I worry. What does worry do? Nothing good or positive.

Do you think my daughter can't feel or read my emotions? Why all the struggle to have her have such a rough syndrome to deal with day in and day out? I will never get the answer from God in this lifetime. I have to truly surrender. Acceptance is at the top of the hill. I reach it in two and a half weeks.

I am at the top of the hill. I see the peaks and valleys. I know that I have my faith, my mind, my spirituality and Cailin. She is here today. She doesn't even know she is sick. So, why should I be carrying around all this worry to her bedside? I drop the worry along the way of the climb. I have been told by a Sharman, "Be crystal clear and do not bring negativity to Cailin." The hospital is a hard place to heal for someone that needs to heal.

Cailin's eyes look right through my soul. There are no accidents in life. She had an agreement with God for this entry and complication. I must trust and surrender that He knows what is best for Cailin and me. Fair? Life is not fair.

He is constructing the peaks and valleys we will be traveling through this life. He is the only one that knows why. How it will all turn out? I release it to Him. I free myself of the worry around me. I reach my hand out and ask for help to my mother and friends. I am inspired by how they respond. Willingness and dedication to obtaining help.

I reach support groups and befriend a mother of a child with Short Gut Syndrome on Facebook. I refuse to not find a connection. Cailin has been a blessing to me. She carries many gifts for me. One is clarity. The clarity of what my life was, what it is now and how to proceed. How do I know this? Through my heart and the way in which my life has unraveled.

My life has been exposed to an entire unit in a hospital, my salon, my friends and family. I am typically a private person in many ways. Well, that was shot to hell. I needed to

Inspired – May 4

change. I have been inspired to write my trials and tribulations of this life experience. I am revealing myself to measures I never could have fathomed.

I am inspired to keep following my heart and my instincts. My sense of knowing is at a higher spiritual level. I must not let anyone distract me from my sense of knowing. This is a gift from God to navigate throughout life with Short Gut Syndrome. Each child is different. My child and I have a connection that runs so very deep. I dream of her complications weeks, months before they arise. One dream that keeps inspiring me is the one when Cailin first came to me in my dreams. Cailin Jane had bright blue eyes and blonde wavy hair and was a baby then instantly flashed to her young adulthood. I hold this dream and vision close to my heart.

Inspiration kicks my butt up, lights my stomach and gets me sharing it. Cailin keeps me inspired by her demeanor and big eyes looking right through me. I feel in my heart she knows what she is here to teach me. God chooses how to create and develop each of us. He chooses to have us enter the Short Gut Syndrome community of life. I step out and place one foot in front of the other knowing he will show me the way.

19 – May 6

I am not taking about inches; I am talking about centimeters. "I want to know how much in length and what exactly is left in her small bowel," I tell Dr. Sensible a few days ago. Cailin had her upper GI study that was expected not to take very long. It started at 8:30 a.m. yesterday and was completed by 7:45 p.m. The "little bit" took a lot longer than anticipated.

"The pace is in your favor," Dr. Sensible says with her accent. She nods her head with it tilted to see my response. She is a good listener. She likes to hear what I have to say and really to see where my head is actually at. As we speak for some time today, she describes of the tribulation on decisions and a general consensus of the study. Radiology is ready to start feeds, Surgery was not opposed and Neonatology wanted to complete the study and review. The consensus is that Cailin has a narrowing in her small bowel where she was reconnected. Dr. Glamorous Gladiator is not surprised and this is common. Dr. Sensible obtained all the information regarding her study then decided to start feeds at one milliliter every two hours. I was thrilled! We have to start somewhere.

Dr. Sensible concluded, "The consensus is that Cailin has 19 centimeters of small bowel left."

I reply, "Well, I was given a close estimation compared to stating that the valve was present when it wasn't. This is very extreme."

She replies with, "Yes, it is. The number is 19."

I was content with how she came through with my request. I let the number go through me and I didn't quiver. Yes, it is certainly a very short amount of small bowel left. Her gestational age was extremely young. Her birth weight was extremely low. Her vitals were low. Her skin was transparent. All the odds were against her, but she is coming home with 19 centimeters. I go through my processes on each bit of information that I am provided with. The scare factor is pretty darn high in the NICU. Although it is time to face the drummer and know that it is Cailin we are talking about. She is the bravest little soul I have ever laid eyes on and she is my daughter. She is a gift from God and she presents many gifts to my life. Clarity is the greatest gift I received through this process.

Just as Dr. Sensible clarifies the small amount left in length of her small bowel, Cailin provided me clarity of about the many who, what and whys in my life. Who is in my life and what do they provide? Why do I choose? I have had many faces revealed to me. Once I was told that people will tell you who they really are, just listen to them. Oh, no, people! People reveal who they really are to you by their actions. I

19 – May 6

have had quite the challenges with revelations of people in my life. The shoes weren't fitting any longer.

Angie and I discuss our recent professional challenges with certain personalities tonight. Clarity is the bottom line, the end of the story, the icing on the cake. Boom! The light goes off in your mind and you see what you are really made of. Time will always tell. The truth always prevails. Cailin's challenge is survival with an extremely short bowel measuring 19 centimeters. Does she know she is sick? I believe no and yes. On an earthly level as a human, absolutely no. Spiritually, absolutely, positively yes! She is an old, old soul. She will look anyone right down to their core. She seeks the truth and has cut through so much fluff and nonsense to just get to the heart of the matter. She has stirred a lot of pots, made the medical staff scratch their heads and clarified my life. The doctors provided the worst-case scenarios, the hard facts and statistics. I am here again. We are up against some tough odds. I have to think back to how positive and faithful I was in the very beginning. I didn't feel I would lose her in my heart. I can get distracted with my research, data gathering and the science of it all. I have a choice. Be grateful that she has at least 19 centimeters. I can change the story. I can believe in her and let God lead the way.

As a mother, you want to know what you are up against. You need to know the facts, but there is a world much larger than all of this. I mean the spiritual side of life. Dr. Eyes gave me great advice and helped guide my mindset. He said, "I have seen things in caring for people that do not have an explanation for." I feel I must keep a bit of a balance. Cailin needs to be medically treated. I do not care to be radical or jump off the deep end and just think spiritually she will just be healed. I can pray, meditate and continue to deepen my desire for evolving spiritually as well as follow the medical program. I truly believe in miracles. Cailin is nothing less than an amazing miracle. So, 19 is our story and we are sticking to it.

Gratitude – May 7

Shedding tears is nothing new to me for the last five plus months. Today was a special shedding of tears, which are of pure gratitude. I reached my hand and heart out for help. For an independent, confident and strong woman it was a new step in my life. I prayed and meditated on how could I possibly handle all of the financial worries. I kept thinking I need a fundraiser. So, here I am today with three evolved fundraisers. My high school pals were clever and came up with an email for "Donate for Devotion." My mom and my friend, Marge, are creating bowling fundraisers for the second week of June. I sit and reflect outside the carwash. A well-needed one, my beloved Pilot has not been cleaned since Cailin's birth. I am off work today, and I planned on getting a few things in order. Two important tasks were washing the car and installing the baby car seat. Grateful to be off work, have a job and see the results of asking for help. Gratitude brings you to a place of serenity. Oddly enough I have been feeling serenity and harmony during all of the challenges. I longed for it enough to seek it out. I sit back and feel this overwhelming sense of gratitude. A wave comes crashing and then just sprinkles amazing contributions. I trusted myself enough to go with what my heart was telling me, "Ask for help!" People have offered to do other contributions along the way. The gestures have been kind, although I have been fighting alongside Cailin for her life. Many made offers that were well-intended, although I have to be clear about what I need and what I do not. Our NICU family has been gracious in supporting me and helping in what "home" for us means and what we will need. The need for support is always brought up. I believe I have support. My support system is small and mighty just like a little girl I know so very well.

The Law of Attraction is occurring right before my eyes. I visualized and absorbed what the feeling would be like to have help. It has arrived and touched me deeper than the visualization I had. I prayed for the guidance and followed my intuition to lead me the way. It works and I will use the prayer and a positive mindset over and over to trek ahead. I hope to show Cailin how to be grateful what life has to offer.

I think of this often between my car rides to and from the hospital. The world keeps spinning and life keeps on going whether you are working through a crisis or not. I am reminded of this daily as I work and listen to my client's challenges and complaints. I have a larger perspective than most, which I am grateful for. It can be lonely at times, although it is a familiar place to me. When I connect with a friend for even a phone call, I am grateful for the time we shared. I have a small handful of supportive friends that I can count on. Some of their names go in my gratitude journal I have been keeping. This journal helps me keep a positive perspective. Each day has its major medical challenges for Cailin. The journal allows me to reflect on the

Gratitude – May 7

positive aspects of the day and certain conversations or people that touched me throughout the day.

I don't know many people that would keep such a journal when fighting for a life. My gratitude journal is dated daily and has around eight various things I am grateful for each day. This process keeps me in a place of gratitude. You have a choice to cry from complaints or cry tears of gratitude. I choose to cry tears of gratitude which are sweeter, more constructive and a much more rewarding way to see your days. We all suffer but you can choose your thoughts and feelings of your suffering. To lessen your suffering and learn about gratitude is highly recommended.

Today I will have a wonderful entry in my journal of gratitude. 1. Cailin having gas sounds, a stool and burping a few times 2. Cailin starting on feeds every two hours of 2 cc. 3. Cailin being weaned down to 1.4 on her fentnalye 4. The sun shining and the crisp air 5. Fundraiser contributions 6. Talking to Brett today 7. Holding Cailin 8. Being off work.

The small things in life are what matter. My 5 pound, 7 ounces small baby girl is what I am most grateful for.

Rounds to Routines – May 18

"Rounds" is a time that the Attendees, Fellows and Residents are updating and discussing each child's issues and needs. It is from 9:30 a.m. to 12:00 p.m. each day. This is the only time I am not allowed to be present at Cailin's bedside. I arrive or call shortly after rounds each day. What changes are necessary? What concerns do they have? The questions are consistent as much as change is in life.

I sit in my dining room with Cailin's baby items to the left and right of me. The transition is coming to wash and place all of her items throughout our home. We are working on routines now. Every other day, she receives a bath. I am allowed to give her a bottle of Elecare totaling 5 milliliters daily. She takes the bottle much better in the afternoon or evening than the morning. Skin care for her little bottom is another major routine. She is to be wiped gently, dabbed in areas if possible and then the essential reapplication to her skin barriers. Her inner bottom is getting a little red. She passes most of her stomach bile and it irritates her skin quite a bit.

Any parent has to change their routines when their bundle of joy arrives. Although my bundle of joy has special needs. I will need to become a pro on many tasks such as skin barriers, soothing her bottom's irritations, Nasal Gastric placement to feed her, feeding monitors, cycling her Total Parental Nutrition and Lipids and monitoring her oxygen. All of these routines will be on top of the normal stress of caring for an infant on a daily basis. I wonder, not worry.

I am asked continuously, "Are you nervous to take her home?" My answer is no! I am not overly excited either. I have many feelings though. They are of complete exhaustion. The deck of cards has been shuffling for the last five months; my hand has been dealt. It is a tough hand, but my hand. Nervous would not be the feeling or the description that I feel in my heart, head and stomach. Oh no!

I feel a sense of major spiritual growth throughout my being. I wonder how will I handle this next phase of our life. Then I hear Big Jer's words replay in my head, "There is no one else I know that can handle this. God has prepared you Carrie, since November." It all makes sense to me. First of all, Big Jer is a very popular lady. So I take her kind words as a compliment and reassurance that she is one of my Earth Angels. She tells me of her trial and tribulations, and I can handle Cailin's medical needs. I believe I can and sometimes I am blown away with where I am in my life.

I take as many naps as possible to rest and regroup for the next phase of Cailin coming home. I rejoice in a very peaceful manner though. There were a heavy handful of times that I almost lost my child. I would communicate to God and her and let go. She would pull through each time. She is a living miracle. There are not medical and logical explanations for how she pulled through so many times. This is proof of the spiritual side of life that many take for granted in their rushed "fast food" way of life. I hear of the daily stresses everyday with the nurses and my clients. I giggle inside quite a bit and show compassion. It all reminds me of how I am still on the plank. I do have a few friends that can relate to me though. For this I am grateful.

The wonders of our routines are pondered by my mother. I remind her that it will be much like her hospital stay with her routines, just in a pleasant environment called home. I plan to incorporate music, fresh air, walks to the park, reading and talking. Cailin is ready to come home. When I speak to her about home she responds with a smirk or smile. I know she hears me and understands what I am talking about. She wants to come home as bad as I want her to. The unit is crowded, noisy and crazy right now. It is filled with many other sick babies. The sad part is the lack of consistent parent involvement. I shake my head and know that most of the babies that receive few visits from their parents will go home much better off than us. You ask if I am angry? No, I know that God gave me a hard hand because I have not lost my faith and this is a huge purpose of my path. It will not be easy by any means. I am to help others in a way and he will guide me to do so. Hopefully, you are reading one means right now.

The long stretch of rounds and routines makes me ponder on some good old-fashion self-reflection. I ask myself, "What have I learned?" I want to share some of the lessons that I have learned. Put your heart first, over your head. Yes, use your logic and don't be an idiot! Your heart is to be warmed and followed. If you are not warmed by a person or situation, stop, listen and follow it. Will this disrupt some of your relationships? Yes, absolutely. When you remove dysfunction from yourself you will have another hard lesson to learn. I discovered just how many and to what degree of dysfunctional relationships I had embedded in my life. They disrupted and caused me more pain and stress on top of Cailin's fight for life. I have slowly forgiven the actions of an aunt, my mother, my father, my sister, my brother, friends that are really just acquaintances and many people's ignorance. Painful? Yep, it hurt to the bone. I cried and cried. The lesson reveals that you are the deciding factor of what you will accept and from whom. Will people be talking, gossiping, judge and make their own emotions a priority? The answer is yes! You cannot change anyone. Letting go is the best solution. Will they show back up? Most likely they will. It is your choice on how you allow them into your life.

I reflect back on the hurtful, selfish situations I have experienced by my sister, my father, a long-term friend, a short-term friend, a boss and a coworker. I see that I have been a huge part of a lesson for them. Though it is their choice to grow and take accountability or not. I will continue to move forward in my life. I will allow the doors that need to be shut to do so. I was a huge enabler and comforter and my choice is to no longer be such a person. Do I love the characters that have hurt me? Yes, I do. Some from a distance. My heart will guide where I feel accepted, treated properly and who I need to spend energy on and with.

I will have plenty of routines while I care for my child. I will have to have my own time to perform "rounds" each day. There will be many questions. What is best for Cailin's health? What I am teaching her? How am I leading my life? I will continue to grow and lower my expectations of others. I will accept others for what they really are, not for what I thought or hoped for. This will only create less drama and more peace. I will commit to surround Cailin with positive people and energy. She has provided clarity for my life and shined a light through many tough lessons. More lessons of life will only unfold throughout each of my days as I am granted to be her mother. In the meantime, I have to get ready for her arrival home.

Ready - May 20

I awake at my usual time for the usual routine of my little mind to start thinking more and more rapidly as each minute passes. I grab my iPhone to contact the night shift nurse, Pocahontas. She answers to disclose in her soft-spoken voice about Cailin's quiet night. When I arrived after work last night, I held Cailin. She spit up quite a bit and pooped right afterward. She was not tolerating the increase of five milliliters an hour. I was concerned that she may not have had a good evening, but that was certainly not the case. Pocahontas reassured me that she was quite restful.

I am relieved and start to doze off again until about 7:30 a.m. I am off work today. I am stiff and exhausted. I rise to fold all of Cailin's clean clothes, receiving blankets and washcloths. I throw on some comfy clothes, brush my teeth, place a headband in and head out the door. I am ready.

I am ready to take my daughter home. I am tired of running back and forth to the hospital, work and home. Home is the next phase for any new parents from the hospital. My story, our story, our next phase is very different from many new parents. We have been fighting side-by-side for just about six months. The light at the end of the tunnel is a few weeks away. This makes it all the more difficult to leave Cailin in that crib at the NICU. She recognizes me then coos, grunts, smiles and cries in a very raspy way. In time, her vocal cords will heal as will the rest of her body. She will keep getting stronger, develop and blossom each and everyday.

I want this all to happen at home. Patience is a virtue. My capacity for patience is extremely large! Cailin is finally off of the pain medicine, Fentanyl. I am happy to see one less tubing attachment. I patiently waited each day to see her withdrawal scores increase as the medical staff weaned her from the medicine. Her withdrawal scores were nothing to be concerned of and resulted in her free of the assistance.

Cailin is such a "good-natured" baby as Ockto, Cailin's nurse, would say. She really is not an unhappy baby. She is easily consoled and comforted. Pocahontas, Cailin's primary nurse, said, "She was just looking around with her hands in her mouth when I came on tonight. It was really, really cute." I love to hear this sort of feedback. At the NICU, those types of comments are rare. Medical and surgical options are the frequent topics.

When I first wake up I am ready for my conversations with Cailin. I can get out of bed and see her and tend to her myself. I want to be able to pull the curtain and let the sunshine on her. I look forward to the fresh breezes coming through our home for her to experience. This world has so much to offer and our choices will be the very small things

Ready – May 20

in life. We will take pleasure more than most do on a daily basis.

The last few times I left the hospital, I filled up a bag with her books. I am trying to bring her belongings home slowly. To the left of me in the NICU, I hear a cry of the big girl next to us. She is going home today. I had a concern of the bedside being occupied right next to us. We are in Isolation due to MRSA. Well, this beautiful term baby has MRSA too. Her mother is only in high school. I believe she is probably a sophomore or junior from what her grandmother tells me. Her grandmother is only 43 years old and is now a great-grandmother. The proud, anxious teenage mother is doing a good job with the baby. Some of her questions are because she is only a kid herself. Her lessons arrive much earlier than mine in the motherhood department. Life is before my eyes once again. I do not judge, I just observe. I can hear all of their information as I read through all the background stress of the other sick babies.

There are no mistakes or accidents in life. This young mother was supposed to arrive on to the bedside next to us. For a lesson to both of us.

She asked me, "How long have you been here with your baby?"

I replied, "Since November."

Our first exchange ended with her mouth wide open and her eyes bulging out of her head. She was pure in showing her expression only to quickly divert back to her beautiful full term daughter. I sit back, rock and soothe my Cailin in my arms and watch our neighbors' short stay unfold before my eyes. I was not quite ready to have the space invaded although this was meant to happen.

Here I have a young teenager that is asking the nurses over and over, "When is my baby coming home?" Her daughter was there for four short days in my eyes. Her stomach was fine, hip is just dandy. Today, she's out the door. This young mother probably felt that those four days were an eternity. Hence her expression to me upon my response of November. She was so pure in her questioning to me and to the nurses. I do not feel so pure these days.

I held Cailin while I watched yet another child be discharged from the hospital. Thankfully, we will be on our way home soon. Our discharge preparation has started since the end of April. I have to master quite a bit of medical knowledge and skills in order to bring Cailin home. She has to be taken care of properly. Our neighbors and us have very different stories yet we share very much in common. Our common threads are motherly love and being ready to go home with our gifts from God, our daughters.

Full Circle - May 22

Dr. Jasmine approaches me before I depart the unit to grab a bit to eat. I smell her perfume long before she arrives to our bedside. It is a very distinct scent that I identify with her. If I smell it 10 years from now her face will pop up in my mind. Jasmine had a couple questions for me one being, "Have you contacted a Short Gut Clinic that you are working with?"

I reply, "Yes, I have already met with Kiddo Hospital and will be working with them. I just need to inform them a week before Cailin will be discharged."

She tells me she wants to have the NICU's dietician formulate the TPN home recipe due to the Lipids, fats, being in one bag. I have my visuals down pat from spending everyday in the unit. Jasmine informs me of the next steps we need to take to have Cailin come home as soon as the Broviac, central line, is put in.

"I wonder if Cailin could go home in two days after the procedure? Well, that is only two days after the operating room and Dr. Glamorous Gladiator would just laugh at us." Jasmine thinks out loud.

I add, "It all depends on how Cailin does after her procedure with her lungs."

"Yes, of course. Though I think she should go home as soon as possible from the procedure." Jasmine, Princess Aurora and I all agree knowing how infection is more likely with a port that large especially in the hospital. We come to an agreement to shoot for May 31, Memorial Day, to be Cailin's discharge date.

I head down to the cafeteria to have a dinner and do a few things on my laptop. I just keep saying over and over in my mind, "Wow, this is less then 10 days away!" The list arrives in my head. I always have a list. The things that I need to get done before she comes home. I need to purchase two new air conditioning units, wash and organize Cailin's essentials, clean all my hardwood floors again, and get a pedicure and manicure. I saved my birthday present from Kiki for the pedicure and manicure as a reward of Cailin's homecoming. I would like to go for a nice steak dinner with my mom. I am not sure if I really have time for that. The list and excitement goes on while my smile increases. Home, she is coming home! I am going to have her home, and I just am so happy!

Jasmine and I have had other serious conversations. She was the doctor to give me the pre-term consult while I was breathing out contractions. I kept telling her, "My baby is coming today!" During my consult, we discussed all the harsh statistics on Cailin's development, complications and challenges ahead as a 23-weeker. I remember distinctly answering the question if I wanted to resuscitate Cailin as,

Full Circle – May 22

"YES!" From that answer to two days shy of six months, we stand by Cailin's bedside to discuss going home.

I go about bathing Cailin and talking to Pocahontas. She taught me a restraint wrap for Cailin when I am inserting her Nasal Gastric feeding tube. We joke about Cailin's fake cries and whines. We have her pegged, but Grandma is gonna get suckered. No doubt about that! I head down to my Pilot to go home and speak to my parking lot friend. He is an Earth Angel that has spoken to me throughout our journey here at the Human Spirit Hospital. I disclose that I hope to have Cailin home by Memorial Day. He says,"What a joy!"I nod my head, drive off and turn up my David Gray CD.

As I turn on Roosevelt, I start to feel my emotions pour out in tears. Heartfelt tears. I am bringing my baby home. I start to have flashes and replays of the difficult times I have experienced along side my Cailin. Jasmine was in most of them. The first consult with all the possibilities, when Cailin was showing signs of NEC, x-rays of Cailin's very immature lungs and homebound plans. She even made sure I was speaking to someone on how to cope with this crisis in the beginning of this journey. She is a caring and compassionate doctor that has touched our lives. I know for certain that is the same truth for her.

I reflect and think of how and where Jasmine was really a large part of our journey. As with a journey, there is not always a destination. I know that the last six months is only one major monument of our journey through life together. The circle of life goes on without one destination. Though the conversation I had with Jasmine today has been a true "full circle" moment for me. There is something so very sacred to me about these moments. It shows how life is full of twists and turns, only to meet up again. I cherish this moment and feel blown away by the reality of Cailin coming home!

All Aboard! – May 25

The Broviac day… the Broviac day… the long awaited day has arrived! The Broviac is Cailin's central line, otherwise known as her lifeline. She will receive all of her medications as well as TPN and IV nutrients, all through this line. This is our long awaited ticket home. We have talked and talked about this day and how I need to learn how to maintain and be fully aware of the signs of an issue. Any issue could arise and cannot be taken lightly whether it is air in the line, a clot or an infection. The line goes into her heart. Things could go badly, very quickly. Princess Aurora has been all over me being informed with literature on how to care for the Broviac and what to look for.

Princess Aurora has been on the ball and rounding up the troops for all the pieces to come together. We need medications, monitors, oxygen, ilex paste, ice packs and a lot of hands to help. Cailin has created a life for us that requires a lot of people to be involved. She knows more people in her short six months than I did for years of my life. She has had many medical professionals looking after her and has an important date today with Dr. Glamorous Gladiator in the operating room.

Cailin has visited the operating room on three occasions already in her short-lived life. She has had a total of five surgical procedures in only six months. I have an uneasy feeling in my stomach when I enter the operating room. Surgery has been a great option in caring for Cailin's bowel issues, eyes, lungs and now a central line placement. When I enter the operating room there is a huge sense of uncertainty. The air is so sterile it can be scary. I know this is a must in helping my daughter survive. So, here we are today. I am not a naïve young mother. Oh, no! I know the operating room is just like the craps table. You have your odds and your small wins. I roll the dice and shout for Dr. Glamorous Gladiator and Cailin to hit the lucky seven today. I get my case number for Cailin's surgery that I can follow in the waiting room, just like the airport. Although we are not going to Vegas we are still gambling for survival and life here in Illinois. The front desk employee is quite friendly to me. She believed for over three months that I worked at the hospital. Not until her last surgery did she realize that I have a daughter being cared for here. She glances at her sheet of paper and writes of my attire, "green sweatshirt, mother - white shirt, grandmother." I give her my cell number. I find a seating area away from most people. I like to focus, meditate, concentrate and pray. I need to be centered without distractions to connect with Cailin, Angels and God.

My mom is on her cell phone, like usual. I guess it is her way of dealing with the stress. I can't run from life anymore. I need to be present for Cailin and myself. I center myself. I focus on my trusty little prayer book. I pray and ask God to give my energy and strength to Cailin. I am tired. I curl up in my ball on the small stiff loveseat, pull

All Aboard! – May 25

my hood over my head and hold my phone in my chest. I breathe deeply in and out. I do my best to relax each of my major muscle groups. I start to drift. I am in the state I need to be in.

"She is over there," the front desk employee discloses to the Nurse Practitioner of Surgery. She looks similar to Dr. Glamorous Gladiator, but in a taller fashion.

The Nurse Practitioner states, "She is so small," in regards to me sitting in a ball on the loveseat. She proceeds to inform me, "The procedure is beginning and should take 20 minutes to one hour." We chat briefly, then she departs. I am thinking I should go to the ladies room. I don't want to leave the space. I am centered.

No quicker than thirty minutes later I am being lead to the debriefing private room number four. Dr. Glamorous Gladiator and her Sidekick, Nurse Practitioner, enter. "Cailin did very well today. She allowed me to do what I needed to do. We were able to enter her thread under the collarbone and have the Broviac port exit the chest. Most likely she will be extubated off of the ventilator. You know her lungs are doing a bit better."

I am so happy and relieved at the same time. We are going home! I can't wipe the smile off of my face, nor should I. I haven't been this happy since I found out I was pregnant. Dr. Glamorous Gladiator wants to be paged when we go home so she can give her a, "Whoo hoo!" I am all over the celebration!

I enter her bedside shortly after the debriefing and an elevator ride. She is not paralyzed! She is not on the ventilator! She has her Broviac! Her eyes are open! I am so happy, relieved and genuinely excited that she is coming home. We are going to make it! Some how, some way we will, just you wait and see. All aboard!

Long Way – May 27

November, December, January, February, March, April and May. The holidays are so long away, the snow and the gray skies. Blue skies, sunlight and heat have arrived. May is creeping its way into June. The first of June is only days away. Time is relevant in seeing how life progresses. Although moments of the last six months are more present in my mind and heart than hours. Moments.

I made a decision that my 23-week gestational baby was going to get a shot at this life. I was given a gift from God. It is not my decision to take a life. God is the shelter of life. Cailin has a challenging life, but it is hers that was granted. Moments, decisions, choices are what direct your tidings. All the plans and motivations will not change your cards. God is the dealer. The house always wins, right? God is the house. He will always win knowing what is best for me, Cailin and our journey. Will it be easy? Heck, no. Life is not easy. Well, if it is to you, then you're not truly growing through life. No, you would be running and hiding. In this day and age, such an act is either overstimulation or isolation. Either way, pure avoidance of your true necessary lessons of life.

A long, long time ago back in November, I had beliefs about life. Here are a few for you to hear again. Blood is thicker than water. Not true. You always have your family. Not true. "Buts" are acceptable. Actually they really are a way to justify and deny yourself or someone else. Expectations will create a standard of your life. You only will create more disappointment. Give and take. There is never an even flow of either, for certain people are givers and some are plain takers. Striving to be independent will make my life easier. That was a joke. I need people more than ever. It is just the type of people I need that is most essential to make my life better. Yep, a long time ago in November, I had those internal cognitive messages repeating and embedded within myself.

Change is the only thing consistent in life. I have changed to know that I have a great relationship with the most important person in my life, myself. I am my best friend. My faith and relationship with God is my backbone, my sense of how to lead my life and my heart. Cailin is a gift for me and each person she touches. I am the blessed one to have a daughter with such a soul capacity as hers.

There are no accidents in life. Things happen for a reason. Now, those are two concepts I truly believe in. Cailin is not an accident; her arrival, her medical journey, nor her spirit. I believe that we make agreements with God upon entering this life as to our mission or purpose is this lifetime. I believe a soul picks their mother. I was chosen by both, Cailin and God. We have a spiritual agreement of how our life will challenge us. She is an amazing soul to have gone through all that she has. Cailin has touched so many people's lives personally, professionally and spiritually.

So what is life about? Life is a gift, a challenge, a journey and a hand you are dealt. You have free will. Although there are reasons you walk this earth and how you should walk it. Each person has different purposes. I believe that Cailin has been here many, many times before. She is an old, old, old soul. I watch her all the time as she looks right through people. She has looked right through my soul many times during her short life already. Her purpose here is being a truth seeker, shedding clarity, teaching courage and bravery. She has taught the medical professionals that margins and stats are only margins and stats. There is more to life. Pure will, fate, faith, purpose and a mission are countered by all their medical knowledge. I apparently needed a large adjustment in my life. I have received so much clarity to my life since Cailin was born. What life is, what is important, how to surround myself with positive forces, clean out the drama in my life and how to get past solid devastating betrayal. A long, long time ago in November, I had no idea of the all the life lessons I would learn. I have been through more than the average person. Although I chose this life and agreed to some tough lessons, I thought my limits were less, I did not value myself as I should of, I was an enabler and a planner that kept planning. My world crashed and crumbled, although I did not. I have grown stronger, yet more humbled right alongside Cailin.

A long, long time ago back in November, I would have never known the twist of fate in my life. I do not regret any of my decisions. I know I was meant for this card, this hand, this life. Boy, have we both come a long, long way. Amen.

Bed 18

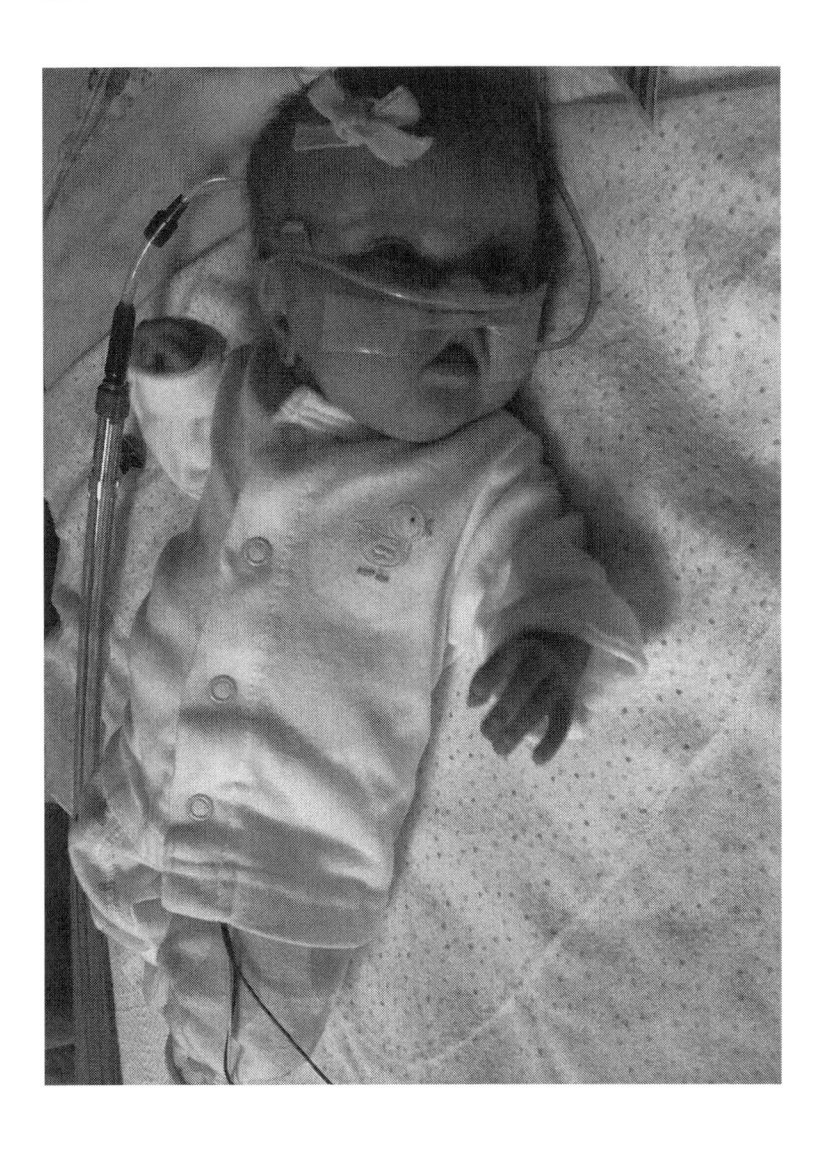

Transition and Transformation – May 29

Princess Aurora is leaning over me to hand me Cailin's formula (5 cc) in a bottle. This is Cailin's daily opportunity to actually drink something and wet her whistle. As Princess Aurora rises up she gasps, "Oh my gosh! I just saw the most beautiful big yellow butterfly!"

I reply, "I wish I would have seen it!"

As I gaze at Cailin, she is bigger than that butterfly. She has gone through such a transformation in six months. We only have days left of her stay her in the NICU.

I am going through a major transition. I will be off work for a bit and caring for Cailin. It is scary enough to take home a newborn full-term child. I have a much larger ticket to home. Cailin is a very peaceful, easily consoled child who smiles and coos just as any other nine-week infant. She is such a good baby. Her medical needs are great. I learned how to care for her Broviac, central line site, and all the medicines she needs. Being a Short Gut child, Cailin can't take any medicine orally due to her malabsorption issues. I will have to have her TPN fluids cycling off for four hours a day and enter her line with saline flushes, medicine and clamping the line off. I am learning about Cailin's daily needs for home. The difference at home is that it is only Cailin and me. I will have visitors to help here and there. Although it is as it was before, Cailin and me. The nurses have confidence that I can do it and so does Big Jerre. I know I can. I also know I have another steep hill to climb. The transformation from a NICU mom to a mom who is caring for medically fragile, complex, amazing child is a steep climb.

Cailin has transformed from a fetus with many medications to a medically fragile infant with medicines and two diagnoses. Cailin has BPD (bronchopulmonary dysplasia, sometimes called chronic lung disease), which is pulmonary, breathing issues due to her being so premature, being intubated for so long in her life and the inability to eat as a full term child to heal better. Lungs have the opportunity to regenerate themselves and do not truly develop until a person is eight years old. In the meantime, she receives oxygen. I check her lungs and heart rate with a stat monitor three times a day and perform breathing treatments two times a day. Her other diagnosis is Short Bowel Syndrome. She has the ability to grow her small intestines due to being born so prematurely. This causes her to be on TPN for 20 hours a day and only 4 cc of formula each hour for a 24-hour period. Cailin will transform and transition to different feeds. There will be a bit of a "tug-of-war." In order to challenge her intestines and stomach, there will be increases in feeds and weans on TPN. Not each addition and wean with work the first time, although eventually Cailin will adapt and grow. I know she will. She has such a will to live. She is a challenger and an educator. She has taught more residents, nurses, fellows and attendees that not every child is typical. There are always a few cases that stretch outside the boundaries. Cailin is just that case.

Every time I ask a doctor or nurse, "Have you ever had a patient with BPD and SBS?"

They respond confidently, "Yes." Then they add with intense eye contact, "Not as severe as Cailin."

I know she is "that child" who blows away doubt and challenges them all personally, professionally and spiritually.

Through the days of gathering more information, learning her new schedule and tweaks in her medical care I end up with a butterfly near me often. I was driving home from the hospital to see a huge butterfly flying between the car in front of me and my windshield for blocks at a time. I know that butterflies do not know how to use their wings for the first time. Then they fly from the cocoon looking more magnificent then they will ever know. I have really attached my visualizations of Cailin's healing and mine as the transformation of a butterfly. It seems to have worked in divine timing. The season calls for butterflies to be so very present. The sight of them touches me more than their beauty. Butterflies will always remind me of our journey.

As we transition to home care, there are three beautiful princesses that primarily cared for Cailin. Princess Aurora was the daytime caretaker. She was always on top of what Cailin needed, what she didn't and when to change both. She was never sleeping on the job. That is for sure! She truly cares for us both. Princess Aurora made sure to get all the things we needed in order for Cailin to come home. She had a checklist and was making sure that all the ducks were in line. Once Cailin's Broviac line was put in, time was of urgency. Princess Aurora touched our hearts deeply. She would flutter around the unit making sure that she was providing Cailin the best of care. She has always been an honest communicator, compassionate, down-to-earth and a great educator. She has helped me so much and taught me how to care for Cailin. Snow White was that calming force and empathetic listener throughout our challenging journey. She would always call Cailin a princess. She found Cailin's personality just humorous. Cailin has quite the expressions on her face depending on the scenario. I will always remember Snow White's gentle eyes and silly giggle. She is one amazing nurse on the unit. Her knowledge base was large and she could handle the pressure of Cailin's ups and downs. Snow White and I would discuss spirituality often. Law of Attraction, reasons and life. I will always remember her kneeling before me with so much compassion about Cailin's diagnosis of Short Gut Syndrome. "Carrie, you and Cailin are paired up for a reason. She has you for a mother and you have her for a daughter with these complications for a reason." I agree, although the parents that are not present or advocating for their children seem to leave with a lighter load. I have seen this time and time again. Snow White was very attentive, caring and loving. She allowed me to sleep at night. Her presence put my mind at ease time and time again.

Our primary nurse was Pocahontas. She was a true angel. Even with her motions she was angelic. Her passion for her career goes beyond a job. She has a heart of gold and gravitates many nurses to her. She is very special. She and Cailin had a bit of a battling relationship. "Cailin, why are you protesting?" Would be her common question as Cailin was fighting her breathing treatments in her face or bath time or an Ostomy bag change. Pocahontas would master all the various arts and crafts of Cailin's Ostomy bag changes. I would create an "inner Cailin world" competition to see whose Ostomy dressing change would last the longest. Pocahontas had a different nickname from me on the unit which was similar to "Chia Pet." Other nurses would say it and we would smile. Pocahontas missed some of Cailin's challenges during a long exotic trip and then an injury. I would always joke of how she was not our primary nurse, but "primarily gone." We would smile. Pocahontas knew she would have the long vacation and roped Snow White into signing up for Cailin's care. That is the type of nurse she was. She didn't want just anyone caring for Cailin during the night shift. She recruited who she thought would do well for us. When I think back upon the first day I delivered Cailin, I think of Pocahontas's soft face and kind eyes. She was present. She was feeling my pain and delicately caring for Cailin. She had her scary moments with Cailin and would giggle to cope. It took me sometime to figure her out at times. Her presence was calm, yet strong. Cailin loved her. Although Pocahontas caught on to her ways.

My gratitude goes out to our three Princesses. They did a tremendous job with Cailin's care and guiding me through this journey. They all had some knowledge of different ways it could of gone. Better and worse. Our Princesses did not just care for Cailin but assisted me through all my tribulations during a crisis. I endured a lot of heartache on top of my daughter being so sick. They had the compassion to give me space, hugs, laughs and pure encouragement when needed. You girls know who you are. Although when you look in the mirror you don't see the picture of yourself as I do. Let me paint it for you. Each part of you is designed for a greater purpose in life. I believe that each of you fly and touch lives more than you would ever truly know. I can speak from experience. There were a lot of phone calls, sleepless nights and restful ones because of you. Don't ever measure yourself short. If you do, then take a step back. Reflect on this experience and know not one person has left your presence untouched for the better. Cailin and I have transformed and are transitioning home because of your day-to-day dedications.

I know Princess Aurora, Snow White and Pocahontas will hold a special place in their hearts for Cailin. They have many years and many babies ahead of them to help heal. I know for certain at various times through their journey of life they will think of Cailin's transformation. There is not one party that has not been deeply touched from this journey. We all have left better people. Cailin sure is something else!

The Dynamic Duo – May 31

Cailin will be having home health care nurses everyday for the first two weeks. I will be having assistance to care for her Broviac line, how to mix her meds and TPN and work all the machines as well. The Scorpio has Cailin on her last day of care at the NICU. She is intense in a soft-spoken way. Persistence is her vice, and I know this will help along the portion of our journey until I have a full-time nurse approved. She is dynamic with her knowledge base. I always get great feedback when I disclose who will be our nurses at home. The Scorpio was always eager to talk to me in the unit and was encouraging about Cailin being on TPN with her diagnosis of Short Gut Syndrome. I liked her, and she appeared to have a great skill set.

The other part of the duo is a tall, slender Gemini. She has an Irish accent that Cailin and I love. We look Polish, but are so proud of the Irish blood we have as well. The Gemini is calculated, cool, calm and collected at all time. Our Gemini arrived to the bedside behind us and I turned to say hello and take a peek. It was one of those moments with our eyes connecting; I have known her before. A feeling of safety came over me. She asks me about Cailin's history and I provide the dates, the surgeries, the ups and downs. She glances and says, "You like challenges don't you." Now this lovely nurse has known me for a few minutes and has hit the nail on the head. You do attract what you need and desire in life. Sometimes we attract things we don't need or want, although there is a lesson. I prayed hard for angels to enter our life. These angels I hoped and prayed for were that of angels whom would enter my home environment, care for Cailin and guide my hands to do the medical caring during our adventures at home.

I believe my prayers were answered. I really saw it from a higher level today. As I went to the bathroom, I asked the Gemini if she would like to hold Cailin for me. I walked away from someone I knew for a few moments. The raving reviews, smiles and reassuring comments helped me see the impression the Gemini has left on people. I trust my gut and heart for my decisions. I walked back to see our beloved Gemini singing and loving Cailin. I felt safe and sure of both the Scorpio and Gemini. Our new dynamic duo.

They have the skill set and hearts. They are eager to get to know her. Take over on the Broviac care and dressing changes weekly. Cailin has some challenges ahead for them. She will point her pointer finger, raise her eyebrows and throw both arms up on her 7 pound self. She will guide us all through the next part of her journey. They are qualified nurses with great personalities. The time, energy and stress they will experience will not leave them untouched. Cailin has entered their lives for many reasons. We will see how and what Cailin teaches our new dynamic duo.

So Long, Farewell – June 1

I had a wonderful evening last night. I left the unit to meet my mom at my condo. Before I departed, I was sure to have The Animal Tamer paged to the nurses' station. She came strolling down only to see my face. She took a deep breath. We embraced in a hug. I wouldn't let go until she did. I can't even put into words all the times and places she helped me through this journey at the NICU. She was placed in my life at the perfect time and in the perfect place. God guides us all in life. This crisis was unbearable for many minutes, hours, days, weeks and months. The Animal Tamer was unbelievably angelic. She is a guide, a true connection on so many, many different levels she has with us. As she pulled away, we both had tears. Tears of joy, and longing for we will not see each other everyday anymore. We will miss each other immensely. She was my breath of fresh air and I know our "Cailin Corner" was just that to her. She is such a special person that I would not write a farewell card to her because I do not and will not let go of her. I gaze over my right shoulder and see none other than the Gemini of the Dynamic Duo passing to depart the unit. One of many full circle moments as we wrap up our stay here. There was such a familiar feeling when I laid eyes on the Gemini just as I did in November to The Animal Tamer. A feeling of familiarity, of knowing, of a previous experience. They are guides with their profession to Cailin and me. Their spirituality and personalities were purposely placed in our lives. I know this feeling all too much.

The Gemini states with her beloved Irish accent, "It is gonna take you an hour to get out of here."

The Animal Tamer turns and replies with tears, "She is a very special person."

I am grateful for the feeling she has for me for I have the same for her.

My mom treated me to a great night. We went to a local rooftop in Oak Park for a steak dinner, a glass of red and good old Key Lime pie. I savor the taste and the feel. I know this is my last evening for a while like this. Our Jem, Cailin's nurse, suggested to do such. I am so glad my mom is doing this for me. We head to the Lake Theatre to see *Sex and the City 2*. I love this movie. I watched all the episodes which allowed me to watch the characters evolve along with their chemistry. The fashion, the twists and turns was a great grand finale. We both enjoyed the evening. On the walk to my Pilot, there was a quiet in the air. A change, a big change right around the corner.

We arrived back to my Pilot, I picked up my iPhone to call the NICU. I was transferred to Holly Hobby, Cailin's nurse. She had just finished up Cailin's bath time. She typically is one of the charge nurses. She always is cheery to me for my 6 a.m. call in.

So Long, Farewell – June 1

"Thank you for being so kind to me all the time when I call in to see how Cailin did the night before," I state.

Holly Hobby replies, "No problem, sweetie. I have to tell you that I will be leaving at 11:30."

I proceed to be surprised and ask, "Who will be her nurse tonight?"

Holly Hobby informs me, "Fate will be the nurse for Cailin's last night."

Wow! Fate was the nurse on duty November 24, 2009. She was on the Labor and Delivery Admission Team. She was in the delivery room when Cailin was born and Jasmine, a Fellow, was trying to intubate a very tiny, badly bruised 23-weeker, my daughter Cailin. Here we have it another full circle moment. Divine timing.

It takes me about an hour to slip into a deep sleep. My mind is racing and I am overly excited. Cailin is coming home! Cailin is coming home! Tomorrow night she will be with me. I will not be separated from her any longer. The time has come. The time is 6 a.m. I rise. I call the NICU and I am transferred to Fate.

"Congratulations, Carrie. How did you sleep?"

"Thank you. I slept really deep. It just took me a while to fall asleep. Were you the nurse on the night Cailin was born?"

"Yes, I was," Fate states.

"What a full circle moment. I thought you were and I wanted to double check," I say.

Fate requests, "Please be sure to keep us updated and send pictures. Sometimes we have people sending us photos of their kids that were here for only five days. There is not one person here that will not remember Cailin. So, please update us. We will be happy to hear how she is doing."

"I will definitely do that. Thanks for taking good care of her on her last night." I say.

"Oh, she will be a spit-fire for you. Cailin had a very good night's rest," Fate replies.

I shower, apply my Mac makeup, blow my hair out, slap on my dark jeans, place on my turquoise shirt and buckle my red shoes on. I am ready to go pick up my girl, Cailin. I am bringing her home!

The stroller is empty and everyone is looking for a baby. On the elevator, a man says, "You forgot your baby."

My mom and I smile and chuckle. The couple turns and asks, "Are you taking your baby home?"

With a smile and much confidence, I say, "Yes."

They reply, "We have a baby in there."

I nod. My mom looks to me as we exit the elevator and says, "Full circle moment?"

So Long, Farewell – June 1

I say, "No, I don't even know them."

I am always riding the elevator with other NICU family and friends. I have ridden this elevator many times to see many babies go home without equipment, by the way.

We turn and head to the NICU. Dr. Balance has a haircut. The second one since I have been there. I guess the weather got to him just like everyone else or maybe he has a child graduating. We exchange hellos.

"Oh, that is a nice stroller. It is all Earth tones." Dr. Balance says.

I respond with, "I like it too. I didn't want a pink theme. Oh, you got a haircut."

He says, "The stroller looks great!"

I say, "It will look better when Cailin is in it and on her way home."

We depart. He is not wishing me luck. He is staring at me hoping that I will handle whatever happens. I see the fear, the compassion and the doubt. It is his job to know that stats and have seen a lot of cases throughout his 20 something years in the NICU. He is a silly, laidback kind of guy regardless. We had many moments up at the NICU. I will not forget him and he will remember us, for sure!

We arrive at 8 a.m. to Cailin's bedside. Princess Aurora is her nurse. She will discharge Cailin on time. I have been in the NICU for over six months at this point. We are leaving on time. Hello! This is never heard of or seen. The children usually start acting up and need to be cared for and monitored. Cailin is not typical once again. Oh, is she my daughter or what? Ha!

Princess Aurora is getting her paperwork all together. The Scorpio is coming to the bedside to assist me setting up her feeding and monitor, oxygen and monitor, disconnecting her TPN. I recall running into a single mother that lost three children prior to her premature infant in the NICU. Her son has Down's Syndrome. She was concerned that he will never be independent. I thought in my head. Well, Cailin will be independent. The other comparison I made was the nice couple that transferred their daughter to our NICU due to being burned during a surgical procedure. I thought how devastating is that? Knowing you are trusting the medical professionals to be safe during surgeries. I see the pictures of their daughter with minor deformities on her face. I think, well Cailin's face is perfectly normal. Here I am today picking up my daughter to take her home. The previous comparisons have made it easier for Cailin and me. Most of the parents on the floor now could compare their card to ours and be grateful. We get Cailin on her portable oxygen. She has a portable tank. She also has a monitor for the oxygen. We have her feeding pump/monitor, feeding bag along with a gastric bag. The TPN and its monitor will be attached to her Broviac at home. We have a solid four hours from detachment time of 10 a.m. to rehook her up and settle in. There is a sense of pressure although it is smooth sailing.

So Long, Farewell – June 1

I have seen many discharges not happen the day they should. The child tends to have an issue arise to cause more medical care and monitoring. Cailin needs both and is stable enough to come home. She hasn't had any surprising episodes this time. She is ready to come home. The NICU staff is prepared and ready for her to come home. They have their t's crossed and i's dotted. That is for sure. They have been working diligently to make this happen on June 1. This is such a symbolic date. Cailin's great-grandmother, Jane Kacen, is celebrating her birthday today. What a treat!

Mariam, Princess Aurora and the Scorpio are working as a team to get all of the last minute transition tasks completed. Princess Aurora leans over to grab the paging/intercom system at Cailin's bedside. She announces that Cailin Kacen is going home and if anyone would like to say goodbye to come over. We are under a time constraint. I didn't imagine the turnout. Joy comes and embraces me. Dr. Wise hugs and pats. Jem is teary and holding me. I didn't think that would happen. Jem, the Scorpio, the southsider Irish chickie, Dr. Bolt, Dr. Wise, Blondie, Joy, Barrington, Raya, Mariam, Oscar, Cherry all pull in for photo shots! Cailin has more supporting forces than I ever knew. We take pictures. We are done and she is standing there with emotion that she is capable of Dr. Vague. She looks at me and smiles. This is her way of rejoicing. I don't embrace her. I didn't feel it in my heart to do so. We lock eyes and that is enough for us. I start to walk and the Southside Irish Chickie is by the windowsill and I stop to hug her. She is Pocahontas and Snow White's friend. She is in the inside! Her big blue eyes were awesome! Her poor head got cut off in the photo shoot!

We stop at the exit sign to take some pictures. My mom is standing back. "Don't you want to get in the picture?" I direct at her. She comes over. My mom has been careful not stepping over boundaries and yet being helpful. She has done a great job. I am very grateful. I leave and don't look back. I want to move forward. I know we have another set of challenges. Our time at the NICU has been concluded. We leave as two very different people. I know for certain we left the staff and changed for the better. I see it in the faces that are taking time out of their work-day to see us off all the way to the door. Conflict brings change. I had my share of it with a very open mouth. Faith conquers doubt. Life is precious and we showed just how precious for the last six months and 8 days. I like that there is that 8 in the equation. Eight is an auspicious number and means eternity.

My mom is behind me and Princess Aurora is too. We take the staff elevators and head down to the hospital lobby. My mom goes to my vehicle to pull it around. Princess Aurora and I see two of my friends in the lobby. Richard stops by and wishes us luck on our new life. Then the Operating Nurse stops by and wishes well too! Princess Aurora turns to me and says, "You have made a lot of friends."

We smile. I hug her and tell her, "I am so happy and so scared."

Princess Aurora says, "Don't be scared. God will guide you each day."

I breathe and we head out to my Pilot and Mom. Cailin is placed in my Pilot with all her equipment. I turn to Princess Aurora and give her a high five. She asks me to call her since she is working until seven. I agree. I sit in the back sit and my Mom takes her girls home.

Un Dia A La Vez - June 13, 2010

I shared what I learned throughout this life experience. I disclosed events, feelings, conflicts, rejoices and moments of progress as they unfolded. We arrived home to start the next chapter in our life. I have a little voice telling me that it will not be in anyway a chapter, but a book. Cailin's journey might just be a book series! She glances at her automobile mobile. I have a strong sense that she knows exactly where we are heading. Home that is! The intensity of the sunlight causes her to be even more alert. She loves her swing so a car ride is a treat for my wee one. We pulled up to my condo to have the Scorpio waiting for us. We were under a strict time constraint to hook Cailin back up to her TPN fluids. I open the door for Cailin. I see her feeding backpack with the monitor, gastric bag and her feeding hanging. Her portable oxygen tank and monitor for her heart and lungs on the floor. I have to be ever so careful with all of her tubing. The most important is her line, Broviac. This is her lifeline. A whole new ball game.

The ball game has bases loaded although we are up against a team of numbers. The opposing team has strong numbers of mortality, sepsis and liver disease. We are the underdog. We have faith, patience, intelligence, love and divine guidance. Our traits are not in numbers. They are in the heart and mind. We have been underestimated our whole journey thus far. What do "they" say about underestimating the underdog? Oh, yeah! You shouldn't. As our Gemini says lovingly with her Irish brogue, "Carrie, you take all those numbers and life-expectancy with a grain of salt. It is their job not to be overly optimistic, but to tell you the worst case scenario." A story all too familiar for us! I have heard it over and over for every single cell, organ and system of Cailin's body. There is something to say for faith, meditation, visualizations, cleansing her life and mental strength. I have not been sick once during the last six months and eight days. I made it to the hospital everyday two to three times a day, worked and kept going with life. Life does not stop no matter what your ball game looks like.

It was my choice to dust off the scraped knees, heal my broken heart and hope for the next time I'm up to bat that I have enough faith in myself and Cailin. I continue to take the bat and do my best to aim before I swing. I might miss a few. I know the same pitches will keep coming at me until I learn the lesson. The lesson of life.

I have learned many lessons. I carry my player, Cailin, up my two flights of stairs with her car seat, tubing, monitors and oxygen. My mom, the Scorpio, and I get her settled. I will be pinch hitting for her. She is "medically fragile" or "critically stable" the docs say. I have many pitches to master.

The first is how to mix her two vitamin vials and Pepcid (for her reflex) to her TPN. How to program the TPN machine, prime the tubing, make sure there are no air bubbles and

Un Dia A La Vez – June 13, 2010

how to hook her up. Secondly, how to mix her Ampicillin (to avoid a kidney infection), how to administer both medications and flush with saline to reduce mixing meds, clogging and crystallizing her lifeline! I have to learn how to mix her 20-calorie feeding formula, put the correct amount in the bag, hook it up to the gastric bag, prime the tubing and set the feeding monitor. I must know how to change and place her Nasal Gastric feeding tube down her nostril into her stomach for feeds. If she is "handsy" and pulls it out then I need to put it in immediately. Thirdly, Cailin's lungs require additional oxygen. She has a stat machine displaying her heart rate and oxygen Os (good range is 95-98). I must administer her Nebulizer for breathing treatments and suction her nostrils. This is a must so her airway does not become blocked with a mucus plug. Her leads are placed, cleaned and attached to a loud machine. My neighbors use to hear the crying spells from my unit. I would cry myself to sleep, when I woke up, really anytime I needed to. I believe you are not a weak player when you cry and show your true self. You are strong beyond measure, really! Now my neighbors hear me talking frequently to my wounded player, loud buzzes, walking my unit all day long and Cailin's sweet cries, moans and presence.

Our team has plenty of bench support. My mom, Gemini, Scorpio, Angie, Brett, Christine, Margaret, Maria and Myrna to name just a few. Everyone is just a phone call away! The first 48 hours of Cailin's arrival was a huge learning curve for the nurses and me. They haven't had a patient on TPN at home in a while. New technology, old tricks and memories. We worked together and all left each day with pure exhaustion. Not as exhausted as Cailin. She is working with no reserves and still works hard to heal and live this life the very best she can. Some of the innings of our adaptation were partly sunny, cloudy and just plain rained out. We made some mistakes saturating her lungs with large saline flushes and Cailin was very loud about something not being right.

My one major meltdown is dealing with tubing and keeping all untangled. Wish me luck! There is no way around being so careful and delicate with moving Cailin and moving about her.

I yelp to my Mom, "How am I going to do this all by myself?"

My mom doesn't say anything as I proceed into my bedroom to regroup. Cailin is feeding off of my anxiety and emotions. I answer myself by the saying that is over my dining room doorway, **Un dia a la vez**. One day at a time. Just as it has been since November 24, 2009. One day, one minute, one hour… whatever amount of time I can handle. I am going to be caring and protect Cailin as a single mother. I am alone as a human here on Earth. As a spiritual being, I am not alone. Cailin and I have angels, ancestors and God all around us. When I am self-doubting, anxious or scared I turn to them all. I pray continuously. I love to communicate with Mother Mary and The Archangel Michael. I often feel a presence when it is just Cailin and me. I still count on my Earth Angels though.

Angie, our Earth Angel, arrives on Friday to help me get to and from Cailin's first pediatric appointment. We arrive to

Un Dia A La Vez – June 13, 2010

the waiting area and pick a far back sitting place away from everyone. We slowly get Cailin organized on the stiff loveseat hospital couch. I have spent many hours in the NICU and OR on this type of furniture. Angie and I are giggling with all of Cailin's "stuff." I am known to carry a lot of "stuff" myself. Like mother, like daughter! I leave Angie and go to check in. We are "that family" The glares and stares from the spectators have begun outside our somewhat safe environment at the NICU. I thought of this type of life a bit. You never know until you have that shoe on. Well, I have "that" pair of shoes on. I am confident. I keep my chin up. I know how far she has come. I choose to carry myself with dignity and grace. I believe God wants me to show people how they should be grateful for the usual baby stuff. Be grateful that your child just has an ear infection, fever, diaper rash or long night. We are the family that helps people to remember to be grateful for health and average daily stresses.

I am checked in and called in by a nurse. Angie, Cailin and I, with tubing, machines and a car seat make a proud walk. I envision this walk the same as the end of the game. Each team lines up to walk past each other and slap hands. No matter who wins or loses you acknowledge the game. The two teams and the players. I jump up in my thoughts and hit my "high-five" to the heavens. I recall the days I would cry the whole way to my Pilot and say to God, "I will cry, suffer, and be heart-broken everyday as long as I can take Cailin home with me." I never envisioned the amount of medical dependency, BPD and Short Gut Syndrome. Just as life unfolds you are only given as much as you can handle at each moment in life. We walk past our Pediatrician that was referred to us by Dr. Sensible back in December. Dr. Curly is peppy and warm. She wears great accessories. As we are taken back to our exam room, I like her immediately. I gasp for air as I look at the sign. Exam Room 18.

Made in the USA
Charleston, SC
15 January 2011